BRIANN DANAE

JACK GIRLZ
ATLANTA

T0349166

MEDIA

WWW.BLACKODYSSEY.NET

Published by
BLACK ODYSSEY MEDIA

www.blackodyssey.net
Email: info@blackodyssey.net

This book is a work of fiction. Any references to events, real people, or real places are used fictitiously. Other names, characters, places, and events are products of the author's imagination, and any resemblance to actual events or places or persons, living or dead, is entirely coincidental.

JACK GIRLZ ATLANTA. Copyright © 2025 by BRIANN DANAE

Library of Congress Control Number: 2024916886

First Trade Paperback Printing: April 2025
ISBN: 978-1-957950-60-0
ISBN: 978-1-957950-61-7 (e-book)

Cover Design by Ashlee Nassar of Designs With Sass
Model: Diamond Simmons-James
Photography by Tommy Bedford
To the extent that the image or images on the cover of this book depict a person or persons, such person or persons are merely models and are not intended to portray any character in the book.

10 9 8 7 6 5 4 3 2 1

Manufactured in the United States of America

Distributed by Kensington Publishing Corp.

Dear Reader,

I want to thank you immensely for supporting Black Odyssey Media and our ongoing efforts to spotlight the diverse narratives of blossoming and seasoned storytellers. With every manuscript we acquire, we believe that it took talent, discipline, and remarkable courage to construct that story, flesh out those characters, and prepare it for the world. Debut or seasoned, our authors are the real heroes and heroines in OUR story. For them, we are eternally grateful.

Whether you are new to BriAnn Danae or Black Odyssey Media, we hope that you are here to stay. Our goal is to make a lasting impact in the publishing landscape, one step at a time and one book at a time. We also welcome your feedback and kindly ask that you leave a review. For upcoming releases, announcements, submission guidelines, etc., please be sure to visit our website at www.blackodyssey.net or scan the QR code below. And remember, no matter where you are in your journey, the best of both worlds begins now!

Joyfully,

Shawanda Williams

Shawanda "N'Tyse" Williams
Founder & CEO, Black Odyssey Media

PROLOGUE

2001

No matter how hard she tried, Hazel couldn't ignore the harsh tone of her father's voice. She could always tell when he was on the brink of losing his temper. It was an action of his that her eight-year-old brain had processed long before now. Her body squirmed underneath the covers, tempting her to peek out of the bedroom she shared with her sisters.

Mia, the oldest at twelve years old, was still awake. Hazel knew it because she hadn't heard her light snores begin. That was the one thing she despised about sharing rooms. Teyona, the youngest at two years old, had been out like a light for the past hour. She'd wake up soon and venture to their parents' bedroom like always.

Glancing towards her big sister's bed, Hazel squinted.

"Mia," she whispered, "I know you're awake. They're arguing again."

Ignoring her, Mia kept her eyes closed and back turned. She hated it when her parents argued and wanted no part of whatever

1

Hazel had up her sleeve. She was always up to something. Sucking her teeth, Hazel tossed the purple comforter off her frame and climbed from the bed. When she accidentally stepped on one of Teyona's toys before furiously kicking it, Mia shifted her way.

"What're you doing?" Mia questioned.

"I'm just taking a peek. Come on."

Curiosity would one day be Mia's downfall, no matter how much her gut told her to stay in bed. The two crept across the carpeted floor in matching pajamas. Their father always wanted twins, and since their mother didn't have any, he settled for them dressing alike. Their massive closet was filled with identical wardrobes, down to the socks. Hazel hated it. She would always change whenever she knew her parents had fallen asleep for the night. They hadn't, and that's why she was up, slowly pulling their bedroom door open to see why not.

"You don't get to stand in my face and shed fucking tears!"

The bass in Matthew Grant's voice traveled down the hall, causing Mia to flinch beside her sister.

Hazel scowled. She couldn't hear her mother's reply, but whatever it was, it caused Matthew's voice to raise an octave. Kimberly Grant knew just how to piss her husband off, but she had taken it too far.

"Is that all you care about? Some stupid notebook pages!"

Mia gripped Hazel's hand and stepped closer to get a look. From their bedroom, it was a clear view down the hall that led to the staircase where they stood. Out of all the places in their 5,300-square-foot home where they could've had this argument, Hazel didn't know why they chose next to their bedroom. Her nosey nature was kind of glad they had, though. That's until Matthew's hand wrapped around her mother's neck.

"Oh my gosh," Mia gasped, clasping a hand over her mouth.

Hazel gritted her teeth, and her palms grew warm.

Matthew's voice was inaudible now. Words spoken close to Kimberly's ear. Her head shook from side to side as she clawed at his hands, her brown eyes pleading with him to release her. The expression on his face iced her core. On the brim of unconsciousness, she could hardly understand his next question but nodded anyway.

Matthew loosened his grip. Kimberly's life flashed before her blurred vision as she tumbled down the stairs of their home. The fall would surely ensue death, and her last thought before blacking out was of her daughters.

Mia couldn't move. The sounds of her mother's vicious fall had her sick to her stomach. Hazel bolted out of the room, not caring if Mia followed behind. She flew down the stairs with angry tears in her eyes. Matthew cradled Kimberly while their evening cleaner called for the paramedics. Soon after, Mia was by her sister's side.

"Wh-What happened?" Mia asked.

Matthew stared at his oldest daughter with tears in his eyes. "She slipped, but she'll be okay. Go back to your rooms."

"But, Daddy," Mia began.

"Now!" he shouted, making Mia haul ass upstairs in tears.

Hazel rose slowly, giving him a stare of death. Her eyes blazed with hate. Mia could believe what Matthew wanted her to believe, but Hazel knew better. They both witnessed what happened, and no one could convince her otherwise. When she returned to their bedroom, Hazel left the door wide open. Mia sat at the edge of her bed, crying profusely.

"I can't believe Mommy fell. Do you think she'll be okay?" Mia asked.

"She didn't fall," Hazel grumbled, angry tears sliding down her cheeks.

Mia hiccupped. "But that's what Daddy said."

"And he's a damn liar."

Hazel's words were cold. Too cold for an eight-year-old. Mia's eyes widened at her use of profanity, and she sniffled but didn't scold her. She only looked on as Hazel stripped from her pajamas, replaced them with a pair not identical to hers, and climbed into bed.

"Haze," Mia called out after she pulled the covers over her head.

Hazel ignored her while crying into her pillow. Mia swallowed her fear, torn by conflicting thoughts and emotions. Matthew instilled in them that trust was to be earned, and Mia believed him. She believed her sister, too, but she never had to choose sides—until today, and she would for the rest of her life.

ONE

JUNE 2023

The rumbling of Mia's stomach was almost as disruptive as the vibration from her cell phone in her lap. She had skipped breakfast and was now paying for it. Her eyes skirted toward her father, who sat comfortably across the table from her. His attention was on Rob, the chief operating officer of Grant Pharmaceuticals, Inc., as he discussed their next marketing campaign.

Mia didn't know why her father insisted on her attendance at these meetings, but here she was. It was obvious her presence was needed. Physically, she was there, but mentally, her mind was on the text message she just received. Without having to unlock her phone, she tapped the screen and eyed the message from her sister, Hazel.

Are you able to give it to me or not?

Biting the corner of her lip, Mia let the screen go black and exhaled. Being the oldest sister came with so much responsibility that she still wasn't used to. At thirty-four years old, she felt more like Hazel and Teyona's mother than she did their sister.

Mia unlocked her phone and quickly typed a response without thinking much about it.

Yes…but this is the last time.

Dots danced across the screen for a few seconds, indicating Hazel was typing, but then they stopped. Instead of sending a message, she reacted to Mia's reply with a thumbs-up. Sighing again, Mia locked her phone just as Rob garnered her attention.

"Any input, Mia?" he asked.

Mia blinked, unsure of what her input needed to be. She hadn't heard a word he said for the last minute or so.

"No. Not at the moment," she replied, hoping her answer sufficed.

When both Rob and Matthew gave her nods, she relaxed. She couldn't wait to return to her office. Being Matthew Grant's first-born daughter was rewarding yet the most stressful title she held. That said a lot, considering she was a clinical pharmacist.

Since childhood, Mia knew she wanted to follow in her grandfather's and dad's footsteps and work in the medical field—not just in it but making an impact in the community like they did and still do. Her grandfather, Matthew Sr., founded Grant Pharmaceuticals in 1985. It had taken over twenty years and sacrifices he would never speak on to get his foot in the door and remain there. Now, it's a household name with multiple healthcare products. The Grants were wealthy—the wealthy who fit right in living in the city of Atlanta. Being in business for nearly forty years hadn't come easy, but it was worth it.

Mia stood from her chair and waited for her father as the meeting ended. He wasn't often spotted at the main headquarters, so many of the employees wanted a minute or two of his time.

While waiting, Mia read over a few of her text messages and smiled at the one from her boo before Matthew called her over. She admired his gray suit that mimicked the hairs dispersed in his low-cut beard and thickly waved fade. Matthew carried his age well at sixty-one, but Mia knew the toll being the CEO of such a profitable company took on his body. His umber complexion held a nice shine, but the stress lines decorating his forehead and the corners of his eyes didn't go unnoticed.

"My Mia," Matthew said, pulling her into a hug.

Mia smiled. "Hey, Daddy."

"Everything going good? We didn't get a chance to catch up before this meeting."

Matthew would be the first to know if things weren't going good. Mia knew that, and so did he. So, she wondered why that was his first question.

"With business?" Mia countered, wanting clarification.

"Of course, with business. Was there another reason your face was in your phone for half of the meeting?" Matthew questioned.

He stared intently with those brown eyes she struggled to read some days. If her father didn't do anything else, he made Mia second-guess many of her words and actions. She cleared her throat before answering him.

"Half of the meeting? Really, Daddy?" She chuckled.

Matthew smirked. "You know what I mean." He got serious. "Handle personal matters on your time. Whoever it was and what they wanted could've waited. Do you think I've gotten this far in life by not prioritizing and focusing on those things that are of less importance?"

Exhaling, Mia willed herself not to roll her eyes. Whenever her father got into one of his moods, a lecture was sure to follow. He wasn't asking the question because he didn't know the answer. She and he both knew it.

"No, Daddy, I know you haven't. But my—"

"But?" Matthew asked, tilting his head to the side.

He hated excuses, and Mia hated being chastised. There was no point in trying to explain anything to him, especially her reasoning for being on her phone. He'd really go off then, and she didn't have time for that. As much as she loved her father, Matthew sure knew how to ruin a good day.

"Never mind. Was there anything else you needed from me? I haven't eaten a thing today, and my stomach is touching my back."

Matthew chuckled as they walked out of the room. "I'd love to take you to lunch, but I'm swamped with meetings all day. There was something I needed to tell you, though."

Mia waited with bated breath. "What was that?"

"I want you to work here full time and quit the hospital."

"What?" Mia questioned with a frown, marring her pretty face. She was so taken aback by his request that her skin grew warm.

"You need to quit that job at the hospital. It serves you no purpose," he replied in a clipped, tense tone that seemingly forbade further questions.

"Quitting would defeat the purpose of you putting me through college."

Mia wanted to say so much more, but she knew her father. He had no other words besides the ones he had just spoken.

"If you think *that's* your purpose, I have failed you," Matthew said, kissing her forehead as the elevator doors opened. "Enjoy your lunch."

Matthew's assistant entered the elevator after him, and Mia watched the doors close. She was seething on the inside. He had planted those thoughts about quitting in her head for a reason, but Mia wasn't falling for it. Yes, she wanted to follow in her father's footsteps, but she didn't want to use her degree solely under Grant Pharms' umbrella. Plus, her work at Emory University in Midtown was only part-time, and she was sure her presence wasn't needed at her father's company that much. He was pushing his weight around like he'd always done. Mia had no problem completing pharmacy school. It was demanding, just like her father, but she was prepared. Still, his controlling behavior unnerved Mia to no end.

Walking across the building to her office, Mia spoke and waved to the staff. She'd grown up running the halls of the building, attending meetings with her personalized lab coat on, knowing one day she would be the CEO of Grant Pharmaceuticals. Until then, she wanted to remain a clinical pharmacist and engage with her community while also contributing to the legacy the men of the family started. It didn't seem difficult to do, but of course, to her father, it was.

Entering her office, Mia inhaled the fresh scent of lavender and lemon that permeated the air, calming her nerves immediately. Going to her floor-to-ceiling windows, she stared out of them, admiring the perfectly manicured lawns, bushes, and flowers blooming thanks to the landscapers and groundskeepers. The main headquarters sat on four acres of land, with ten other office locations throughout the US. Mia dedicated the other half of her time during the week to the two local pharmacies in the city. She had been doing it for years now, feeling that's what she was meant to do as a Grant, but now, she was having second thoughts.

Before she could dwell on the what-ifs, her phone vibrated with an incoming call from Hazel. Mia thought about declining it but knew there was no point. Knowing her sister, she would text her, telling her to answer.

"Hey, Haze," Mia answered, walking to her desk and sitting in the chair.

"Hello to you, too, my dearest sister. How is your day?"

Mia chuckled. "It's boring, and I'm starving. Did you get my text?"

"Yes. That's why I was calling. When do you work again?"

Sighing, Mia swiveled her chair and typed in her password to unlock her iMac.

"Why, Haze? I already told you—"

"I know what you told me, but I'm desperate, Mia," Hazel groaned. "I just need you for a few more months until this painting gig comes through."

Mia squeezed her eyes shut, hating the predicament her sister had placed her in. She was jeopardizing not only her career but also the family's reputation.

"I work Thursday," she answered, giving in. She could never flat-out tell her no.

"Okay. I'll come by once you get off. Thank you."

"You're welcome," she mumbled before blurting, "Daddy wants me to work here full-time."

Hazel scoffed. "I don't know why you sound surprised. You know you're his favorite daughter. It'd make his day to have you up under him."

"Don't say that. He loves all of us the same," Mia defended.

"I'll let you think that. I thought you liked your job at the hospital?"

Mia bit into her bottom lip, eyeing her email notifications. "I do. I love it."

But you want to please him, is what Hazel wanted to say. Instead, she opted for a response that wouldn't piss her or Mia off. "Well, do what you do best."

What the hell does that mean? Mia thought to herself.

"Yeah…I will. Are you stopping by the house tonight for dinner?" Mia questioned, just as someone knocked on her open office door.

Her face lit up when she saw her boyfriend standing there with food and flowers.

"Unfortunately. It's the one day of the week I have to tolerate that man," Hazel grumbled.

"Well, I'll be happy to see you. I have to go, though. Jarel just brought me lunch," Mia announced as he placed the vase of flowers on her desk.

Hazel said goodbye, and Mia stood from her chair to greet her man properly. Grinning like he'd just made her day ten times better, she wrapped her arms around his neck. She inhaled deeply, loving the cologne lingering on his skin.

"You look happy to see me," Jarel chuckled.

"I'm always happy to see you," she said, poking her lips out for a quick kiss.

Jarel obliged, kissing her lips and giving her ass a squeeze. The hunter green dress she paired with black heels hugged her curvaceous frame. Pulling away, she looked over his crisp white button-down and navy blue slacks and smirked. Jarel was so handsome to her with his waves and low fade. His full beard and creamy caramel skin were a bonus, along with his height. Considering her five-foot-five stature, Jarel's six-foot-one build was what gained her attention when they first met.

"I brought your favorite," he said as she opened the stapled paper bag.

"Thank you, babe. I've been starving all morning."

Mia squirted some hand sanitizer in her hands before pulling out the plastic containers filled with vegetable fried rice and bourbon chicken. It was a quick yet fulfilling meal that would hold her over until dinner at her parents' later that evening. She ate in silence for almost two minutes before coming up for air.

"Have you eaten?" she asked him.

"Not yet," Jarel replied. "I don't really have an appetite."

Mia paused and placed her spoon down. She immediately detected the sadness in his voice. Whenever Jarel's mood seemed shifty, she knew he had just come from seeing his sister or was on his way to visit.

"Any changes?" Mia asked.

Jarel flexed his jaw and shook his head. It wasn't easy talking about the condition his sister, Evelyn, was in. Her life changed within the blink of an eye, placing her in a coma. From what he had told her when they first got together three months ago, she'd been rushed to the hospital after having a stroke and had been in a coma ever since. It was so unfortunate, and Mia didn't know what she would do if something so traumatic happened to one of her sisters.

"None yet, but I'm hoping something changes."

"I am, too," she responded with a saddened sigh. Wanting to change the subject and the dampened mood, she said, "You look really handsome today."

His charming smile let Mia know her compliment lifted his spirits. "Yeah? How good?"

Mia blushed when he licked his lips and invaded her space. There wasn't a thing shy about her, but Jarel made her feel that way. She loved it. Having dealt with a shitty man in her past, the attentiveness and care Jarel gave her had her on the verge of falling in love. They weren't quite at that stage yet, but Mia could see them reaching it soon.

"Babe," she giggled as he kissed her neck. "My food is going to get cold."

The last thing on Mia's mind now was her food. Jarel and his roaming hands had taken up residence there.

"I suddenly have an appetite," Jarel spoke lowly in her ear while trailing his hands up her thighs.

Mia's chest rose and fell as her legs spread against her will. She'd never had office sex before, but there was a first time for everything. She shuddered as his hands crept higher. Craning her neck, she closed her eyes, ready to let him relieve her of the day's stressors. That's until a throat was cleared across the room. Mia's eyes popped open, and she tugged her dress down. Jarel stood straight, trying to mask his erection.

"Yes, Brittany?" Mia questioned in a snappy tone before dialing it down. It wasn't her fault she'd gotten caught trying to get freaky or that she had taken her office phone out of meeting mode. "Sorry. How are you doing?"

Brittany, the third-floor receptionist, smiled brightly. "I'm doing good. My apologies for interrupting. We have a student and their parent here to discuss this summer's internship program."

"Oh, yes! Okay. I'd love to meet with them. Give me about ten minutes, and please walk them back," Mia said.

"Will do!"

Brittany headed back toward her desk while Mia tidied up hers. Jarel watched with an amused grin as she stuffed a few more bites of food in her mouth.

"What?" Mia asked, replacing the lids.

"Nothing. I like watching you get in your zone."

Mia smiled. "What can I say? I love my job. Are you headed back to work?"

"Yeah. I have a few things to knock out before I call it a day."

As a data analyst for a manufacturing company, Jarel was well equipped with problem-solving. That was a characteristic Mia's last man didn't bring to the table. In fact, he hadn't brought much. She tried to overlook it and ended up getting her feelings hurt. This relationship was nothing like her last, and she was so grateful for Jarel.

"Okay. Well, I'll text you when I'm wrapping up for the day. We're having dinner at my parents' house this evening, so I can come by later if you want."

He pulled her into him by the waist. "I do. Dinner with your people is a weekly thing?"

Mia nodded. "Mhm. Every Monday. Maybe you can join me one of these weeks."

"Yeah…maybe I can," he replied with a smirk, loving the sound of that.

The progression of their relationship was moving at a pace he could manage, but he knew Mia wanted more. Dinner with her parents was definitely more, and he was looking forward to it now that she put it out there. Jarel gave her one more kiss before making his exit.

Quickly, Mia pulled out a compact mirror from her purse, examined her teeth for any leftover food, and popped a mint into her mouth. It was back to business as usual, but it wouldn't be for long if her father kept on with his shenanigans.

TWO

As Hazel placed her belongings back inside her bag, it took everything in her to keep her frustrations at bay. This was the third local art shop she had stopped by today, and they all had turned her down. A person with less determination would've given up by now. Not Hazel, though. She had goals to reach and a point to prove.

"What'd they say?" Karter, her boyfriend of two years, asked as she climbed in the passenger seat and slammed the door shut.

Hazel huffed. "Sorry, but we're currently not taking any local art at the moment. You can try back in a few months," she said, mocking the woman behind the counter. "I don't get it. If you're a local art store and want to support local artists, why not accept their work? Do I have a *do not fuck with me* sign on my forehead or something?"

Karter knew her question was rhetorical, so he didn't respond to that. Instead, he gave her a better option.

"You need to hit your sister up," he suggested.

"I did. She works Thursday. But how much longer do you think this is going to work?"

Karter frowned as he pulled out of the parking lot. "What you mean? As long as we want it to. You want that studio space, don't you?"

She sucked her teeth. "Yeah, but I'm not trying to jeopardize Mia's career."

"Since when?" Karter chuckled. "We *been* doing this shit, and ain't nothing happened. Your art shit is going to take off, but you need money now. You know what you gotta do to make some quick cash, or did you forget?"

"I haven't forgotten," Hazel grumbled.

"A'ight. Shit is good then. Yo' daddy is a fucking millionaire and got you out here struggling. Fuck 'em."

Though his words were harsh, Hazel couldn't help but agree with him. At thirty years old, she didn't think this was what her life would be like. It wasn't horrible, but you'd think the daughter of Matthew Grant wouldn't be in such a bind. Unlike Mia, Hazel didn't choose to follow in their father's footsteps. She was deemed the rebellious child—the daughter who couldn't get her shit together and went against everything the Grant name stood for.

Hazel couldn't care less about her last name. She loved her sisters and mother, but her father was a different story. Matthew did nothing for her because she chose to do her own thing and not seek a degree or work in the medical field like her siblings. Hazel thought he would at least support her dreams as an artist, but she learned early on that if it wasn't his way, there was no way. She was starting to see and believe that more than ever.

With a gift for painting and anything artistic, Hazel found solace in front of a canvas on most days. With each stroke of her brush, she put the worries of the world behind her. However, as much as she enjoyed the craft and had since she was a little girl, it didn't pay the bills—not a majority of them, anyway. That's where selling pills came into play.

It hadn't been her first option when she needed some quick money, but it had been profitable, thanks to Karter. When she broke her left wrist months ago, limiting her physical movement, Hazel almost fell into a depression. Thankfully, it wasn't her dominant hand, but the pain was still overwhelming. She was prescribed Percocet for the pain, and once that subsided, Karter convinced her to get a refill and sell the rest.

One of the perks of having a sister who worked at a pharmacy their father owned was having access to her drugs of choice. Well, in a way. It took some convincing for Mia to agree to add some extra pills to her prescription. Mia was going against every code of ethics and was almost convinced her sister had become codependent on the pills. Hazel couldn't tell her she was selling them. Not right away, anyway. After a few months, Hazel asked her to pocket a popular weight loss pill that had gotten a huge buzz.

"Are you sure you're not on drugs, Haze?" Mia questioned lowly as she walked around her sister's loft.

Hazel almost laughed. "I'm positive."

"It's okay if you are. I know a few treatment programs that—"

"Listen. I'm not on drugs, okay? I've been selling the pills for some extra money."

Mia drew her head back. "What? Why the hell would you risk your freedom like that? Not just yours, but mine, too. Are you fucking serious?!"

Tossing her hands up, Hazel walked away from her. Mia was always with the dramatics. She chucked it up as her being the only child for four years.

"It's not that serious, Mia."

She rushed behind her into the kitchen. "Maybe not to you, but my entire life is on the line. I thought your paintings were selling. Are you behind on rent again? Wait…" Mia quickly paused. "Is Karter making you do this?"

Her question was asked in a whisper, and Hazel rolled her eyes.

"Why does everyone think I'm incapable of thinking for myself? No, Karter doesn't have me doing anything. I stopped taking the pills once my wrist felt better and decided to sell them. My art is selling, but guess what doesn't stop? Bills."

"Of course, they don't, but that doesn't mean you have to turn into a drug dealer like your boyfriend," Mia scoffed.

Hazel laughed loudly. "You should hear yourself right now."

"I'm being serious, Haze. Is it money that you need?"

"Obviously. I want the pills, though. Can you keep getting them for me?"

Mia scratched the back of her neck. She didn't like this one bit. Hazel had already made her add a few more to her bottle under the impression that she actually needed them. Doing anything more was too risky, but it made Mia curious.

"How much money are you making off them?" she asked.

"Enough," Hazel answered, crossing her arms. "What? You want a cut?"

Mia thought about it for a second and shook her head. "No. I was just wondering. You can always ask Daddy—"

"The man who wouldn't even help me through art school or pay for anything I've asked him for? Is that the man you're speaking of?"

Sighing, Mia grabbed a bottle of water from the fridge, twisted off the cap, and drank.

"I don't know why there's so much tension between you two. I don't get it."

"You and I both know why."

Hazel's brown eyes narrowed, pinning her sister in place. She analyzed her for a reaction, but one never came. The reaction she was looking for never did, which was why there was somewhat of a strain between them. The unspoken truth from Hazel and the foggy memory of a lie she was told from Mia lingered in the air like a thick cloud of dust.

Deep down, Mia felt somewhat responsible for how Matthew treated Hazel. So, she felt the need to step in. Whatever Hazel needed, Mia did her best to look out for her.

"Whatever, Haze. What's this weight loss drug you're talking about? I'm only helping you out because I love you and know it's been rough. But if any backlash comes from this, you better never mention my name."

Hazel stepped her way and kissed her cheek. "Of course not, sis. I'd never rat you out."

"I'm 'bouta bend a few corners. You want me to drop you off at home?" Karter asked, snapping Hazel back to the present.

"Yeah, you can."

Weaving through the Atlanta traffic, Karter headed to the side of the city where Hazel stayed. When she first moved out of her parents' house at nineteen to rent an apartment with a group of friends, she quickly learned that having multiple roommates wasn't for her. Granted, she and her sisters had shared rooms while growing up, but that was different. You never truly know someone until you live with them, and Hazel quickly found that out.

Unbeknownst to Mia, pills weren't the first drug of choice Hazel had sold. Before dating Karter, she was in a relationship with another well-known drug dealer who got caught up and went to prison for some years. In his absence, he left behind product that couldn't go to waste, so Hazel got to it. She'd mainly sold the weed to students on campus; everything else she left to his homeboys.

Unlike her college boo, who let her pocket the cash to help pay her bills and whatever else she wanted to spend it on, Karter wasn't on that. Some days, she felt he was hustling backward, barely wanting to contribute to her needs. She wished he could've provided more for her, and then she wouldn't have to go to her sister for help.

It is what it is, Hazel thought, telling herself it would all pay off one day.

Karter pulled up to her building and parked near the entrance. "I'll see you later on tonight," he offered, leaning her way for a kiss.

What she thought would be a quick smooch turned into a tongue-wrestling match that left Hazel breathless. Pulling away, she licked her lips and smiled. *Did he know I'd been thinking badly about him?* she thought to herself, admiring his handsome rugged look. Karter was the bad boy she heard her cousins talk about growing up. The one they said you should stay away from, and if you didn't, not to take them seriously. Hazel hadn't listened.

She rubbed her fingers through his soft sponge curls and brushed a thumb over his bushy eyebrow.

"You sure you just want to see me later on?"

Karter smirked. "Yeah. I was just giving you a lil' somethin' to occupy your mind other than what's on it right now. You gon' be good. I'ma make sure of it."

Hazel didn't like the sound of that.

"Don't go and do anything crazy, baby. We're already pushing it."

"I'm not. Gon' head in the crib."

She eyed him for a few seconds more before pushing her door open. His answer didn't sit well with her, but she didn't have time to dwell on it. Karter was a grown man and was going to do whatever he wanted to do.

Like always, he waited until she was safely inside before pulling off. Her phone rang as soon as she inserted her key into the lock. Rushing inside, she placed her belongings down and grabbed her phone out of her purse. Hazel watched as her younger sister's name flashed across the screen. She didn't bother to answer her call, already knowing why she was hitting her line. Teyona would call every Monday to make sure she would be at the family dinner. Out of them all, she was the only one who seemed to care if she attended. Not showing up was not an option, though.

She let the call go to voicemail before getting in her zone. After turning on her favorite lo-fi station, Hazel opened the windows to let a cool breeze inside. Stripping from her clothes, she tossed on a pair of black spandex shorts, an oversized Falcons t-shirt decorated with specks of paint, and fuzzy socks. Once she pulled her long twists, which extended past her butt, into a bun, she was ready to get to work.

Dinner wouldn't last long if she didn't exert her energy and bask in her calmness before this evening. Eyeing the brick wall aligned with her new set of paintings, she smiled. Hazel was okay with a local store not being interested in her paintings for now. She had a loyal clientele through her website and social media platforms. Until her big break came through, she would keep risking it all, no matter the cost. It's what she had to do to prove a point—not just to herself but to others, specifically her father.

"This is my dream. I'm not giving it up," she said proudly.

THREE

"I understand this is a summer course, but your grade still matters. All of you are here for a reason, so I expect nothing less during these next two months. I'll see you all tomorrow," the professor said, ending class.

Standing from her seat, Teyona stretched and let out a big yawn. "This is about to be the longest eight weeks of my life."

"Girl, who are you telling? During the damn summer at that," Marisa, her classmate, said as they headed out of the building.

Taking summer courses hadn't been part of Teyona's plans, but she had to knock out a few courses to graduate on time next school year and not have a heavy workload. The iced matcha latte she drank during the drive to campus had worn off long ago, and now, she needed a quick pick-me-up to continue with her day.

"You act like you had plans," Teyona snickered.

"I do have a job. Everyone wasn't born into money like you."

Teyona stopped walking. "Are you trying to be shady? Because that was so uncalled for."

The sun beamed down on her smooth brown skin as she tucked strands of her fresh silk press behind her ear. Teyona's quizzical expression made Marisa shake her head. "I wasn't trying to be shady. C'mon. You know that," Marisa voiced, her eyes pleading for understanding.

"My family having money has nothing to do with me, so I'd appreciate it if you didn't bring that up again."

Her tone was even and direct. Whether Marisa was trying to be shady or not, Teyona didn't care for her comment. Money wasn't everything. In fact, she sometimes despised how much of it she was connected to. It brought out the ugliest side of people, and she knew that firsthand.

"Okay, girl. You don't have to worry about me ever mentioning that again. Anyway, what are you about to do?" Marisa asked, wanting to change the subject.

Exhaling, Teyona began walking again. "Catch me a nap before meeting up with my family later on. You?"

Afraid Marisa would ask to tag along, Teyona opted out of telling her that she was about to meet with her best friend, Cymone, to get a pedicure. They were cool but not that cool.

"Grab a quick bite to eat before I have to clock in to work."

"Oh, okay. Well, I hope you have a good shift. Don't let any rude customers piss you off," Teyona chuckled.

Marisa wasn't going to make any promises. Being a waitress wasn't the best job, but it paid well.

"I'll try not to. See you later!"

Waving bye, Teyona headed to her vehicle. One of the luxuries of walking campus in the summer was the slim crowd of students. Wanting to venture away for college but not too far, Teyona applied to the University of Georgia and was accepted. Athens was only an hour and a half away from her parents' home in Buckhead—two hours or more if there was traffic, and there was always traffic. She didn't mind it, though.

The drive gave Teyona time to herself, and the distance from her family allowed her to grow into a young woman without being under their watchful eyes twenty-four-seven. Unlike Hazel, Teyona took after Mia and was in school to become a nurse. She'd taken a year off after graduating high school because she was indecisive about what she wanted to do next, but she got it together.

Her father left her no choice. The pressure of figuring her life out weighed heavily on her, especially because she came from such a successful family. Some days, she wished she could've had the attitude and personality of Hazel, who did what she wanted to do and didn't care what anyone thought. Teyona wasn't at that place in her life yet. She was still seeking validation from a person who never gave it.

With her mind now on her sister, Teyona called Hazel like she did every Monday. She could've sent her a text, but hearing Hazel's voice always made her smile. Being the baby of the family had indeed spoiled her, so the frown she sported once Hazel didn't answer was warranted. Deciding to leave her a voice note, Teyona navigated to her text messages.

"Hazel," she sang and chuckled. "Hi, sister. Knowing you, you probably just watched my name flash across your screen. Do we have to do this every week? You know I'm going to call, so you might as well answer. Since you didn't, I'm forced to leave you a voice note. I just left my last class for the day, and now I'm on my way to get my nails and toes done with Cymone. You better be at Mommy and Daddy's for dinner or else. Love you! Bye!"

Teyona tapped the blue arrow to send her voice note before telling Siri to call Cymone. She answered on the third ring, letting her know she'd be pulling up to their appointment on time. With traffic flowing and thankfully no wrecks, Teyona made it to Nail

Spa Haven with ten minutes to spare. She learned about the Black-owned spa from a friend a few years ago and was so impressed with their service that she'd been going ever since. Cymone arrived minutes later, hopping out of her car with a big grin.

"That smile on your face tells me everything I need to know," Teyona smirked, locking her doors.

"Girl, whatever. You don't know shit," Cymone laughed, running a hand over her ponytail.

She had to redo it, thanks to her boyfriend tugging it while getting a quickie in. Teyona eyed her best friend since middle school, loving how her bright pink activewear popped against her rich, dark skin. You'd think she had been to someone's gym, but that was far from the case.

"Mhm. You look cute. Your skin is all glowing. The gym trainer must've done you right," Teyona joked as they walked inside the building.

"Worked me out so good. I can't wait for this massage."

They chuckled while getting checked in. The spa offered more than manicures and pedicures, and Cymone was more than grateful. While she got her fifty-minute massage, Teyona got a fill, and then they both were seated beside one another for their pedicures.

"I always tell myself I'ma switch up the color on my toes, but I can't stray away from pink," Teyona voiced.

"You already know what I'm getting. White toes for the win. How was class earlier?"

"Same as it always is. Stressful but worth it. I had to check one of my classmates."

Cymone snaked her neck to the right. "For what?"

Hesitating, Teyona contemplated her next words.

"We were talking about having to take classes over the summer, and I said something about her not having anything to do anyway. She went on to say that everyone wasn't born into money like me, so she has a job. She said it real snappy, too."

Cymone's eyes tightened as she frowned and replied, "Okay… but what does your family having money have to do with taking classes?"

"Nothing at all. Maybe I shouldn't have said she didn't have anything else to do." Teyona shrugged.

"Nope. Don't do that. I know you probably said it in a joking manner, yet she felt some type of way. She doesn't even know you like that to be talking crazy."

One thing Cymone hated was for someone to come at her friend a certain way.

"She doesn't, but maybe she was just making an observation. I mean, my family does have—"

"Why do you do that?" Cymone fussed.

"Do what?"

"Make excuses for people's corny behavior. I'm not going to go in on you like I normally would because we're in public, but just know you're going to hear my mouth later."

Teyona sighed. "Yes, Mom," she said, making Cymone roll her eyes.

"Girl, whatever. How is your mama, by the way?"

Cymone's question brought a genuine smile to Teyona's face.

"She's doing good. I'm going straight there when I leave here." Thankfully, her parents only lived fifteen minutes from the spa.

"Yeah, I know. It's Monday," Cymone replied.

"You should come over for dinner. I know my mom would love to see you. It's been a minute."

Cymone chuckled. "Is your dad going to be there?"

Teyona nodded.

"Oh, well. You know he doesn't really care for me, so I'll come by another time when he's not home."

Teyona wanted to pout about her refusal but knew there was no point. When she had first invited Cymone over to her house in the eighth grade, Teyona hadn't mentioned anything about the set of rules Matthew wanted everyone who entered their home to follow. Being the outspoken teenager she was and wanting to thank Kimberly for such a good meal, she did so, not expecting the backlash she would receive from speaking to her.

Matthew had snapped at her so viciously that Cymone promised never to ask to spend the night again, and she didn't unless Teyona was absolutely sure he'd be out of town. The man spooked her but, thankfully, didn't run her away. For that, Teyona was grateful. Cymone was her only friend who she could trust with her entire being.

The incident happened years ago, yet Teyona hadn't noticed much change in her father. Especially not when it came to his "rules" and their mother. Queasiness settled in Teyona's stomach at the thought, and she took a sip from her mixed drink. The tequila and pineapple mixture probably wouldn't settle it, but it would damn sure help calm her now rattled nerves.

Once their pedicures were finished, they tipped and headed out. As they approached their vehicles, Teyona spotted a piece of paper underneath the windshield wiper on her driver's side. Figuring it was a club flyer, she snatched it up, ready to toss it in the trash bin nearby.

"They knew not to put that mess on my car," Cymone said.

Teyona squinted at the paper, realizing it wasn't a flyer. It was a folded handwritten note that kicked her heart rate up a few notches. Trying to keep her composure, she scanned the parking lot for any sign of the culprit behind the words.

"Oh…it's a note. What does it say?" Cymone asked, oblivious to Teyona's trembling hands.

"Girl, just someone's number and them telling me to call them." She chuckled nervously. "They must've seen me when I pulled up earlier."

The little white lie rolled off her tongue with ease.

"That'd be too cute if some of these men nowadays weren't creeps. Had they really been about it, whoever they are would've walked up to the car."

"Or came inside to speak," Teyona added with a chuckle.

"Okay! Now that's the energy I like. Maybe. I'd have to be in that position to find out."

The friends shared a laugh before making plans to link up over the weekend and then getting in their cars. Cymone pulled off first, leaving Teyona with her thoughts. Unfolding the note again, she read the words a second time and wondered who they were meant for.

Those responsible will pay.

She wasn't sure who and what had to pay, but she hoped the anonymous person found whomever they were looking for. To Teyona's knowledge, it wasn't her.

FOUR

Being married to Matthew Grant was the one thing Kimberly regretted in life. She hadn't always felt that way and never thought she would. The man staring disgustedly at her from across the bedroom wasn't the same man who she fell in love with at eighteen years old and professed her love to before God, their family, and friends. That man had long ago disappeared, and so had the woman she'd been.

The man barking orders at her as if she wasn't his wife was unrecognizable. It used to pain her to know their marriage had failed, but Kimberly no longer dwelled on it. There'd been too many lies spoken, too little respect shown, and too much time wasted for her to care about him or their broken union.

To the public eye, Matthew Grant was an impeccable leader, committed activist, reputable CEO, doting father, and loving husband. He made it all look good on paper and in front of the camera. The public must've been wearing blindfolds. Kimberly was sure of it.

"Did you hear what I just told you, or are you playing deaf today?" Matthew snarled.

Gracefully, as she'd always been, Kimberly smiled. She wasn't in the mood for his shitty attitude, especially today. Grabbing her phone, she opened a text-to-audio translator app and tapped on one of her pre-saved responses.

"I heard you," the automated voice said.

Matthew sucked his teeth. "I'll be glad when you stop using that thing. You don't want to speak to me yourself?"

Still smiling, Kimberly cocked her head to the side as if to say, *You already know the answer to that.* And he did. Matthew asked the question as if he weren't responsible for her having to use the translator in the first place. He took delusional to a level Kimberly had never witnessed before.

"Fine," he grumbled. "We should be able to talk as husband and wife, but you'd rather have a damn robot to communicate."

Kimberly's fingers flew across her screen as she typed a new message to deliver.

"The same wife who has a separate bedroom from her *husband.* You can't possibly be talking about me," the voice said.

Matthew clenched his jaw. "I'm not having this discussion with you…or that damn robot. Your daughters will be here shortly, and you need to look halfway decent upon their arrival. I'll be in the den if you need me. Hopefully, you don't."

Kimberly watched his back as he sauntered out of her bedroom, almost bumping into Teyona on the way out.

"Hey, Dad," she spoke cheerily.

"Hello," he said dismissively, but she was used to it by now.

He acted as if speaking to her would end the world, and Teyona hated it, but she long ago stopped causing a fuss behind his behavior. It would never change.

The fake smile Kimberly used with her husband left her face as she eyed her youngest daughter. Out of all three girls, Teyona resembled her the most. She even styled her hair like her mama's, wanting to feel a deeper connection. Their dark brown silk-pressed hair was parted down the middle, framing their cinnamon-complexioned faces. Kimberly's heart filled with pride whenever she thought of or saw one of her daughters, but Teyona was her baby. Her heart moved to a different beat when they shared space.

"Hi, Mommy," Teyona grinned, removing her purse from her shoulder.

"Hi, pretty girl," Kimberly replied in her slow, soft-natured tone.

Teyona could never get enough of hearing her mother's voice. She considered it a privilege because Kimberly didn't use it with just anyone. After years without hearing it, her mother's words sounded like the sweetest lullaby.

Leaning over the bed where her mother was perched in a white silk robe with her back against the headboard, Teyona kissed her cheek. "You look gorgeous. Ms. Lisa did your hair?"

"Yes. Now I can look like you," Kimberly teased.

"I really am your twin. How are you feeling today?"

Teyona made it her duty to check her mother's mood. She could only imagine what she dealt with behind closed doors.

"It's Monday, my girls are…will all be here soon, and I'm alive. I'm feeling good," Kimberly answered, truly happy, if only for the moment.

"You sound like it. Wish I could say the same," Teyona mumbled, dropping her eyes.

Kimberly grabbed her hand. "Talk to Mama," she said, patting the spot beside her.

Teyona didn't want to burden her with her fears about her future, the strain between her and Matthew, or the note she received. It wasn't her weight to carry. She twiddled with her thumbs, giving a smile that didn't reach her brown eyes.

Hoping to reassure her mother, Teyona quickly signed with her hands, letting her know it was nothing she wanted to talk about right then.

Kimberly smirked. Whenever they didn't want to speak verbally, they used sign language. Kimberly hadn't been the same after the tragic incident that seemingly broke their family. The fall down the steps resulted in a severe head and brain injury that led to her having aphasia. As a previous educator in the school system, she faced a loss of language and an inability to express herself.

Not being able to communicate with her children, friends, family, or colleagues effectively crippled Kimberly like no other. Her entire world was flipped upside down, and relearning and understanding written or spoken language took longer than she expected. Not because they couldn't hire the best of the best speech-language therapists but because Matthew only allowed her to get better when he decided it was time.

Leaving her fate in his hands had gone on for years with empty promises to help her improve never coming. Kimberly's family, especially her sister Nicole, stayed on Matthew's case about her well-being and the help she needed. Nicole could only do so much since she lived in another state. With no one to dictate to him, Matthew had the last say.

He would hire and get rid of a therapist every sixty days, forcing Kimberly to get reacclimated with another stranger. By this time, Hazel was old enough to advocate for her mother. Though he didn't want to, Matthew finally hired a nanny years after Kimberly's *accident*. If he had it his way, no one besides him, the girls, the chef, and the cleaning staff would be allowed in the home. He didn't care to have family trotting around, poking their nose in their business.

Unbeknownst to Matthew, the nanny he hired was fluent in sign language. Hazel picked up interest and learned it quickly over the years. She taught her mother when Matthew wasn't home and then taught Teyona, who was the youngest and didn't fully understand why Kimberly never spoke. She still didn't know the severity of her mother's disorder, but she could sense the cause was nothing good.

Signing back, Kimberly told her that whenever she was ready to talk, she was there. Teyona smiled and held out her hand. She had to change the subject before she spilled her guts.

"Do you like my new design?" she asked. The youngest child syndrome made her seek validation not only from her parents but also from almost everyone in her life.

Kimberly nodded. "I do. Have you spoken to your sister?"

"I called her earlier, but she didn't answer," Teyona replied, already knowing the sister she was talking about.

Pursing her lips outwards, Kimberly nodded. "Okay. I'm sure she'll be here. I'll be down in a little bit."

"Okay. I love you," Teyona said.

"I love you more, pretty girl. Don't ever forget that."

Nodding, Teyona excused herself from her mother's bedroom and headed downstairs. She always wondered why her parents suddenly slept in separate living quarters of their home. When she asked, Kimberly told her it was the key to *their* marriage lasting. Though Teyona found that odd, as she realized none of her friends' parents had separate bedrooms, she didn't bother to ask again.

While Kimberly was getting dressed, Hazel pulled up to the gated home. Much like her personality, her burnt orange Jeep Wrangler stuck out like a sore thumb amongst the other elegant vehicles lining the never-ending driveway. Matthew grunted every time he saw the truck. She entered the house's side entrance, repeatedly telling herself she'd keep her witty remarks to herself this evening. Hazel would have never stepped foot in their home if it had not been for her mother.

"Well, well," Teyona taunted, spotting her. "Look who it is."

Hazel smirked. "Shut up. Yes, I saw your call and listened to your voice note. You knew I'd be here."

"And *you* know I'm going to always check. Mommy asked about you."

"She's getting dressed?"

Teyona nodded. "Mhm. I hope Kayla fixed something good today. I haven't eaten since this morning."

Their parents' chef, Kayla, was hired a few years ago and, surprisingly to everyone, has stuck around. Hazel assumed it was because of her love for cooking and the pay; she knew the atmosphere couldn't have been the reason. Her once vibrant, welcoming childhood home now felt suffocating. The tension and gloominess were thick enough to choke a person.

"Hello," the sisters heard come from Mia in a sing-song tone.

Hazel rolled her eyes. "Here she goes acting delusional like her fucking daddy."

"Stop." Teyona laughed, slapping her arm. "One of us needs to act like we enjoy being here."

"It for damn sure won't be me," Hazel said.

Mia made her way to them and smiled. "What're y'all looking like that for?"

"No reason. You're in a good mood," Teyona assumed.

Swinging her razor-sharp bob, which stopped right above her shoulders, Mia replied, "I like Mondays. It sets the tone for the week. Plus, I get to see my favorite sisters in the world."

Hazel smirked as she playfully kissed their cheeks, and they hugged. "We're you're only sisters."

"So you say," Mia said before walking off.

Alarmed, Teyona snatched her back by her arm. "What is that supposed to mean?"

"Oh my goodness." Mia laughed. "It was a joke. You two need to relax."

Teyona released her arm, and Mia continued on her way. Her words wouldn't have shaken Teyona up the way they had if she hadn't received that note on her windshield. It had her rethinking everything.

"You okay?" Hazel asked her.

Teyona nodded. "Yeah. Do you think she was joking?"

Hazel shrugged. "Who knows? Come on. Let's get in here before we have to hear his mouth more than either of us wants to."

She walked off, leaving Teyona to follow behind her. Though she looked forward to dinner with her family, she wished today was one of those days she could sit out.

As they took their respective seats at the marble table with cream upholstered chairs meant to seat twelve, Kimberly strolled into the dining room. Her floral rose scent permeated the air as her floor-length kimono fanned out as she walked. The butterfly print resembled what she felt like but couldn't yet be, which was free.

"My beautiful daughters," Kimberly spoke, feeling herself get emotional.

"You look and smell good, Mama," Hazel complimented.

Kimberly blushed. "Thank you."

"And I love that kimono," Teyona added.

"I don't know why she insists on wearing a robe at the dinner table."

Matthew's disapproving comment made Kimberly clench her jaw before quickly replacing it with a grim smile. She never acknowledged him or his words, which further pissed him off, but she didn't care. He ruined the mood before Kayla could even place their drinks down, but what was new?

An uncomfortable silence fell over the table as everyone ate. The baked chicken thighs, spring salad, sauteed veggies, and mashed potatoes were a hit. The only thing Hazel liked about Mondays was that she didn't have to cook or eat out for dinner. There'd be plenty to take home, as well, since Matthew didn't eat leftovers and didn't want them in the fridge.

Unable to handle the deafening quietness and sounds of forks scraping the plates, Teyona spoke. Her nerves were getting the best of her, so she talked about what she loved the most.

"I'm so happy I'll be graduating in the fall," she beamed, wanting her father to acknowledge her accomplishments. Mia beat him to it.

"I am, too! You've worked so hard," Mia praised.

She was extremely proud of her for pushing through.

"You've worked hard, too, Mia. Tell us about the internship program you've been working hard on," Matthew interrupted.

"Um…" Mia hesitated.

She wasn't in the mood to discuss work or take the spotlight off her sister. This wasn't about her right now, but of course, Matthew made it.

"Is there a problem?" Matthew questioned when he didn't hear her say anything more.

Mia cleared her throat. "N-No. I'm just not in the mood to discuss it. Plus, I wanted to hear more about Teyona's upcoming plans after graduation. I'm so proud of you, sis."

Teyona tucked her hair behind her ear. "Thank you. It's because of you that I even made it this far."

Matthew cleared his throat, expecting her to acknowledge his contribution. Teyona glanced his way but couldn't find the words to speak.

"As if I'm not the CEO of the best pharmaceutical company," he said, stating the obvious.

The sisters all eyed one another as their father continued eating. They ignored him, which was nothing new in his presence. He had convinced them that he sometimes talked to hear himself.

"How's the painting going?" Mia asked Hazel, who cut her eyes her way.

Mia knew exactly how it was going, so for her to bring it up made Hazel's blood boil. Her question wasn't maliciously asked; she just wanted to keep the conversation flowing and off of her and Teyona.

"Fine. Tey's best friend just bought some prints the other day," Hazel responded.

"She didn't even tell me. They'll likely get hung up in her shop," Teyona said, speaking of Cymone.

"I don't know why you still hang with that girl," Matthew scoffed. "She has nothing good going for herself."

Teyona blinked rapidly. "Yes, she does, Daddy. She's one of the best lash technicians in Atlanta and even travels sometimes," she defended.

"So you say."

Knowing it'd ensure an argument if she said anything else, Teyona quieted. Her pained eyes connected with Kimberly, and she smiled. Signing, she told her that Cymone was the best in the city and that she was glad she had a friend like her. Teyona signed back thank you. The entire table flinched when Matthew banged his fist on the marble table.

"Cut that signing shit out while we're at the table. I've told you all that more than enough times."

Mia's eyes widened. "Daddy," she said slowly.

"Hush, Mia. I'm not trying to hear anything you have to say," Matthew spat.

Oh, now he doesn't want to hear her speak, Hazel thought.

She chuckled angrily while Mia shook her head and focused on her plate. There was only so much she could take before she went off.

"You have something you need to say?" Matthew questioned, his eyes snapping her way.

"Don't I always? That's my problem. So you say," Hazel said, mocking him.

Teyona smirked. *Get him, sis!* she thought to herself.

"That's your damn problem. Plus, a plethora of things I'm sure you wouldn't want me to air out."

Hazel smirked. "Well, father dearest…sadly, that says more about how I was raised than anything. If you want to get technical, the problem is you."

Mia gasped. "Hazel. That's enough."

"Is it? Had he learned how to communicate with his wife like the rest of us, he wouldn't feel so left out. But that would have been too much like right. You're so quick to jump to his defense, and *that's* the problem, too. Open your damn eyes," Hazel hissed, pushing away from the table and standing.

"Wait. You're leaving?" Teyona blurted.

"Yep. I can't do any more of these fake dinner dates unless he's gone. Mama, I'll call you later," Hazel said, kissing Kimberly on the cheek.

With a pep in her step, Hazel ventured to the kitchen to make her a to-go plate and was out the door. While Mia and Teyona looked stunned by her actions, Kimberly didn't look the least bit fazed. She had a smirk on her face and wanted to laugh loudly when Matthew looked her way.

"All of that because I asked you to use your words," he grumbled. "All you had to do was listen."

Listening to you is what got me where I am today, Kimberly thought.

Each daughter's dynamic with Matthew was completely different and not in a good way. Mia cowered at him and didn't realize it. Teyona tolerated him for the sake of seeking his affection, and Hazel wanted to straight up say fuck him. Unfortunately, Mondays would no longer be Kimberly's favorite day of the week, all thanks to her *husband*.

FIVE

At four in the morning, Mia lay awake in bed, her mind a whirlwind of worries that kept her from finding even a moment's peace. Her last shift of the week at Emory started at 7:30 a.m., and there was nothing more she wanted to do than call off. The week had dragged on, and she had this nagging feeling in the pit of her gut.

With how things ended during dinner on Monday, Hazel's words continued to echo loudly in her head. They had never gone through a rough patch as siblings, but she could always tell there was something Hazel despised about her. Yes, she loved her sister and always had her back, but that wasn't enough to shake off Mia's ill feelings. As the eldest, she was the one they were supposed to turn to for guidance and support, yet she didn't feel like they'd be willing to come to her. At least not Hazel.

Jarel's unsettling behaviors added to her heightened emotions. The side of the bed he slept on was empty, and Mia knew it was much too early for him to have left for work. It was the second time she'd awakened to his absence this week, and Mia was tired of it. If he didn't want her there, she would gladly go home.

Not wanting to make any assumptions or snoop around to find out where he was, Mia lay there and waited. There had to be something wrong for him to venture off during the night. Mia's uncertainty gnawed at her as minutes stretched into what felt like an eternity. She replayed recent conversations and encounters, searching for clues to the enigma that shrouded Jarel's actions. Something felt off, a subtle shift in his demeanor that she couldn't pinpoint. Was it merely her imagination running wild, or was there truly cause for concern? The questions lingered, casting a shadow over her otherwise tranquil morning.

Mia's thoughts drifted from Jarel back to her sisters. She couldn't help but wonder if there was something more she could do for them, but she wasn't sure what. Being the oldest placed a weight of responsibility on her shoulders that was hard to lift.

Solutions eluded her as sleep once again found her. By the next time she woke up, Jarel had returned to bed and nestled himself behind her. His cold hand slid up her stomach to cuff her breast, and Mia shivered. His presence brought a sense of familiarity amidst her doubt. Yet, as he gently pulled her closer, grazing his lips against her neck, she couldn't shake the uneasiness.

"Where'd you go?" she asked softly.

Mia wasn't sure if she wanted the truth or just an answer. Her question lingered like a whisper in the air. She felt him tense, and Mia's suspicions only deepened. Jarel didn't want to discuss his whereabouts. He knew he had to soothe her worries, though.

"To grab a drink of water from the kitchen," he said, clearing his throat.

The feeling of his scruffy beard as he kissed her neck made her spine tingle. Mia swallowed hard, forcing herself to let it go. Thus far, Jarel hadn't given her a reason not to believe him, so she wouldn't start.

Turning her head, they shared a passion-filled kiss. Though sensual, their embrace was filled with tension. The weight of unspoken words hung heavily between them as Jarel climbed atop her. Mia was afraid to open her eyes and look at him. Her past relationship had practically traumatized her, but she refused to turn a blind eye again. Her heart couldn't handle it.

"Look at me," Jarel coaxed.

Her eyes peeled open as he lifted her thighs. Jarel aligned the head of his dick at her center, and her eyes fluttered as he entered her. His strokes were antagonizing slow, making Mia arch her back and softly moan. His length stretching her walls felt both comforting and fraught with underlying caution. Mia pulled him in for another kiss, yearning to erase the distance between them and the mystery of Jarel's faraway demeanor.

His strokes were no longer gentle, and the lovemaking they started with had turned into intense pounding. Jarel's fervent sex skills were one of the reasons why Mia needed to find out what the issue was. There was no way she was giving up back-to-back orgasms again. When her body tensed, Jarel pulled out and lowered his head.

"Baby!" Mia squealed, loving the way his warm tongue lapped up her juices.

His tongue flickered over her clit before he suckled it into his mouth. Jarel was a pleaser, that was for sure. Whatever uncertainties she had about them were slurped out of her. Coming up for air, Jarel licked his lips and slid back inside of her.

"Get out of your head. I'm not going anywhere," he said.

Mia's mouth opened slightly as he poked at her G-spot.

"Tell me you hear me," he encouraged.

"I hear you," she moaned. "I hear you, baby."

Ten minutes later, Jarel pulled out and released on her stomach. He rolled onto the side of her, releasing satisfied exhales. Mia lay there, knowing she needed to get up and ready for work. The quiet intimacy of the moment gave her time to question where his truths lay and, if revealed, what they would unravel.

There's no way he was only getting a drink, she thought before climbing out of his bed.

Even though her heart was saying one thing, Mia would leave it alone for now. There was no use in searching for something that didn't want to be found out.

*After working her shift at Emory, Mia ended her evening by closing down the shop at Grant Pharmacy. The location was perfect for their customers, with a favorite mix of shops and restaurants to dine at nearby. She waved bye to the last employee before locking the door, flipping the sign from 'Open' to 'Closed,' and pulling the gate with a lock. She forbade anyone from trying to get a neon sign that she had to switch on.

Mia exhaled as she tidied up the counter before pulling down the metal shutter. She couldn't wait to get home, shower, and climb into bed. Eating a decent meal didn't outweigh how exhausted she was. Despite the fatigue weighing her down, there was a sense of accomplishment in having helped numerous customers with their needs throughout the day. It made what she had been doing and what she was about to do not seem as bad.

"It's for a good cause," Mia said, convincing herself.

It was the only pep talk she needed. An hour and a half flew by before she was leaving out of the back door that locked automatically. Though the neighborhood was considered safe, she kept her head on a swivel while walking to her car. Before she could pull her door open, a hand clasped over her mouth, forcing the scream she wanted to let out back down her throat.

"Give me everything in your purse," a male's voice said.

Mia didn't recognize the voice immediately, but when the person chuckled and released her, she was fuming.

"What the fuck, Karter!" she yelled, throwing a fist into his defined chest. "Have you lost your fucking mind?!"

He tossed his hands up, still grinning. "My bad, sis. I thought yo' sister let you know I'd be pulling up on you."

Mia held onto her chest, feeling as if she were about to pass out. "No, she didn't tell me anything about you faking like a damn robber. I could've shot you!"

"With what? You ain't even got yo' heat out, let alone ready to blast that muthafucka. Why y'all bitch-ass pops got you leaving out of here by yourself anyway?"

On the days when Mia planned to steal drugs, she sent the security home early. Matthew wasn't foolish enough not to have some muscle there when she closed down shop. Had Karter truly been robbing her, Mia would've been out of luck. Her gun was in her purse and unprepared to be used. Karter had caught her slipping, and now she wondered why he was there in the first place. She dismissed all of his questions and asked one of her own.

"Why would my sister send you? *We* don't do that," she hissed.

"Change of plans, I guess. You'll have to ask her that. All I know is I'm here to collect."

Mia gritted her teeth. She didn't dislike Karter, but something deep down told her the reasoning behind Hazel selling pills was all his doing. His flashy jewelry, crisp designer clothes, and overall dope boy persona couldn't convince her otherwise.

"I don't like this," Mia grumbled, scanning the parking lot. "Where the hell is your car?"

Karter chuckled. "I parked around front. I ain't know you were coming out the back."

"So, you thought to almost scare the piss out of me? How old are you again?" Mia cocked her head to the side.

"You lucky it was just me."

Mia huffed. "Right. Get in. I'm not doing this standing outside."

Karter gladly walked around to the passenger door and hopped in. Going inside her purse, Mia pulled out multiple clear baggies of pills, each marked with a different colored marker to indicate which pills were what.

"So, can you tell me what all of this is for? I mean, aren't you a drug dealer?"

Karter smirked. "I don't know what that is, baby. I'll have yo' sister call you. Good lookin' out," he said before hopping out of the car.

He'd never gotten opp vibes from Mia, but Karter could never be too sure. She was asking him shit that had nothing to do with him. He was running an errand for his woman because that's what you do in a relationship. All of that other shit Mia was spitting could miss him.

Pulling out her phone, Mia dialed Hazel. She needed some answers and quick. It was one thing for her to be giving her pills, but for Karter to pop out at the pharmacy was taking things too far. She had already manipulated their system's inventory to receive more drugs and hadn't gotten caught, but it was only a matter of time.

"Please leave your message for—"

Mia hung up as soon as the call went to voicemail. Frustration festered in her bones as she burnt rubber out of the lot. With the morning she had, a good night's rest surely wouldn't be coming.

SIX

Hazel wasn't the typical image of a drug dealer. Her lithe frame, striking beauty, and eccentric style gave off hipster vibes, not a hustler. That was far from the case. She led a double life for a while now, seamlessly navigating between her clandestine dope boy aspirations and the façade of normalcy she presented to the world on canvas.

Her mind was calculated, operating with a finesse that always kept her one step ahead of the game—that is, until she got greedy and careless. She was unaware of how the man before her found out about her dealings. Her first mind was to point the finger at Karter, but she knew there was no way he'd turn on her like this.

"I'm not sure what you want from me, but I can guarantee you have the wrong person," Hazel stated.

"Hazel Grant. Thirty years old. Currently, an aspiring artist based on the paintings everywhere," he assessed.

She sucked her teeth. "Common knowledge."

"Is it commonly known that your mother and father are murderers?"

Her blood ran cold. "What are you talking about?"

The man chuckled. "So they're still keeping secrets, huh? What a shame."

He walked back over to where he'd been sitting but continued to stand. Hazel hated that she had let him in her home. Donning black jeans, a white crew neck tee, New Balances, and a black baseball cap pulled low over his eyes, he claimed to be the maintenance man she requested. Yet, she should've known better. One, because he smelled of fresh cologne and wasn't dressed the part. Two, because she'd just made the request over the phone while entering her building an hour ago. They never showed up that quickly. Third, because her building didn't have any Black maintenance men. Hazel made the mistake of thinking he was a new hire.

"My parents are law-abiding citizens whom this community happens to love very much," she defended.

He chuckled. "I must've heard incorrectly."

Digging in his back pocket, he produced a few pictures and held them out. Hazel gasped at the images before trying to snatch them from his hand.

"Ah-ah-ah, not so fast. That's not how this works. See, your mom here has something I want, but you…," he said, dragging his gun down the side of her cheek, "…are going to get it for me."

"Or what?" Hazel spat, gritting her teeth.

She was a woman of few weaknesses, her resolve as strong as the steel of the cold gun against her face. A vulnerability lurked underneath the surface of her tough exterior, and he was determined to exploit it in the most sinister of ways. Kimberly and her sisters were her Achilles heel.

"Or let's just say this not-so-picture-perfect image Atlanta and the world have about the Grants will be broadcast everywhere. I can see the headlines now. Matthew and Kimberly Grant of Grant Pharmaceuticals arrested for murder. Preceded in death are three daughters. Pow!"

He faked as if he let off a shot, and Hazel ducked.

Cackling loudly, the man shook his head. "See how easy that would've been? I'm no killer, though. At least not yet."

Hazel's chest heaved as she watched him walk toward the door.

"I can't let you leak those images."

For her mother's sake and image, Hazel would do whatever. She didn't care what happened to her father, but judging by those images, Kimberly was an accomplice. If Matthew went down, so would she.

"Get me what I want, and they'll be a distant memory," he said.

"But I don't know what it is that you want."

He smirked. "We'll see each other again soon, and I'll let you know. Until then, it was a pleasure to meet you. I hope my unexpected visit didn't ruin anything."

Hazel wanted to tell him to go fuck himself, but she was in no position to get slick at the mouth. The man who didn't bother to give her a name left just as quickly as he came. Reaching under her couch for her gun, Hazel rushed to the door to lock it after slamming it closed. Going to her curtains that were open to allow the sun to peek through, she quickly closed them, too. Her place of peace had been compromised, and it had her on edge like crazy.

For minutes, she sat on the couch, replaying his words. They were laced with so much malice that she did not doubt he would ruin their family—well, the piece of them that was still holding on, anyway. Her heart sank as images of her parents flashed through her mind. She couldn't help but wonder what other secrets had been carefully concealed throughout her life.

She knew one, but this revelation rocked Hazel to her core, shattering the illusion of her perfect mother. Everyone had flaws, but murderous ones were pushing it. Whatever the cost, she was going to protect her mother. Kimberly had already gone through so much turmoil at the hands of a man who vowed to love and cherish her; this news getting out would surely send her to her grave.

Bang! Bang! Bang!

The boisterous knocks on her door made Hazel leap from her couch. With her gun off safety, she inched toward the door.

"Who is it?"

"Your damn sister," Mia spat.

Hazel frowned and twisted the locks before pulling the door open. Mia barged in, unaffected by Hazel's perplexed expression.

"Have you and Karter lost it? My job, Hazel? Listen…if you're on drugs or owe somebody, you gotta tell me something because this shit—"

Mia paused, finally seeing the gun in her hand.

Hazel looked down and shook her head. She was still out of it from her unwanted visitor. Walking to the couch, she slipped it underneath the cushion.

"Don't worry about that," she said, making Mia cock her head to the side.

"You're carrying a gun to answer the door, and you want me not to worry? Okay, fine, I won't. But you had better tell me something or my involvement will end today. I can't even believe you got me caught up in this mess," Mia fussed.

You haven't seen a mess yet, Hazel thought.

No way she could tell Mia what had transpired minutes before her arrival. There were too many missing pieces, and Mia had so much more to lose than she did if she got her involved too soon. Hazel was going to figure it out, but until then, she came up with a little lie that would hopefully keep Mia off her back.

"Okay," Hazel sighed. "I owe some folks some real serious money, and selling the pills is the quickest way to pay them off."

Mia's chest tightened as Hazel revealed the gravity of the fake situation. Her instinct to protect her sister kicked in. Regardless of the risky path she had chosen, she was ready to ride for her.

"What type of money are we talking about?" Mia asked.

Hazel came up with an astronomical number that made Mia cough. Hazel almost laughed but held her composure.

Clearing her throat, Mia stood from the couch and entered the kitchen. Her first thought was to grab a bottle of water, but then she spotted a bottle of tequila and made her choice. Grabbing two shot glasses, she came back into the living room.

"I need a few shots. Do you want one?" she asked, pouring up.

"Might as well."

They clinked glasses on the table before tossing back-to-back shots. With determination etched on her face, Mia looked at her younger sister. She wished she could've saved her from the evil ways of this world, but it lurked too close to home to protect her from it.

"Whatever you need, I got you. Just don't leave me in the blind, okay?" Mia asked.

Hazel nodded. She hated she was doing exactly that, but it was for Mia's safety. Despite the day's events and the sudden danger lurking in the shadows, their bond stood firm.

As they huddled together, plotting their next move, Hazel couldn't help but marvel over the fact that the secrets they continued to accumulate all began with their father. If anyone deserved to get blackmailed for their secrets, it should've been him, and Hazel was going to make sure of it.

SEVEN

No matter her age, Teyona lived for a field trip day. Surprisingly, the ones in college were just as exciting as the ones she had gone on in elementary and middle school. She enjoyed this one much more because it could set her up for her career as a nurse. Taking a tour of a hospital she wanted to apply to work at after graduation was the mid-week pick-up she needed.

"I can't thank you enough for taking me on an impromptu tour." Teyona chuckled.

"Of course," Danielle, the residency coordinator, said. "It's not often I receive those types of emails, but I'm always excited when I do. There's not always room in the schedule, but I try my best to accommodate."

Teyona nodded, adjusting the folders and paperwork in her hand. "I figured I'd give it a try and see what happens. It doesn't hurt to ask, right?"

Danielle smiled. "It doesn't at all. Even if you don't decide to work here full-time once you graduate, we'd be more than happy to have you as an intern."

Beaming, Teyona nodded. "I'd love that."

"I would, too. With all your father has done for the health of our community, it would be an honor to have his daughter walking these halls."

Teyona struggled to keep a smile on her face. All day, she had wondered if Danielle knew who she was and who she was related to. Using her father's name to get into places or receive better opportunities wasn't how she got down. Teyona worked hard for everything she acquired. To know she would only be given this chance because of her last name soured her stomach.

She had chosen to tour this particular hospital because it was non-profit, highly preferred by women, and the care the staff provided was immaculate. Teyona hated that she would now have to set her sights on another area hospital, but she would.

"I can imagine. Thank you again. I'll be in touch," she said with a quick wave goodbye.

Exiting the hospital, lost in her thoughts, Teyona came to the conclusion that no matter where she went, Matthew Grant's name would always come up. She was tired of living in his shadow, especially when she didn't feel like much of a daughter to him anyway. His biggest contribution to her had always been monetary instead of the love and support she craved.

Still deep in her reverie, mentally processing what just occurred, Teyona almost missed the familiar face as she exited the building.

"Jarel!" Teyona called after him.

Jarel's expression tensed for a moment, caught off guard by the calling of his name.

"What's up, Teyona?"

"Hey. Not much. Just came from taking a tour," she said with a tight-lipped smile. "You?"

"Visiting my sister. It was good seeing you." His words were rushed, mimicking his movements as he walked off.

Puzzled, Teyona's brows dipped. She'd met Jarel a few times before now, and he had always come off as relaxed and down to earth. Mia always sang her praises about how good he treated her. His abrupt departure seemed strange, though. Before Teyona thought anything more of it, she shook off her confusion. After all, this was a hospital, and he seemed to be in a rush. She made a mental note to ask Mia if everything was okay later on.

Making it to her car, Teyona looked at the time and inwardly cheered. She still had time to grab a bite to eat before heading to her next destination. No matter how busy her schedule, she always made time to squeeze in an appointment with her therapist. Pulling out of the parking lot, she traveled to the nearest Chick-fil-A. After ordering, she made the fifteen-minute drive to her therapist's office and finished off her meal before entering with five minutes to spare.

"Hi. How can I help you?" the receptionist asked politely.

"Hello. I'm here to see Mrs. Morris. I have a two o'clock appointment."

"I'll let her know you've arrived. You can have a seat."

Teyona smiled, and before she could sit, the door to the office opened. Mrs. Morris smiled brightly and waved her over.

"Hey, Teyona. Come on in."

No one knew she was seeing a therapist, not even her best friend or sisters. She decided to do it on her own to figure out her emotions without the validation of others.

Mrs. Morris lowered the lighting to Teyona's preference and sat in her black chair. It's been three weeks since they last met, and she couldn't wait to see what had progressed in her life since their last session. Teyona had a lot on her mind. It was evident by the way her leg bounced as she sat perched on the cyan-colored loveseat.

"How has your week been so far?" Mrs. Morris asked.

Teyona smiled faintly at the Black woman in her mid-fifties.

"Hectic as always."

"Hectic or busy because you're a student?"

She chuckled. "A mixture of both, I guess. I worked on the assignment you gave me last time."

Mrs. Morris was happy to hear that. When she gave her clients homework, she usually had to ask them about it. Teyona volunteered the information, and that was a good sign.

"And how was that for you?"

Sighing heavily, Teyona dropped her eyes before mumbling, "Hard."

"And what was hard about it?"

She shrugged but still answered. "Admitting to myself that no matter what I do, I'll never be good enough."

"Good enough for yourself or good enough for your father?" Mrs. Morris questioned.

Opening up about her rocky relationship with Matthew was difficult, but she was trying. She'd been trying. That's why she was there wearing her heart on her sleeve.

"Both," she replied, her voice barely above a whisper. "I know I said I'd work on not seeking his approval, but he's my father."

Her eyes pleaded with Mrs. Morris for understanding.

"I understand. Does seeking his approval hurt more than when you don't?"

"Yes," Teyona said and nodded. "At least when everything is stuck in my head, I'm not left waiting for him to say anything. But then again, I am. Some sort of praise for how proud of me he is or how lucky he is to be my father would be nice. Something."

"Are those the words he uses with your sisters?" Mrs. Morris questioned.

"Not with Hazel, just Mia. It's like because she's the oldest and followed after him, he's prouder of her than of us. It's hurtful."

Sniffling, Teyona shook her head. She wondered if Matthew knew the harm his consistent emotional absence had caused. It left a void in her life. It was a void she'd spent years trying to fill, only to be left disappointed. With a voice that trembled slightly, Teyona recounted instances where her attempts to connect with her father had been met with indifference. She described the ache of longing for his attention and validation, only to be met with silence or a fleeting nod before he resumed his pursuits. The worst of all was comparing her to Mia.

They were nothing alike, yet Matthew overlooked the fact that they were their own person. Despite the constant disappointment, Teyona perpetually strived to earn his affection, believing that if she tried hard enough, she could bridge the gap between them.

Mrs. Morris listened attentively, offering her comforting presence amidst the brewing storm of emotions. With gentle encouragement, she guided Teyona to delve deeper into her feelings of frustration.

"What will his validation of the woman you are and your accomplishments do for you?" Mrs. Morris asked.

The question jarred Teyona for a split second.

"It'll let me know he cares. I guess show me that he loves me."

"I won't say he doesn't love you, but his actions show you what he cares about."

Teyona huffed. "I know, but maybe… I don't know. Maybe if I stood up to him, told him how I felt, and that he needed to be there for me more, maybe it would change something. He can change. People change all the time," she said, her words laced with a mixture of despair and hope.

"They do…when they're ready to change."

The finality in Mrs. Morris's words caused an ache to fester in Teyona's chest. She hadn't lied. People only change when they feel the need to or if it benefits them. Matthew knew his behavior bothered his daughter, yet he never changed. It was a reality check that Teyona began to understand more and more the older she got. Her self-worth didn't have to be defined by her father's approval.

"Yeah," Teyona sighed, agreeing, "you're right."

"How is your relationship with your mother?"

Her face lit up. "That's my girl." Teyona chuckled. "It's more than I could ask for now."

"Now?" Mrs. Morris questioned.

"Um, yes. She hadn't always been there. I mean, she was in the house but like a shell of herself. Sick most of the time. Stayed in the room most of my childhood."

Mrs. Morris scribbled notes on her white pad. Noticing Teyona's mood shift, she wanted to delve deeper. Her words seemed to fill the office with an air of melancholy. Kimberly's *sickness* is the real reason Teyona wanted to become a nurse.

"How did her absence make you feel?"

Teyona pondered for a bit. She wanted to be truthful with herself and Mrs. Morris, too.

"Lonely. I had to depend on my sisters to care for me and rely on my dad to do what he did, I guess."

There were too many moments she tried blocking out of her head. Therefore, she couldn't make sense of it all. There were whispered secrets from her sisters that she was never included in. There was the caregiver who worked around the clock with her mother and then never returned one day. There were arguments between her aunt Nicole and Matthew that kept her from seeing her cousins for months at a time.

The walls of the Grants' home contained many hidden secrets. The most evident one, which Teyona still questioned, was why her mother hadn't spoken for years. She could vividly remember having to relay messages, when allowed, through paper or the caregiver. When she was of age to speak full sentences to her mother, Kimberly would either smile or write her a note back to communicate. When she asked her sisters what was wrong, they simply told her, "Mommy is sick." That much was evident.

Teyona wanted to know how and why her mother had gotten sick. Her questions and concerns were the same as Cymone's, which was why Matthew didn't care for her. The moment she thanked her for a good meal and Kimberly only smiled, Cymone asked the others sitting at the table why she didn't speak. No one answered except Matthew, and it wasn't the answer she was expecting.

"You don't come into my house questioning my wife or my family. Enjoy the meal, and be grateful you're sitting at a table with us," Matthew snapped before picking up his fork.

Cymone's mouth hung open as her eyes scanned the table. Mia's head was down, uncomfortably pushing her food around on her plate. Hazel's eyes bore into him with disdain like none other, while Teyona's was filled with embarrassment and regret. She looked toward the only friend she had been able to make and keep and mouthed, 'I'm sorry.'

Thankfully, Cymone didn't scare easily. She spoke her grievances about Matthew to Teyona and kept her distance from the home as much as she could. Teyona hadn't forgiven him for the way he treated her friend. Of course, an apology was never issued either.

They continued their session, and Teyona felt more empowered by the end. Mrs. Morris gave her the same homework from last month, adding an extra assignment.

"Whenever you start to feel like you need validation from your father, I want you to write or type out that you are enough."

"Every time?" Teyona asked.

"Yes. Even when you want to share some good news with him or even speak, and he doesn't acknowledge you, remind yourself that without his acceptance, you are enough."

Teyona inhaled and exhaled loudly. "Okay. I think I can do that."

Mrs. Morris's brow lifted, and Teyona chuckled.

"I *will* do that."

"I know you can, and you will. Today's session was great. Schedule with Lonna for your next one."

Teyona thanked her and exited the office. She felt drained yet lighter than she had an hour prior. Though the pain lingered, a glimmer of understanding was now taking root within her, thanks to Mrs. Morris's empathetic guidance. The journey to self-discovery wouldn't be easy, but she knew it would be worth it.

The weight of her thoughts was no match for the intense craving she now had for an ice cream cone. After any therapy session, good or bad, she treated herself to the creamy dessert. Slipping into the driver's seat, she let out a long exhale and a yawn. Just as she started her engine, her phone vibrated, indicating an incoming call from the culprit behind her stressful days.

Seeing her father's name on display flooded her with anticipation *and* apprehension. She couldn't help but wonder what he wanted. With a hesitant swipe, she answered his call.

"Hey, Daddy," she said, trying to mask the curiosity in her voice.

"Hey, baby girl," Matthew greeted. "You busy?"

Teyona's brows dipped. He hadn't called her that in…she couldn't remember the last time those words greeted her ears. *He wants something*, she thought.

"Um, no. Not at the moment. What's going on?" Teyona asked.

"I know it's last minute, but I need a favor from you."

She was right. He called for one reason and one reason only.

"A friend of mine has a son who's in town and needs a date for a big event this weekend. I owe him a favor and figured you'd like to go. I already set you up an appointment with Sheryl at Vanity for a dress-fitting, and I'm sure you can style your hair nicely."

Teyona sat stupefied by his demands and need for her immediate attention. As he spoke, she felt torn. On one hand, she wanted to maintain the strength she had just found during her session, carving her own path without feeling indebted to him. On the other hand, there was a deep desire to appease him. Maybe then, she could mend the strained relationship that had plagued them for years. Caught in an internal struggle, Teyona found herself wavering, unsure of how to respond.

I am enough.

The little voice in her head wasn't that strong yet. It faded as she quickly made her decision. She mustered up a calm tone, forcing her inner turmoil to diminish.

"Okay, Daddy. I'd love to help you out. Can you send me all of the information?"

"That's my girl," Matthew said. "I'll have my assistant email you all the details."

The smile in his voice made Teyona's day. Deep down, she knew saying yes would likely earn her some fleeting approval from him——perhaps a moment of connection she so desperately needed.

As the call ended and she pulled out into traffic, a sense of unease settled in her stomach. It was a reminder of the delicate balance between familial obligation and personal autonomy that she grappled with daily. Everything she'd just unpacked during her session had been zipped back up in a suitcase with one phone call, and Teyona didn't even realize it. For now, she pushed those daunting thoughts aside, focusing on the road and date for the weekend. She hoped he was at least handsome.

EIGHT

Thankful for an off day, Mia relished the chance to unwind with a glass of her favorite red wine. Slow sips let her savor the rich flavors that danced on her palate. She sat comfortably in a plush armchair by the open window that faced the manmade pond in her backyard. The soft glow and warmth of the late afternoon sunlight were appreciated, providing the perfect backdrop for much-needed relaxation.

She had a day to herself for once, yet her mind wandered. Her past relationship had her questioning everything in her current one, and she couldn't shake the feeling that something was wrong. Mia scrubbed her mind, replaying conversations and situations that occurred during the last five months of knowing each other.

Maybe we moved too quickly, she thought. Then, another thought hit her. *Or he was looking for someone to lean on while going through so much. Am I a placeholder?*

The thought forced her to gulp her wine, clearing the glass. Jarel using her seemed so farfetched, but Mia wouldn't put it past him. Men were men. They got what they wanted from one woman and moved on to the next. She hoped that wasn't the case with

Jarel. He was different. He was attentive in a way that Mia adored. He could also become distant, blanketing her with a coldness she wasn't fond of.

Just as she made up her mind to bring her issues to the forefront, the ringing of her cell phone snapped her out of her zone. Her eyes glanced to where the device sat across the room on her kitchen counter. Her first thought was to leave it there, but with a huff, she stood to retrieve it. Seeing that it was Teyona calling on FaceTime wiped away her pang of guilt for even considering ignoring the call.

"Hey, sis," Mia answered.

"Mia. Oh, my goodness. I'm so glad you answered," Teyona said in a slight panic.

Immediately, Mia became worried. "What's the matter? And why can't I see your face? I'm staring at the ceiling."

When she picked up the phone, Teyona greeted the screen with a gorgeous face of subtle makeup and a head full of loose curls.

"You look so pretty," Mia gushed. "Where are you going?"

"On a date. It's with one of Dad's friends' sons to a charity event dinner. How should I wear my hair?" Teyona asked.

Her sister's rapid response surprised Mia. She wasn't aware they had hashed out whatever problems they had between them. Knowing that's not what her sister called for, Mia got back to the subject at hand.

"Let me see what dress you're wearing," she said.

Teyona shuffled to her massive walk-in closet and flipped her camera around. The black, strapless, midi tube dress with ruffled trimmings at the end was sexy yet still classy. She planned to pair it with black five-inch stilettoes and a gold clutch.

"That dress is cute," Mia acknowledged.

"Thank you. It came from Vanity. Daddy had Sheryl pick me out a few to choose from."

Now Mia had more questions, but she refrained from asking. "That was sweet of her. Part your hair down the middle and let one side drape your shoulder. Show off those shoulders and shimmery neck."

Teyona snickered. "Shoutout to RiRi's body butter for the glow."

"Right." Mia giggled, reminding herself to restock her jar. "So, who is the date with?"

"His name is DeShaun. The mayor's son."

Mia's eyes stretched with curiosity. "Oh."

Teyona stopped what she was doing to stare at the screen. She had propped up the phone on a pile of shoe boxes she needed to organize.

"Oh, what? Please don't tell me anything bad about him," Teyona stressed.

"No, no," Mia reassured. "It's nothing bad. I don't know anything about him. I was just wondering how Daddy managed to link up with the mayor."

Teyona pursed her lips. "Now, you and I both know he knows everybody. What does he always say?"

"I'm respected and well-connected everywhere I go," the sisters said in unison before cracking up.

Matthew would forever remind his daughters of his rank and pull throughout the city and numerous states. He talked as if he were really pushing drugs—no pun intended. Owning a pharmaceutical company allowed him to bump shoulders with the elite, and he wanted his daughters to do the same. He usually reached out to Mia for formal events and outings, but now it was Teyona. Mia couldn't help but wonder how that came about.

"He gets on my nerves, but I love him. He said it's a favor, so I'm going just to enjoy myself," Teyona said.

"I'm sure it'll be over quickly. Does DeShaun have any plans for you guys afterward?"

Teyona smirked. "I hope so. I mean, if he wants to. He's fine, Mia."

She blushed, making her highlighted cheeks lift.

"I know that's right. Send me his information so I can look him up."

"I will. What're you doing? It's your off day," Teyona acknowledged.

She had texted her sisters earlier about wanting to relax for the day and not to bother her. They ignored her anyway and blew up the group chat with sisterly talk like always. Mia didn't mind it. She loved their bond and hoped it never faded.

"I'm just relaxing, waiting for Jarel to come over," Mia said.

"I meant to tell you that I ran into him the other day."

Conflicted, Mia was hesitant with her next words. She already had doubts about their relationship and wasn't sure if she wanted to be proved right.

"Oh, yeah? Where at?" Mia questioned.

"I was leaving my tour of one of the hospitals by my school, and he was walking in. Is everything okay with his sister? That's who he said he was going to see."

Mia moved her face out of view so Teyona couldn't see her frown. From her understanding, his sister was in one of the hospitals in Atlanta, not Athens. Hating that she always tried to see the good in people, she figured they must've moved her. Her gut was telling her otherwise and to seek answers. Truthful ones that didn't pacify her for the moment.

"She's in a coma," Mia voiced.

"Oh no. That's why he was in such a rush. I hope everything is okay."

"Yeah, me too," Mia grumbled.

Jarel was lying about something, and Mia promised herself that today would be the day she figured out what and why.

"I need to finish getting ready, but thank you for helping me," Teyona said.

"You're welcome. Send me pictures of you two. Who knows, he may become your little boo thang," Mia chuckled.

Teyona laughed with her. "He might. I'll be sure to send you pictures."

The call disconnected, and Mia leaned against the countertop. Her oval-shaped French manicured nails tapped against her empty glass as she thought about the words Jarel needed to hear.

"Mia, get it together. You're thirty-four. Do not let this man play in your face. Ask him what you need to ask him, and let it be that," she said aloud.

Before time passed, giving her room to change her mind, the doorbell rang. The resounding chime rattled her nerves. Heavy steps led her through the kitchen and foyer of her massive home. Having a house built from the ground up in her late twenties was an accomplishment she never took lightly.

If only it felt like a home, she thought.

Approaching the door, she exhaled before unlocking it and pulling it open.

"Damn. You look good," Jarel acknowledged.

Mia's hardened expression softened at his words. Her tan two-piece lounge set showed off her toned stomach and subtle curves.

"Thank you," she said as he crossed the threshold.

Pulling her in by the waist, Jarel kissed her neck and hugged her tightly. He smelled divine and looked even better, dressed casually in cargo shorts and a black polo shirt. Mia tried not to let his appearance throw her off her game. It lasted for only a few seconds once she spotted the plastic bag from Target in his hand.

"You brought them," she acknowledged.

"Yeah. You said you wanted a game night, so that's what we're having. I brought some wine, too."

Turning on her heels, Mia smiled. It was going to be hard staying mad when he made it so easy not to be. Making their way to the kitchen, Jarel followed behind her. Removing the games from the bag, he handed her the wine next.

"Should we order pizza and wings? I wasn't in the mood to cook," she said.

Jarel nodded. "Yeah, that's cool. You should've told me. I could've picked some food up on the way here."

"Where were you coming from?" Mia blurted, her eyes glaring at him.

Her question held more meaning than Jarel knew. He reared his head back, confused by her accusatory tone.

"The crib. Why'd you say it like that?"

"Look," Mia exhaled, ready to hash things out. "You've been moving strangely the last few weeks, and I just want to know what's going on. Is there something you need to tell me?"

"Something like what, Mia?"

"Are you cheating on me?" she asked.

Jarel's demeanor didn't change upon hearing her question. He shook his head and walked around the island. Grabbing her hands, he turned Mia toward him. Lovingly, he cupped her face in his hands.

"Baby, you have to get out of your head. No, I'm not cheating on you. What even made you ask me that?"

Mia licked her lips. "The other night when I woke up, you weren't in bed. You said you were getting a drink of water."

"Is that unheard of during the middle of the night?" Jarel asked. "I was thirsty."

Feeling ridiculous for bringing it up, Mia shook her head. "No, but I just… I don't know."

His inconsistencies tugged at Mia's conscience, urging her to confront him about the apparent deception. Yet, hesitancy held her back, coupled with the desire to preserve the semblance of normalcy in their relationship. She couldn't just let it go, though.

"And then my sister told me she saw you at a hospital in Athens visiting your sister. I thought you said she was in Atlanta?" Jarel's eyes glossed over, and Mia's heart sank. *I went too far*, she thought.

"We were thinking about moving her to a new hospital. My family beat me there, and I was rushing in to meet them. Everything going on with my sister has me stressed out, and I forgot to tell you."

Soothingly, Mia rubbed her hand up his arm. "I understand, baby. I was just worried. I'm sorry for even bringing it up. That was selfish of me."

"It's fine. You had suspicions and wanted answers," he said, kissing her forehead.

"I can't imagine the stress your family must be under. If there's anything I can do, let me know," she told him.

Jarel let her know he would and went back to unbagging the games. While Mia had questions, Jarel had a few of his own.

"Speaking of family, how long have you worked for your father?"

"Ever since I graduated college and got my degree. I've been working at the pharmacies for a few years now. Why?"

Jarel smiled. "Just wanting to get to know you a little better. You haven't taken many days off since we've been together, but I can tell you need them. Tell your old man to give you a break."

Mia giggled. "According to him, there are no breaks."

"Do your sisters work there, too?"

His question made Mia's smile drop and her stomach churn.

"Um, no. Well, not yet. I think Teyona plans to work at one soon. Hazel does her own thing."

Jarel nodded. "That's what's up. It takes a lot to keep a family business afloat."

"Yeah, it does," Mia said, clearing her throat. She had to change the subject quickly. "So, what kind of pizza do you want?"

Mia tuned out after he rattled off his preference to her. While placing the delivery order, her head pounded with questions. She knew Jarel wanted to get to know her, but why those specific questions?

I mean, we were talking about work, but what the hell? I need to call Hazel.

She couldn't help but think Jarel was onto them.

Later that night, while Jarel showered, Mia eased out of the bedroom and dialed her sister's number. It was late, but this was Hazel's favorite time of day. The quietness of the night left space for her creativity to run wild.

"Hello," she answered.

Mia could hear the lo-fi music in her background.

"We have to stop," Mia insisted with a hiss.

"What happened now?" Hazel asked with a sigh, placing her brush down.

Peeking over her shoulder, Mia listened to see if the shower was still running. Confirming that it was, she continued.

"I can't lose Jarel behind this. I think…I think he's on to what we've been doing."

"And how the hell would he know that? You're just being paranoid. Did he say something?"

Mia shook her head, though Hazel couldn't see her. "No. Not necessarily. We were chatting about work, and he asked if you or Teyona worked at the pharmacies, too."

"And you made up in your mind that he knows. Is that what you're saying?"

Sighing, Mia leaned against the wall. Jarel had been the best thing to happen in her life in a long time. He was respectful, strait-laced, educated, family-oriented, and adored Mia. Her illegal activities had her looking at him sideways when he should've been the one with the suspicions. Mia didn't want him to think anything less of her, especially after tonight.

My sister needs me, though.

"Yes, but I'm being silly. I thought he was cheating on me, but he's not. I'm just all over the place. And then I'm worried about you," she said, sighing again.

"Please don't worry about me. I'm fine," Hazel urged. "Jarel is a good guy, so don't go fucking it up because you're comparing him to your past. What you need to do is get some dick and then some rest. It's clear the week you had has you tripping."

The sisters giggled. Just then, the shower cut off.

"Shut up," Mia laughed. "But you're right. I'm tripping. I'll call you tomorrow."

"Talk to you later," Hazel said and hung up.

Locking her phone, Mia stepped back inside her bedroom and slid under the covers. The bathroom door opened, and Jarel stepped out with a towel wrapped around his waist. His bare chest, sprinkled with fine hair that led to his bulge, made Mia erase every doubt in her mind about them.

"I was thinking about something in the shower," Jarel said, making her focus shift from his body to his eyes.

"What about?"

She watched as he moisturized his skin and wondered if tonight had changed his mind about them. Mia hoped not.

"I want you to meet some of my family," Jarel said, surprising her.

She tried not to let the elation show on her face.

"Oh, okay," she chirped, clearing her throat.

"A few of them will be in town next weekend," Jarel explained. "We can all go to dinner so they can meet you."

Mia's heart raced as he spoke so casually about meeting them. While the prospect of getting to know them excited her, skepticism washed over her in waves. The suddenness of the invitation left her questioning the timing.

Why now? she pondered, remaining quiet. *Is there a hidden agenda behind his spontaneous gesture?*

"What's the matter?" Jarel asked, noticing the uncertainty on her face.

"N-Nothing. I'm just a little nervous."

Jarel walked over to her, invading her space. "You're an important part of my life and have been here during one of the most difficult times. We're building something solid between us. So, I feel it's only right my family gets to encounter my special lady."

Mia smirked. "You think you're so smooth. Have they asked about me?"

"All the time. They say you've got me gone," Jarel said, kissing up her neck.

Mia's eyes closed in response to the pleasurable sensation.

"And…I can't lie, baby. You do."

Her breath hitched when his hand maneuvered between her legs. Jarel's words instantly turned her on, creating a wetness that his fingers gingerly played in. He was testing her waters, hoping they were on the same page and ready to dive deeper.

"You have nothing to be worried about," he whispered, sealing the invite with a kiss on her lips.

Mia embraced the idea of him wanting to grow closer. There was no way she could tell him no now, especially not when his fingers slipped inside of her. Whatever worries she had would be laid to rest tonight.

Never had Teyona been happier to do a favor for her father. Though she'd gone against everything she learned in therapy, tonight had been worth it. She sat at the table poised and elegant, holding a glass of champagne and inconspicuously watching the guests mingle. Her eyes searched for her date of the evening in the crowd, and it didn't take long to spot him.

DeShaun Hill stood out like a boss among workers. From the moment they entered the ballroom, it was apparent he was someone people loved. They flocked to him in numbers, seeking his attention, wondering where he'd been and who he'd been with. Teyona found it amusing, seeing as though Matthew labeled him a troublemaker. Obviously, it was the good kind of trouble, and she wanted some.

Despite his so-called reputation, there was an intriguing air about him that drew her in. When the Suburban truck pulled up in front of her home, Teyona didn't know what to expect. DeShaun told the driver to stay seated as he got out to open her door. She loved a gentleman who practiced chivalry. Many claimed it was dead, but Teyona didn't think so. If she had, DeShaun was proof it still resided in the good ones…or the bad ones who knew good.

During the ride, they engaged in conversation that flowed smoothly, exchanging witty remarks and subtle glances that hinted at their mutual attraction to each other. DeShaun's mahogany complexion, crisp straight back braids that passed his shoulders, towering height of six-foot-three, and athletic stature made it hard for Teyona to stay on track. Matthew should've never asked her to do him a favor because she wanted to do DeShaun, literally.

Under the bright lights, opulent surroundings, and noisy chatter, Teyona captured his gaze. He winked and said a few more words to the man he was speaking with before walking in her direction. Teyona picked up her flute, hoping it would help shield her hungry eyes. His tailored suit matched the color of her dress. The jacket was unbuttoned, showing a crisp white button-up and his trim waist. Teyona just knew he had an eight-pack in hiding.

"That glass can't disguise the way you keep eye-fucking me," DeShaun whispered in her ear once he sat down.

Teyona choked on a laugh of embarrassment. "Excuse me? I was doing no such thing."

Her feigned innocence made DeShaun grin and his dick hard. He could see it all in her eyes that she wanted him. He wanted her, too, but now for other reasons than he planned. The good girl fake-dating the bad boy for an appearance wasn't going to work for him.

Draping an arm over her chair, he leaned into her and said, "Yeah? What you call it then?"

Teyona wanted to answer him, but the smell of his cologne, which she'd fallen in love with upon first sniff, made her head fuzzy and her nipples tingle. His warm breath against her ear wasn't helping either.

"I was just watching you fake like you were interested in whatever that man was talking about," Teyona replied.

"I was interested in getting back over here to you. You made tonight bearable."

She swooned but quickly checked herself.

"Glad I could help," she offered, shifting in her seat.

Taking the hint, DeShaun put some distance between their bodies but kept his arm where it was.

"This was a favor, huh?" he questioned.

Teyona nodded. "Yep. What'd my dad owe yours?"

"Fuck if I know," DeShaun scoffed. "Knowing them, it was probably some shady dealings. All he ever wanna do is make it seem like we're this perfect family. Yeah, right."

With pursed lips, Teyona picked up her glass and drained it. She couldn't agree more.

"Tell me about it."

He couldn't help but wonder if she harbored the same grievances toward her father as he did his. DeShaun wouldn't put it past her. Being the child of such prominent men in the community came with responsibilities neither of them wanted.

For instance, attending charity events for the youth, knowing that money was being placed elsewhere.

"Nah, you go first," DeShaun encouraged.

Teyona side-eyed him. "Right here?"

"Yeah. Not unless you trying to go somewhere else. We can ditch this shit for real. It'll be over in like an hour."

She considered it but quickly decided to stay. If her father heard she left the event early, all her efforts to make him proud would have been pointless. Knowing him, he probably had eyes on her to make sure she didn't leave. Plus, being out with DeShaun would keep her mind off of the eerie week she had. Another note appeared on her windshield that read, *It can only be a secret for so long.* Someone had to be playing a prank on her, so she brushed it off…at least for now.

"I only agreed to be your date because I wanted to please my dad," Teyona said with a heavy sigh. "Pathetic, right?"

"Yeah," DeShaun said, making her jerk away from him.

She wasn't expecting him to callously agree with her.

"Damn. Tell me how you really feel," Teyona hissed.

"Pathetic 'cause I'm on the same shit," he offered.

Teyona simmered down and relaxed her back against the chair. She didn't know where he was going with the conversation at first, but now she was even more intrigued. They already had a strong connection, and she wondered if their childhoods had been similar.

"So you didn't want to be here tonight? The crowd seems to love you," she surmised.

"I'm a college athlete. They love me for the player I am and who I'm connected to. They couldn't give a fuck less about DeShaun Hill, the man."

His voice held a degree of anger that tugged at Teyona's heart. She wanted to know the man he spoke of, to peel back the layers of who he was without the titles.

"I'd like to get to know the real you," Teyona said.

DeShaun smirked and shook his head. "Nah. I'm a fuck-up."

"And I'm a fuck-up fixer."

That got a laugh out of him. His dimples denting his chocolate cheeks was another trait of his that Teyona was growing to love. With ease, he had made an impression on her and didn't have to try hard.

"My dad might need to hire you then."

"No disrespect, but hell no. I already feel like I work for mine. I'll pass."

DeShaun glanced her way. "That bad?"

"Worse," Teyona said, facing straight ahead. "I had no idea who he was setting me up with," she said, wanting to change the subject.

"Had to do your research, huh?"

Teyona nodded. "Yep. I judged you at first. I didn't think we'd have anything in common."

DeShaun chuckled as he nodded to someone across the room. "No sugarcoating shit. I like that. What's the verdict on me now?"

Teyona was still trying to feel him out, but the articles she read online hadn't deterred her from a good night. Although DeShaun had gotten into some trouble away at school for having a gun, Teyona didn't see anything wrong with that. He was using it as protection, but of course, when your father is the mayor, people don't see it that way.

Outside of the news articles, Teyona had found herself scrolling his Instagram and searching his name on Twitter. She gathered that he was a well-known basketball star with a roster of women whom he didn't seem to settle down with. Teyona hated the rabbit hole she fell down reading the tweets, but had she not, she would've had a wall up all night. She thought he would be a weird, preppy kid whose dad wanted her to help him get out of his shell. Teyona had nothing against those types of guys, but she wasn't the woman for that particular job.

"You're different," she answered, and DeShaun glanced her way.

"What else?"

His question was spoken with authority and curiosity, making Teyona eager to answer him.

"And nothing could've prepared me for you. You're…a lot. In a good way."

She bit her bottom lip, bowing her head. DeShaun scooted his body back closer to hers.

"So everything you read about me didn't run you off?"

"No," she breathed, feeling flustered.

"That's too bad. I like runners. They give me something to chase."

His words were whispered way too sexually, and Teyona couldn't handle it. She was beyond ready to leave now. DeShaun and all his bad-boy energy could take her wherever; as long as she was with him, she didn't care where they went. Teyona just knew he had the girls at his school going crazy. He was a beast on the court, and she could only imagine how he performed in bed.

When a man and woman came to speak to him, Teyona wanted to thank them. She needed to put some space between them for a few minutes. When she stood, DeShaun stopped his conversation.

"You sneaking away?" he joked, making her smirk.

"I'm sure you'd love that, but no. Going to the restroom. I'll be right back."

DeShaun nodded and kept his eyes on her as she walked off. She wanted to turn around and catch him staring, but she kept forward. With her silver clutch in her hand, Teyona navigated through the crowd. She spotted a few familiar faces and waved, but it didn't stop her strides. They'd have to catch up when she returned from the ladies' room.

Her steps quickened as she approached the door. A restroom attendant stood outside, ready to be of service if needed. Teyona gave her a gracious smile before entering. The smell of lavender and linen graced her nose as she pushed open the door to a stall. With expert flexibility, she unzipped her dress, carefully lowering it to relieve herself. Squatting, she handled her business and rezipped her dress. After washing her hands, applying some hand lotion from her clutch, and making sure her hair and makeup were intact, she exited.

"Oh. I'm sorry. Excuse me," Teyona said to a woman who was coming in.

When she noticed who it was, her face lit up.

"Mrs. Marie. It's so good to see you," she said, greeting one of her mama's old friends.

The women hugged, embracing each other like long-lost family members. Mrs. Marie's eyes pricked with tears as she pulled back, taking Teyona in.

"My gosh, Teyona. You're gorgeous, honey. How have you been?"

"Thank you. I've been good. In school to be a nurse," Teyona said proudly.

They scooted off to the side so they wouldn't be in the way.

"I'm so happy to hear that. I always knew you'd grow up to be amazing, just like your mother. How is she, by the way?"

"She's doing good. She'll be happy to know I ran into you."

Mrs. Marie smiled somberly. "Yeah, I hope so. Our friendship ended on rocky terms. Does she still write in those journals?"

Teyona gave her a puzzled expression. "Um, I'm not sure. I'll have to ask her."

"She's the reason I was able to start my journal company and help the youth. Getting those thoughts out on paper truly does help your mental."

"Do you have a business card? I'd love to support you."

"Of course. One second," she said, going inside her purse. "Here you go."

Teyona stuffed it inside her clutch. "Thank you. It was so good to see you. Maybe one day you and my mom can mend your relationship."

Mrs. Marie smiled, but it didn't reach her eyes. They were sad, leading Teyona to wonder what happened between them.

"I think that ship has sailed, but she'll always be in my prayers."

Teyona stood there for a few seconds, letting Mrs. Marie's words marinate. She always wondered why she didn't see any of her mother's friends around anymore, especially when she was younger. It wasn't noticeable until she was about five or six, and she no longer saw any familiar faces throughout the home. Her aunt Nicole would be there most of the time, but she even stopped coming around.

And what journals was she talking about? Teyona thought as she approached the table.

DeShaun was still in his seat, texting on his phone, but locked it when she sat down. Teyona wondered what he had planned for the rest of the evening. She wasn't blind to the fact that multiple young women had approached him throughout the night.

"You good?" he questioned.

Teyona nodded. "Yep. You?"

"Yeah, I'm straight." He leaned close to her ear, causing Teyona to suck in a sharp breath. "You look good as fuck tonight. Wearing the hell out of that dress. I know this was a favor for your pops, but I'ma have to personally thank him for letting me borrow you for the evening."

Teyona shuddered. She didn't know what type of spell DeShaun was trying to put her under, but it was working. All she could do was lick her lips and grin. She, too, was going to have to thank Matthew. For once, she felt like he deserved it.

As the night came to an end, Mayor Hill approached them by the exit. Teyona immediately felt DeShaun tense beside her. Taking her by surprise, he took her hand in his.

"Son, leaving so soon?" he asked.

DeShaun nodded. "Yeah. Gotta get my date home at a respectable time."

Mayor Hill set his eyes on Teyona. He was clad in a navy blue suit that made his hazel eyes pop. DeShaun's were the same hue. He was tall like him, too, sporting a salt-and-pepper curly low haircut with a beard to match. He stuck his hand out, and Teyona used her free one to greet him.

"Lovely young lady, thank you for accompanying my son tonight. He didn't give you any trouble, did he?"

Teyona smirked as DeShaun scoffed.

"Not at all. He was the perfect gentleman," she answered.

"That's what I like to hear," he said as a photographer approached them. "Let's capture a few photos."

DeShaun looked at Teyona. "You good with that?"

She nodded. "Sure. I don't mind. Just don't be telling people I'm your girl," she joked.

He smirked and pulled her closer to him. "Not yet."

They snapped a few pictures. Teyona knew her phone was going to be blowing up once the images were posted online, but that was okay with her.

"Enjoy the rest of your evening," Mayor Hill told her before pinning his eyes on his son. "DeShaun, meet me at the house in the morning so we can debrief."

His voice was stern, lacking all the passion he had when speaking to Teyona. She found that odd but realized he and her father were more alike than she thought. Matthew often spoke to her in the same dry manner.

"Yeah," he grumbled.

As Mayor Hill walked off, Teyona couldn't help but whisper, "Debrief? Are you his secretary?"

Her joke wiped the scowl off DeShaun's face. He laughed as they headed out the door. Their driver for the evening was waiting outside of the truck.

"That's how he be acting. Like I need to check in with him every time I make a move. Shit is annoying."

At least he cares, Teyona thought, keeping her words to herself.

DeShaun opened the back door for her, then helped her climb in. Removing his suit jacket, he slid in beside her and closed the door. Sitting back, he undid a few top buttons of his shirt, revealing a single gold chain. He sighed, and Teyona caught a glimpse of his tattoos as they passed under the street lighting.

She licked her lips, contemplating her words. "I enjoyed my night."

"Did you expect not to?"

"Honestly, I wasn't sure. Most of these events are boring. A bunch of fake smiles, laughs, and horrible food."

DeShaun chuckled. "You ain't lying. This one was cool, though. I love seeing the youth go after their dreams."

"Did you always want to be a basketball player?" Teyona asked, interested in his life.

"Nah, not always. I was just good at it, and my dad thought keeping me busy would keep me out of trouble. So, here I am."

He was pleasing his father.

"Well, at least you're good at it. It'd suck if you were a shitty player," she expressed.

DeShaun smirked. "You right about that. What about you? What you in school for?"

"Nursing."

He let out a low whistle. "I know that's hard. Salute to you."

"Thank you. I still have some years to go, but that's fine."

"What made you wanna get into that field?"

She peered out the window, unsure of how much she should share. Her heart suddenly became heavy with her reasoning why, but she wasn't ashamed. DeShaun felt like someone she could trust.

"My mom was always sick when I was younger. As a little kid, I wanted to take care of her and make her feel better, but I never knew how. I promised that when I got old enough to go to college, I would become a nurse and be able to look after her no matter what."

"Damn," DeShaun breathed, impressed like hell. "That's admirable of you. Is she still sick?"

"No, but the mission still stands."

He nodded, finding himself liking her even more. Had DeShaun not been burdened by his father's relentless expectations and desire for him to be perfect, he would've chosen another career path. Aside from hooping, he was obtaining a degree in business and administration. It'd always come in handy, regardless of the career he chose after graduating.

A wave of sadness hit Teyona as they pulled into her neighborhood. It invaded her senses, making her realize she didn't want their night to end. Their shared experiences forged a bond in a short amount of time. It transcended the superficiality of the initial favor, making Teyona want to confide in him more.

DeShaun felt the same. Despite their different backgrounds, he was drawn to her in such an uncanny way that he was ready to extend his stay at home. That never happened. Their family dynamics' complexities gave them a newfound sense of understanding. Underneath all the glitz and glamour were two souls trying to find their way and break free from the shadows cast by their fathers.

Teyona exhaled once the SUV parked in front of her home. DeShaun told the driver he could stay in the car. He exited and helped Teyona out, leading her to her front door. She peered up at him, trying to read his expression, but fell short.

"Thank you for tonight," she said as if he did her a favor.

"It's nothing. Glad to be of service," he joked. "Thank you, too. For real."

Teyona smirked. "You're welcome. Do you want to come in?"

He licked his lips, and she knew he was about to say yes.

"Nah. Don't wanna turn the good girl bad," he said, smirking.

"I can't be good forever."

Leaning forward, she kissed his lips before he could respond. DeShaun's tongue slid into her mouth as he gripped her around the waist. His lips were soft, just like she imagined them to be. When he pulled away, Teyona groaned lowly. The kiss ended too quickly for her liking, but she was glad one of them had some self-control.

DeShaun smiled, licking his lips…savoring her taste. "Goodnight, pretty."

Teyona blushed. "Goodnight."

She entered her home and locked the door behind her. Smiling, she held a hand over her racing heart. Teyona wanted him to stay the night for more reasons than one. DeShaun had gotten her mind off of the reason they met, and he seemed like he wouldn't mind protecting her. Not just her heart but all of her.

With a potential stalker leaving her notes and lurking somewhere, she didn't want to be alone. Telling her family, especially her father, would only make her feel like she had done something wrong. So, she kept the notes to herself. It was clear she wasn't the only person in the family with secrets.

NINE

The words on Hazel's MacBook screen were starting to blur, and her eyes burned. For hours, she'd been on Google searching for any information that would link her parents to a murder. She wasn't exactly sure what or who she was looking for, but she was too invested. For the man who entered her home to make such a drastic claim, he had to have more proof than some pictures.

Once she finally sat back and thought about it, the people in those photos could've been anyone. Photoshop was a thing. If her parents had committed such a crime, shouldn't they have been in jail? Then, she wondered what it was her mother had that the man wanted.

For days, Hazel didn't bother to leave her loft. Plagued with stress and an overwhelming sense of trying to figure out what the hell was going on, she stayed locked away. She hadn't picked up a paintbrush in three days, and her curtains had remained closed. Karter continuously asked her what was wrong, but she didn't let him in on what had happened. Until she could put some things together that made sense to her, Hazel wasn't uttering a word. The only place she knew she could get answers from was the source itself: her mother.

"I can't just walk in there and ask her if she and Daddy murdered someone," she muttered.

Slamming her MacBook closed, Hazel stood from her round glass table and stretched. She wouldn't come right out and ask, but she could snoop around the house for clues.

Just as she stepped inside her room to get dressed, her phone rang. Her movements halted, and the hair on her arms stood up. The anticipation of hearing from the man with more information had her on edge. Noticing it was one of her regular customers calling, she exhaled and picked up.

"Yeah?"

"Hey, are you free to meet me in like thirty minutes?"

Hazel checked the time. "Sure."

"Oh, um, do you have any of those weight loss pills still? I want to try them out."

"Mhm. How many?"

The girl told her the quantity, and they hung up. Hazel wasn't sure about the side effects of the pill called Abnazol, but it obviously was working. It was going crazy on the streets. She had sold the same amount of it as she did the other pills. On a good month, she had to ask Mia for more. Speaking of her sister, Hazel made a mental reminder to drop by and check on her. Mia's call to her a few nights ago didn't sit well in her spirit, but she didn't have time to think about Jarel. She had bigger fish to fry.

After getting dressed, she drove to the other side of town to meet her customer. With the stash she was collecting, Hazel was sure she would be able to purchase an art studio in no time.

Back-to-back customers called before she could make the drive to her parents' house. When she finally arrived, she parked her jeep in the back, hopped out, and used her key to enter the side entrance. The house was quiet, which wasn't unusual. It was a weekday, and Matthew wasn't home. Had he been, Hazel wouldn't have made the trip. Taking the steps to the second level, she knocked on her mother's bedroom door.

"Come in," Kimberly called out.

Her face lit up when she saw her second oldest. After Hazel left the dinner table that evening, Kimberly had only heard from her through a few text messages.

"Hey, Mama."

"Oh no. Something must've happened for you to be here visiting me," she joked.

The two embraced, and Kimberly hugged her tight.

"Don't be like that. What're you in here doing?"

Hazel took in her mother's bedroom and felt at peace. It was so serene with cream, gold, and white decorations. The California king bed sat in the middle of the room, while a huge vanity sat to the right of it. Hazel could remember always sneaking to play in her mother's makeup or sitting on the bed and drawing her while Kimberly did hers. It was back when life was easier... so she thought.

"I just got off the phone with your auntie. Probably about to go to the study and read a book. What're you doing over this way?"

Kimberly eyed her daughter, sensing the heaviness she was carrying. She wouldn't force her to divulge, though.

"I needed to get out of the house, so I figured I'd come and see you. It's nice outside. We should go for a walk. Do you like being cooped up in here?"

Giggling, Kimberly shrugged. "It's fine. I'm used to it."

Those four words caused a pang of anger and hurt to surge through Hazel.

"That's the problem," she mumbled.

"What was that?"

"You shouldn't be okay with feeling like you're trapped here, Mama."

Kimberly placed down the brush she was using to put her hair in a ponytail. "Is that what you think I feel like?" Hazel nodded. "Yes. Why haven't you left him? He's not good to you."

Seeing her daughter's eyes swell with tears broke Kimberly's heart. The immense amount of love Hazel had for her mother wouldn't just let her sit idly by and keep her feelings at bay. Her father was an asshole and had been for years now. His controlling ways disgusted her. That's why she didn't come around. He held no power over her, and Matthew hated it.

"Oh, honey," Kimberly said, taking Hazel's hands into hers. "It's not that easy. Your father and I have been together for a long time."

"So what? You don't even like him," Hazel grumbled.

Kimberly snickered. "I like him some days."

"And that's not how marriage should be."

"You're not going to always like your spouse or the things they do, Hazel. That's not realistic."

Kimberly sighed. She wasn't prepared to have this conversation, but it looked like it would take place anyway. Hazel had a lot on her mind and needed to get it off.

"I know that, but he's taken you through so much. He's the reason you were sick."

Dropping her hands, Kimberly turned away from her. "Don't say that."

Her voice was low and her words strained as if she couldn't bear hearing Hazel speak that way. Hazel sat down next to her on the plush bench.

"It's the truth, Mama. It's been years, and you're better now. You don't have to hide anything from me," Hazel urged.

What Kimberly did hide, Hazel heard throughout her childhood. The arguments turned one-sided after she was diagnosed with aphasia. It's as if Matthew turned into another man. They'd heard him fuss and curse out folks regarding business, but he never raised his voice at their mother, who had difficulty speaking and processing others' words for years. It hurt Hazel like no other, especially when their aunt Nicole explained the cause of it all.

To those on the outside looking in, Kimberly's fall was an accident. Hazel wasn't convinced and hadn't been since she was eight. Her love, respect, and perception of her father hadn't been the same since. To her, his image was all a façade, and no one could see it.

"I never wanted our family to be as strained as we are," Kimberly expressed sadly. "When I was diagnosed with aphasia, I couldn't understand what was happening. Everyone around me seemed to talk at me, not to me. A lot of them, especially your father, would speak for me. Because I couldn't verbalize how I was feeling, they talked down on me or ignored me. It was easier for me just to be quiet and out of the way."

Years ago, Kimberly wouldn't have been able to speak those words without crying. She had to show her daughter she was strong and always had been, especially for them. It took some time, care, and patience to return to this place.

"But that was never you," Hazel said. "You'd always been so outspoken and brightened any room you stepped into."

Kimberly smiled, loving how her daughter picked up on her personality traits even as a little girl.

"Trauma changes you, baby. It makes you become a shell of the person you've grown to be. Everything around you begins to look different, even the people you once knew. Not being able to talk or understand people was frustrating, but it showed me people's true selves. When you don't have the words or the way to connect one dot in your brain to another, you start to question your existence. I didn't know who I was anymore. Not a woman, a friend, a sister, a wife, or a mother."

Hazel sniffled, trying her best to conceal her tears. She'd never heard her mother express how she felt or what she had gone through.

"Seeing you girls' confusion every day was just like mine," she sadly chuckled. "Y'all didn't know what was going on, and neither did I."

Kimberly's mind drifted to the brutal moments during her healing phase. She felt so lonely, and Matthew didn't help cure the feeling. He only intensified it, leaving Kimberly to easily put herself in a box.

It was year three after her injury, and Kimberly's speech hadn't improved much, but she was trying. She missed her old life, her friends, and her job. Though she didn't have to work, Kimberly loved being a professor. She missed it more than ever. The days of taking her girls to the park, helping them with their homework, and asking how their day went were long gone.

"Would you like a cup of tea?" Rachel, the speech therapist, asked Kimberly slowly.

She nodded her head.

"She doesn't even like tea," Matthew insisted. "Why would you tell her you want a cup of tea when you drink coffee?"

Kimberly's head turned his way. Though her words made sense in her head, they didn't come out as quickly from her mouth. Her disorder required patience from others, something many people, including her husband, didn't possess.

"Remember, her brain processes words differently from ours. Just because she answered yes, it doesn't mean that's what she meant," Rachel reminded him.

Matthew scoffed. "If she'd use her damn words, we'd understand."

"No need to get frustrated. Imagine how she feels."

Rachel had worked with many families whose loved ones suffered a stroke or brain injury. Her mission was to improve their ability to communicate, no matter how long it took. Getting the family or caregivers to grasp the concept that the person with aphasia has to relearn everything was difficult. Not every person fully recovered and went back to speaking fluently, but some did.

"Do you like coffee?" Rachel asked, being sure to speak slowly.

Kimberly opened her mouth to speak but quickly closed it. She glanced at Matthew, who had a scowl on his face. Feeling overwhelmed, Kimberly glanced around their kitchen. Spotting the pot of coffee on the warmer from earlier, she pointed to it. Rachel's eyes followed where she was pointing, and she smiled.

"So, coffee. That's good you are using your hands. Mr. Grant, hand gestures are another way she can communicate with you."

"You can call me Matthew," he said with a bit too much charm in his voice.

The smile he gave her made Rachel shift uncomfortably in her seat and clear her throat. Sensing something was wrong, Kimberly looked at her husband.

"Don't…um, y-you—"

"Don't what, huh? You can't even get your words out. You'd be better off not speaking at all. Especially to me."

Rachel gasped as Kimberly's eyes watered. His hateful words restricted her breathing, forcing her to stand from her chair and rush off abruptly.

"Mr. Grant, that was uncalled for and highly disrespectful. Your wife is trying her best, and as her husband, you should be her strongest support system," Rachel fussed.

Matthew smirked. "I should?"

"Yes, you should."

"We wouldn't be in this predicament had it not been for my wife's behavior. So, excuse me if my efforts aren't enough," he said, standing from the table.

He started to walk out of the kitchen but turned around. "And make this your last day coming here. You're fired."

Rachel couldn't believe what had just happened. She shed a few tears as she gathered her belongings and left the home. Kimberly was seemingly stuck in a situation where her husband determined her improvement. She felt ill for her but didn't know what to do. Kimberly felt the same.

Warm tears coated Kimberly's cheeks as she stood in front of her bathroom mirror. Jumbled thoughts swam around in her head, but she couldn't get them to formulate sentences that made sense. Matthew had reached a low that bruised not only her ego but her heart, as well. It was bleeding with no signs of stopping.

"Mama," Hazel's sweet voice called out from the door.

Kimberly glanced her way and quickly dapped her face with a towel. She waved her inside.

"I drew you a picture," Hazel said, handing her the drawing.

Kimberly's eyes lit up. The picture was of her, Mia, Teyona, Kimberly, and a dog they didn't have at the park. It was so detailed that it brought on another round of tears from Kimberly. These were happy ones. Hazel remembered one of the therapists recommending drawings to help with communication, and she would draw at least two pictures daily for Kimberly.

"That's our dog in the future," Hazel pointed out.

Grinning, Kimberly hugged her and kissed her cheek. Reaching for a piece of paper, she wrote her response. The words gradually came to her in a slow manner, but it felt better to get them out by pen than by mouth.

"Thank you," Hazel said, reading her scribbled words. "You're welcome, Mama. I love you even if you can't talk, but I know you will again one day."

Those were the words Kimberly wanted to hear from her husband, but she was glad her daughter said them. Since Matthew didn't want to hear her voice, Kimberly vowed never to speak to him again if she didn't have to.

The memory unlocked a time that Kimberly thought she would never grow through. Thankfully, she'd made a full recovery. There were instances where certain words were hard for her to pronounce, but she practiced them. She didn't let her language disorder control her life anymore; she controlled it.

"What happened to you is where I got my love for drawing," Hazel told her.

"I know. If there was one good thing that came from it, it was you finding your passion and purpose." Kimberly smiled and asked, "Are you still thinking about getting your studio?"

Hazel nodded. "Yes. It's just taking a bit longer than I'd like, but it's fine."

"How much is it?"

"No, Mama," she said, shaking her head. "I don't want you to give me money."

"You're my child."

She laughed. "Yes, your grown child who wants to do this on her own. Is that okay with you?"

Kimberly pinched her cheek. "I guess it is. Thank you."

"For what?" Hazel's brows furrowed.

"For always being you and loving me no matter what."

Hazel's bottom lip poked out. "Awww, Mama. Don't make me cry."

"I'm serious, Hazel. I know you're grown and capable of making your own decisions, but always remember who you are. Whatever life throws your way, don't let it turn you into someone you don't want to be or recognize when you look in the mirror."

Nodding, Hazel said, "I won't."

"Good. Was there something else you needed to get off your mind?" Kimberly asked, hoping she would open up.

Out of all her daughters, Hazel challenged her the most—not in an argumentative way, but in a way Kimberly wished she knew how to get through. Hazel had things she kept bottled up, but today's conversation was the start of her twisting the cap.

"There was something else, but I can't think of it now."

Hazel knew what she wanted to ask her, but after the conversation they just shared, she didn't want to overwhelm her mother. Asking about a murder that may or may not have been true would surely trigger her.

"Well, when you remember, you know where I am," Kimberly said, kissing her cheek. "Make sure you eat something today."

Hazel laughed. "What're you trying to say?"

"Nothing that your stomach hasn't already said," Kimberly said, snickering. "Close my door on your way out."

Hazel didn't realize she hadn't eaten anything but a bagel until her mother pointed it out. She planned to scrounge through their fridge and pantry for goodies to take home with her. What was the use in stopping by if she didn't take a parting gift? After heading down the steps, Hazel paused. Her initial plan was to get information out of her mother, but that didn't happen. Though she got a better understanding of Kimberly, that's not what she was there for.

She glanced up the steps and then down the hall where Matthew's office was. She knew her mother never went inside it and wouldn't decide to do so today. He'd made it clear that it was off-limits, but Hazel was about to change that. She walked slowly down the hall and took a deep breath before opening the door. Quietly, she stepped inside and left the door cracked so she could hear anyone approaching.

The air seemed to drastically change as she took in her surroundings. It was charged with a mix of curiosity and apprehension. If she found something, anything, she'd be happy, but the other part of her was scared. Finding out secrets not meant to be found out was dangerous.

Her eyes swept the massive room, which held an aura of mystery. Drawers were neatly aligned, and shelves were stacked with files and books. Everything seemed to be meticulously organized, reflecting Matthew's disciplined nature. The house cleaner was the cause of the neatness. Hazel wasn't there to admire the orderliness, though. She needed to uncover secrets if any existed.

Her eyes landed on his desk, which seemed out of place with its scattered papers and envelopes everywhere. He spent hours engrossed in work there, so she knew there had to be something worth looking for. Hazel's heart raced as she pulled open drawers, fumbling through manilla folders. She bypassed a bunch of paperwork for Grant Pharmacy and mundane papers, coming up empty-handed. Exhaling, she moved onto the top of his desk. She would've tried to go through his desktop but didn't want to lock the computer.

While shifting through the piles of papers on his desk, Hazel's breath hitched when she came across a letter from the bank. It was issuing a new credit card but didn't have Matthew's name on it. The name was one Hazel didn't recognize, one that certainly didn't belong to her mother or any immediate woman of the family.

"Who the hell is this?" Hazel mumbled.

Confusion gripped her momentarily, and then a sinking realization dawned. Matthew was living a double life. The assumption wasn't farfetched considering the type of man he was. But a cheater? Hazel needed more proof. Quickly, she pulled out her phone and texted Mia.

What's Dad's assistant's name?

So far removed from her father's business, Hazel had no clue who was who or what roles they played. The room's silence amplified the sound of her racing heartbeat as she held the credit card. Waiting for Mia to reply had her on edge, and she scrutinized whether the plastic card held all or some of the answers to her question.

It's Daniel. Why?

Thanks! Hazel replied and locked her phone.

She couldn't tell Mia what she'd been up to just yet. This new information may not have meant anything, but she wasn't sure yet. Just in case it did, she was going to keep it to herself. Infidelity was an accusation she didn't want to throw around. A part of her yearned for an explanation—a reasonable excuse to absolve him and her mother of any wrongdoings.

Before she placed the paper back in its rightful place, Hazel snapped a picture of the front of the card. With heavy breaths, she stood and exited the office. Her thoughts were all over the place, with conflicting emotions. Confronting Matthew would be more of a risk than she was willing to take, especially for her family's sake. This would put the nail in the coffin.

Hazel couldn't ignore her findings and pretend she never stumbled upon them. Her loyalty to her mother wouldn't let her. She had to do some research. The weight of this unknown person weighed on her heavier than any pills she sold, and she refused to let the fear of the unknown paralyze her. Being blackmailed was much more terrifying. For better or for worse, the truth awaited her somewhere, and Hazel was determined to uncover it no matter how devastating it might be.

TEN

The day had finally come for Mia to meet some of Jarel's family, and her nerves were bubbling over. She'd had all week to prepare, yet the time did nothing to settle her nervousness. At her age, you would think preparing for a date to meet her man's family was normal, but it wasn't. Mia felt so far removed from the dating game that she struggled with the new playing field.

"I need you to calm down," Angel, one of Mia's dear friends, instructed via FaceTime.

She laughed, trying to mask her jitters. "I'm trying to. I don't know what to expect, so my mind is all over the place. I can't shake this nervousness for anything."

"It's completely natural to have that feeling. Meeting the family is a big step in any relationship, but you can't compare this to your last."

Mia sighed, knowing she was right. She'd been reiterating the same sentiments all month.

"I'm not," she said.

"Good." Angel smiled. "This is something fresh."

"What if they don't like me?" Mia asked.

"You're not going there to impress them. Be yourself. I've never seen you like this. Do you love him?"

Mia pondered her question before saying, "Is it too soon?"

"Awww, friend," Angel cooed. "There's no time limit on what our hearts feel. That's why you're a nervous wreck."

She chuckled. "Yeah. Ridiculous."

"No, it's normal. Have you told him yet?"

Mia shook her head. "Not yet. I don't want to run him off. I'll see how today goes and then go from there."

"Good. You're speaking some positivity. Trust me, they're going to love you. Jarel fell for the sweet, loving person you are, and his family will see that, too. You have nothing to be worried about. Now, finish getting ready. Turn on some jams and try to relax."

"Thank you, Angel. I'll let you know how it goes."

Despite Angel's comforting words, those annoying butterflies continued to flutter in her stomach after they hung up. The thought of making a good impression on Jarel's family had her second-guessing every aspect of herself. Shaking her nerves as best as she could, she finished getting dressed.

For once, Mia used some of her PTO for the day. She wanted to give Jarel's family her undivided attention without having to leave early for work. It was something she would've never considered in the past, but change was good. She was adjusting to her relationship, and that thought alone made her smile. With her mood lifted, she turned up Cleo Sol on the speaker and waited for Jarel's arrival.

As the car hummed along the familiar streets, Mia stared out the window. She drank a glass of wine before leaving the house to calm her nerves. It helped some, along with Jarel's soothing touch. He held her hand as he drove, stealing glances at her when given the chance.

"You over there looking like I asked for your hand in marriage," he joked as they stopped at a red light.

His handsome smile did little to quell her nerves.

Mia chuckled. "At least I'd already know the family by then."

"True. You don't have anything to be nervous about. My cousins are chill. You look good, too. I tell you that?"

She blushed and nodded her head. "Mhm. But thank you again."

After trying on four outfits, Mia finally settled on a nude short-sleeved button-up, denim skinny jeans, and black Michael Costello heels. Her makeup was subtle, her lips matching her shirt, and her bob was lightly curled. It was a casual outfit for a lunch date, and she hoped the food was good. She didn't have an appetite, but it'd give her a distraction just in case the vibes weren't right.

Jarel gave her hand a gentle squeeze before bringing it to his lips for a kiss. She appreciated his silent reassurance. With everything he'd been going through and her apprehensiveness about them, Jarel still made time to show her that she meant something to him. She glanced his way, noticing his unwavering confidence, and wished she could borrow just a fraction of it. He didn't seem nervous at all, knowing the timing was right.

As they pulled into the parking lot of *Murphy's*, Mia exhaled. She had heard great things about the restaurant, particularly the service and drinks, so that caused some ease. The parking lot was filled with cars, but thankfully, Jarel had made reservations. Finding a parking space near the entrance, Jarel backed in and parked. He climbed out and walked around to Mia's side to help her out. After adjusting her shirt, she placed her YSL purse on her shoulder.

"You ready?" Jarel asked.

Mia smiled. "Yes."

He kissed her cheek and grabbed her hand, leading them to the door. Jarel let the hostess know their party should already be seated. He didn't let Mia know how many of his cousins would be in attendance today, but as they approached the square table and she spotted two people, she exhaled.

Okay. Two cousins aren't bad. At least it's not a table full.

The man stood, and he and Jarel embraced. "Relly Rel," he joked as they slapped hands.

Jarel smirked. "Don't start, man."

The woman beside him waved, and Jarel bent to hug her. "What's going on, Sharon?"

"Not much. Hi, I'm Sharon," she said, introducing herself.

She stuck her hand out, and Mia nervously shook it. "Hi, I'm Mia."

"Let me get around to the introductions," Jarel said with a chuckle while pulling out her chair.

The two sat, and he commenced with the greetings.

"Ricky, Sharon, this is my lady, Mia. Mia, these two are my favorite cousins."

Sharon sucked her teeth. "Your favorite for now. Don't let him lie to you. There's a bunch of us, so he tells us all that."

Mia chuckled. "It's nice to meet you both. Is this your first time in Atlanta?"

She found herself asking the question with ease, feeling no nervousness. Her openness was due to Sharon's welcoming personality and warm smile.

"No. We've been here a few times. You from here?" Ricky asked.

"Yes. Born and raised."

Sharon blew out a breath. "Whew. I couldn't do it. How do you deal with the traffic?" she asked in a whisper, making Mia laugh.

"I'm used to it, but trust me, it can be a migraine some days."

A waitress came over to take their drink orders. Though she was grown, Mia didn't want to ask for a glass of wine and seem like a lush, especially with it being the middle of the day. Mia hadn't gotten a chance to look at the menu, so she asked for a glass of water. The rest of the party placed their drink orders, with Jarel adding an appetizer of fried calamari to start them off.

Their drinks were brought out, and the appetizer was served shortly after. Mia chewed on the tender, perfectly cooked squid and politely smiled as she listened to the cousins catch up. Her introduction to them wasn't going as badly as she thought it would.

"So, Mia, how did you two meet?" Sharon asked.

Jarel leaned back in his seat and shook his head with a smirk. "You don't have to answer that."

Chuckling, Mia sipped some of her water. "No, it's okay. It was actually all by accident."

"Is that right?" Ricky asked.

Mia gazed his way, trying to detect if his words were said playfully or if he was being sarcastic. When she saw him grin, she continued.

"Yeah. I was doing a favor for someone and happened to be in front of him at the coffee shop."

"Let me guess…he offered to buy your drink?" Sharon grinned.

Mia nodded and looked at Jarel, who had a sheepish grin on his face. Listening to her tell them about their first encounter put him in a mood. He couldn't say for certain which one yet, but her eagerness to share intrigued him.

Mia laughed. "He did. Well, he first suggested I try their drink of the week and then proceeded to pay. He's been a gentleman ever since."

Taking ahold of his hand under the table, Mia intertwined their fingers. She couldn't wait to thank him.

"Awww," Sharon cooed. "That's so sweet. It's like something out of a romance novel."

"I'm more of a thriller type of reader," Ricky enlightened the table. "I like shit that keeps you on edge."

As he spoke, he stared directly at Mia. His gaze, paired with his words, made her highly uncomfortable. She analyzed his face for a hint of a grin like before, but there wasn't one. Mia's nerves returned, erasing the calm confidence she once had. She didn't know what it was about Ricky. He seemed pleasant on the surface, but an undercurrent of tension lurked in his brown eyes.

She broke their stare and focused on Sharon. At least she was still pleasant in her approach. Their food orders were taken and brought out shortly after. Mia's conversation ceased, and Jarel couldn't help but lure her back in. He sensed her disconnect almost immediately.

"Your food good?" he asked.

She nodded. "Yes. You want to taste it?"

"Nah, I'm good, baby. Enjoy it."

Sharon cleared her throat. "Jarel told us you're a pharmacist. That's an amazing job to have."

Mia finished chewing and nodded. "It is."

"How long have you been doing that?" Sharon asked and glanced Jarel's way when she heard him sigh heavily. "What's that for?"

"I'm sure she doesn't want to talk about work on her off day," Jarel assumed.

Mia waved him off. "No, no. It's fine. You're okay," she assured. "I've been in the medical field practically all my life since that's what I was raised around. I've been a pharmacist for almost ten years."

Ricky whistled lowly. "Sheesh. You're a vet, then."

"I wouldn't say all that," Mia denied bashfully.

Jarel smirked. "Talk yo shit, baby. You're doing your thing out here."

She appreciated him hyping her up, but Mia couldn't fully accept the praise—not with the way she'd been moving. There was nothing honorable about stealing from her father, let alone jeopardizing her career and others' lives. She felt like a fraud sitting there smiling and quickly wanted to change the subject.

"I mean, I'm doing okay. It's nothing compared to your strenuous job," she acknowledged.

Ricky sucked his teeth. "This man don't be working for real. Fake computer whiz," he cracked, making Mia giggle.

Jarel could only shake his head with a grin. "Whatever, man. Back to you and this potential girlfriend you were telling me about."

While they got invested in their discussion that Mia didn't care to listen in on, she excused herself to the restroom.

"I'll be right back," she said, standing. "I need to use the ladies' room."

"Alright. Don't be trying to sneak off," Jarel joked.

She kissed his cheek. "Never that."

He watched her strut away, finding it hard to peel his eyes off her curves. Ricky snapping his fingers broke his concentration. Facing his cousin, Jarel didn't miss the glower he and Sharon were wearing.

"What?" he asked.

"Don't tell me you're falling in love with this lil' short-haired bitch," Ricky hissed, clowning Mia's bob.

Jarel's nostrils flared. "Don't play with me. You know I'm not."

"I can't tell," Sharon added, speaking in a low tone. "Baby, this, and letting her kiss you. Did you forget what you're supposed to be doing?"

Jarel drew his head back, finding their pouncing to be quite disrespectful.

"How can I forget when I have to be around her every day? Don't question my motives and the way I'm moving. What? I'm supposed to be callous toward her the entire time?"

Sharon sighed. "No, but damn, Jarel, stick to the fucking script. She's hiding something, and we're trusting you to get to the bottom of it."

"Maybe we should just off this bitch," Ricky stated nonchalantly.

"No," Jarel hissed louder than he meant to. Clearing his throat, he shook his head. "That can't happen. At least not yet. I'm close. Just give me a little more time."

Ricky cocked his head to the side. "Time to figure out what she's hiding or time to fall out of love with her? You strapping up?"

Sharon gasped. "Please tell me you're not fucking her."

Jarel closed his eyes, and Sharon's watered. She couldn't believe this. Jarel sleeping with Mia was never part of the plan, but it was inevitable.

"We're grown and in a relationship, Sharon. The fuck did you expect to happen?" Jarel questioned.

"A *fake* fucking relationship," she spat. "You were supposed to keep your dick in your pants."

"Yeah, well, so much for that," Ricky said, chuckling. "He can't even keep his heart off his sleeve. All I know is you better not fuck this up. Tighten up or else."

Ricky's words were spoken in finality, and Jarel clenched his jaw. The friendly lunch meeting with his cousins wasn't to pacify Mia's worries. It was for them to feel her out and see why Jarel was slow-poking on the job. While Mia was doing everything she could to keep their relationship blossoming, she had no idea it was all a façade.

Deep down, Jarel hated that things had come to this, but his back was against the wall, and he needed answers. Just like she had secrets, so did he. Only his would break her heart, leaving it shattered for good.

The work week rolled around, and Mia was back at Grant Pharmaceutical's main headquarters. Flowers had been delivered to her office an hour prior. Now, she couldn't stop thinking about Jarel. Their lunch date had gone without a hitch, and Mia graciously thanked him afterward for a good time. Her worries were a thing of the past.

With her eyes glued to the trees outside the large window, she imagined a life with him years from now. They would come home from work and tell one another about their busy day while relaxing and enjoying each other's company. Depending on the day of the week, she'd have a glass of wine or a smoothie. She could see herself getting pregnant, basking in the joys of motherhood.

Mia spun around in her chair, smiling at the thought. Their future was brighter than ever in her eyes, and she loved it. She and Angel gloated over the successful lunch date and jokingly began to plan Mia's wedding. Last week, Mia would've thought she was getting ahead of herself, but Jarel had secured his position in her life and heart. She had finally come to terms with letting her past expectations go because they no longer mattered—only now and the future did.

The blaring ring of her office phone jerked her out of her lovely daydream. Mia's nose scrunched as she eyed the number, seeing her father calling. She thought he was away at a conference.

"Mia Grant speaking," she answered professionally.

"My lovely daughter. How are you today?"

She smiled. "I'm doing good, Daddy. I didn't know you were back from your business conference."

"Landed a few hours ago. Wrap up whatever you are working on for a few minutes. I need to see you in my office," Matthew said.

His voice was composed but carried a weight that made Mia's stomach churn with uncertainty.

"Okay. I'll be right up."

Mia hung up and wondered what he needed from her now. She would've appreciated a heads-up about him being in the office but should've known better. Matthew Grant moved at his own speed and to the beat of his own drum. He didn't even let his wife clock his moves. So, of course, his daughter couldn't.

In case she needed to take notes, Mia grabbed her notepad, pen, and iPad. She never knew what he would spring on her, and she wanted to be prepared. Unplugging her phone from the charger, she headed out of her office and locked the door with a press of a button. She took the elevator to the fifth floor and walked down the hallway. Mia took a deep breath, preparing herself for whatever conversation lay ahead. She knocked twice on the open door before entering his office.

"Hey, Daddy," she said, trying to sound as casual as possible.

Matthew faced her and grinned. "Hey. Shut the door, please.

Mia gulped and pushed the door closed. On shaky legs, she took a seat in front of his oakwood desk. The office emanated a rich smell of leather, oak, and cinnamon. She usually liked this smell, but today, it made her feel a bit queasy. Whatever this conversation was about couldn't be in her favor.

Matthew sat behind his desk with his eyes glued to his desktop screen. His expression was unreadable, a trait he mastered in his early teens. After a few clicks, he sat back and placed his folded hands on his desk.

"So, have you made your decision?" he questioned.

Mia's brows dipped. "My decision on what?"

"Quitting the hospital."

"You…were serious?"

"Did you think I wasn't?" Matthew countered.

Mia's heart sank at his words. She hadn't taken their conversation in the hall that day into consideration. In fact, she removed it from her mind the same day. She couldn't believe he was asking her this.

"Yes," she answered lowly and cleared her throat.

"I should've made myself clearer. You've been working here part-time for a while now, and I think it's time for you to consider stepping into a full-time position. Your skills are valuable to the company and shouldn't be utilized anywhere but in the family business."

Mia hated how he tried to make his proposition sound good. Ultimately, she knew if she accepted this role, it would only make her unhappy. She had no problem working at the hospital and dividing her time between the pharmacies. What was so urgent that she needed to be at the main headquarters?

"Daddy, I appreciate the suggestion, but I'm not sure I'm ready for that kind of commitment yet."

"Suggestion?" Matthew asked in a tone that made her squeeze her eyes shut.

"That's what it is," Mia replied, her voice wavering slightly.

Matthew chuckled. "It absolutely is not. I believe you're capable of taking on this responsibility. Are you not?"

"Yes, but not right now. It's not something I had in my plans so soon," Mia expressed.

Matthew exhaled and leaned forward. "Mia, you have a gift for this work," he said, his tone becoming more insistent. "I've known it since you were a little girl. I've watched you grow and excel in every role you've taken on here and out there. It's time to start thinking about your future and the legacy you want to build."

A surge of frustration flowed through Mia. She loved her father and respected his dedication to the company, but she had dreams and aspirations of her own—ones she had set aside once before.

"I know you want what's best for me, but not like this. Not right now. I don't want to be pressured into a decision I'm not ready for or will regret in the long run," she said, her voice tinged with irritation.

Matthew chuckled. It wasn't a humorous one, but one that caused the air to thicken with tension so strong, Mia could've choked. She wasn't willing to budge on her decision, no matter the pang of guilt she felt. Someone besides Hazel had to stand their ground against their father, and she was glad it was finally her.

"So, you not wanting to accept this position is because of regrets?"

Mia nodded.

"And you're not ready to make a commitment to *my* legacy, but you're ready to commit to that guy you've been seeing?"

Her mouth gaped open at his audacity.

"That's different. My work life and home life are separate."

"Ah," Matthew exhaled with a smile. "It is *now*. Remind me again why that is."

Mia clenched her jaw as her eyes turned to slits.

"I'm not going there with you, Daddy, and you know it," she hissed lowly.

"No, no. Let's go there so I can clearly understand why my flesh and blood is choosing a man over what I've built to set her, her children, and her children's children up for life. Enlighten me, please, Mia."

Matthew was getting under her skin, and she hated it. His taunting ways made Mia sick to her stomach. He knew why she had separated her work and home life. If he really wanted to know, he was part of the reason.

"Working here will limit my free time, which I barely have. How do you think a relationship is supposed to last if you don't make time for it? That's why my last one didn't work out. I prioritized work before him, causing a strain in our relationship."

"You think things with this guy are going to last because he sends you flowers to the job?" Matthew asked condescendingly. "Wake up, Mia. There's more to life than chasing after some man."

"I'm not chasing after him!" she shouted.

Matthew's eyes widened, and he drew his head back. "Lower your tone when you're talking to me."

"We don't have to talk anymore. This conversation is over," she said, standing to her feet.

Angry tears pooled in her eyes as she stormed toward the door. Her father's next words made them drip from her eyelids and down her cheeks.

"You can walk out that door, but let me remind you of something, my dearest daughter. Everything you have is because of me. That home you live in, those cars you drive. Hell, even the job at the hospital. This company would be nothing without me, and neither would you. Your last name is Grant, and if I were you, I'd start acting like it before it's too late."

"Is that a threat?" Mia questioned with a hiss, her back still turned.

"It's a promise. I expect to see your face at the dinner table this evening. Now, see yourself out of my office."

Fuck the family dinner and you.

Not caring if she damaged something, Mia swung the door open and stormed out. She couldn't believe he just threw in her face what a father of his stature is supposed to do. It wasn't as if she had done anything wrong. All because she wanted to live her life, he threatened to make it a living hell. Mia was furious and hurt beyond belief.

Before now, she thought their relationship could weather any storm. There wasn't anything anyone could say about her father that would make her feel any different about him or how she was raised. Now, Mia was having second thoughts…about everything. She didn't know what Hazel meant that day in the kitchen about opening her eyes, but she did now. The rift between them felt palpable, and she knew there would be no common ground anytime soon.

Entering the code to her office, Mia pushed the door open before slamming it shut. She flopped down in her chair and put her work phone on busy. Her feelings were so hurt that she couldn't help but let out a scream of frustration in the palms of her hands.

"This is so unfair," she cried.

When her phone vibrated with a new text message, she grabbed a few tissues to wipe her face. With blurry vision, she saw Hazel's name on the screen and opened the messaging app.

Will you be at the dreadful dinner tonight?

Sniffling, Mia typed back: *I don't want to be, but yes. Do you need anything?*

Whaaat! You don't want to be there? It must be about to snow.

Mia laughed, grateful for her sister's sense of humor.

I don't. I'll have to tell you what's going on later.

Okay. I'm sure whatever it is can't be that bad. Love you, sis.

I love you, too. Oh, I have those for you.

Good looking out.

Exiting out of the app, Mia locked her phone. In a matter of minutes, her spirit had been slightly lifted, but she was still angry. She wasn't sure what her father had up his sleeve in regard to her decision, but she had something in store for him. Since he claimed he gave her the life she had now, she was going to make sure she was able to maintain it and on his dime.

ELEVEN

"**Y**ou always do such a good job on my lashes, friend. Thank you," Teyona said, placing the handheld mirror down.

Cymone smiled as she cleaned up her station. "You're welcome. What're you about to get into?"

Teyona wiped under her eyes, brushing off the left-behind lashes. "I want to go home and take a nap before my study session later. I'm hungry, though."

"I wish I could take a nap," Cymone groaned.

She had a full schedule and wouldn't be off until later in the evening.

"When's your last appointment?"

"Six. She's just getting a fill, so it shouldn't take long. What you plan on eating?" Cymone asked as Teyona adjusted her crossbody purse.

"American Deli sounds too good right now."

"Yes," Cymone groaned. "A ten-piece hot with lemon pepper sprinkles, extra wet, and crunchy.

Teyona cracked up laughing. "No, you didn't just recite your order like I work there."

"Girl, you made me hungry. Don't forget my peach lemonade drink, either. I'm about to DoorDash me some. My next girl doesn't get here for another thirty minutes."

"Okay. Call me when you're leaving out."

Cymone told her she would, and Teyona walked out of the suite. She couldn't wait to get home, and thinking about the drive made her roll her eyes. That was the only downside to living in Athens—having to travel to the city for everything else. School was her main priority, so she didn't mind on most days. It was those days like today when she wished she lived closer.

While walking to her car, her eyes fluttered against the weight of the freshly applied lashes. She always went for a natural look since she didn't naturally have any, and they always felt foreign. Shielding her eyes from the afternoon sun that painted the sky in hues of amber and gold, she hit her locks and slid inside. An exhale escaped her before she yawned and relaxed in her seat.

"I'm not making that drive. Let me see where Hazel or Mia is," she muttered before grabbing her phone.

Although she could've just popped up at one of their houses, Teyona decided to call first. She didn't want to assume they would be home and make a blank trip for no reason. Dialing Hazel's number first, she should've known she wouldn't answer. Normally, she would leave her a voice note, but Teyona wasn't in the mood. She knew her sister saw her calling. Thankfully, Mia answered on the second ring.

"Hey, Mia," she greeted.

"Hey, sis. What's up?"

Teyona yawned again. "Nothing much. Are you at home? I was gonna stop by and take a nap. I don't feel like driving home."

"On the rare occasion I am here, you want to take a nap," Mia replied with a chuckle, not the least bit annoyed. She was happy to spend some time with her little sister.

Teyona giggled and pulled out of the parking lot. "Like you care. Had you not been, I would've used the spare key."

"I moved it," Mia joked, then laughed. "Where are you coming from?"

"Just got my lashes done. Have you eaten? I'm in the mood for some wings."

Mia snuggled deeper under the covers. "I'm not hungry. Thanks, though."

"You're welcome. You sound like you're in the bed. Are you sick?" Teyona questioned with concern.

Mia chuckled lowly. "Sick of your father. That's about it."

Teyona's eyes widened some. She had never heard her talk like that about their dad, but she should've known it was coming. At dinner on Monday, Mia had been the quietest. When Matthew did try to engage with her, she never replied verbally. All he received were head nods or tight-lipped smiles. Teyona wasn't sure what had transpired between them, but the shift in their relationship was eye-opening.

"Oh, wow. He has been a bit overbearing lately. Is everything okay with you guys?"

Mia wanted to tell her no but didn't want her worrying. Their strained relationship wasn't her burden to carry.

"Yeah, we're good."

"Well, okay," Teyona mumbled, glancing in her rearview mirror.

She squinted, noticing the same black Ford Fusion had been following her since she left the parking lot. Not wanting to think someone was following her, Teyona turned down a street that ventured from her destination. When the Ford turned with her seconds later, her heart rate quickened.

"Tey, you hear me?" Mia asked.

"I…I think someone is following me," she whispered.

Her tongue was heavy, and her throat felt clogged.

Mia sat up in the bed. "What do you mean someone is following you? Are you sure?"

Teyona nodded, and a shiver ran down her spine as she pressed down on the gas pedal. The Ford stayed on her trail but didn't increase its speed. That didn't matter to her. The fact that it was making every turn she made had her unable to breathe. Her grip tightened on the steering wheel.

"Yes, I think so," Teyona said.

"Hey, okay. Take a deep breath, and don't panic."

Mia's reassuring tone cut through the rising panic like a lifeline, but Teyona drowned it out. Her focus was on the car and what its mission was. She hated that she just noticed and didn't know how long they had been on her tail.

"Teyona!" Mia shouted, now out of bed and rushing to put clothes on.

"Y-Yes. I'm here," she answered, her eyes darting to the rearview mirror again.

"Are they still following you?"

She glanced in her mirror and back at the road, hoping she didn't crash into anything. The residential neighborhood she was in was quiet, and she would cause a commotion had she wrecked. When the car pulled into a driveway some homes back, she choked out a loud exhale and parked on the next street over. Holding a hand to her chest, she breathed in deeply as tears pricked her eyes.

"Send me your location," Mia demanded.

Teyona gulped. "It's...It's fine. They weren't following me. I guess they were in a rush somewhere."

She said the words, trying to convince herself, but failed. The thought of someone being after her crippled her with a fear she had never experienced before. Between the notes left for her and now this, which she wasn't going to brush under the rug, things were too suspicious.

"What the hell, Tey." Mia breathed, relief flooding her veins. "You can't scare me like that. I thought someone was trying to rob you or something."

"I'm sorry."

Teyona exhaled, sitting back in her seat. Her eyes bounced to her side mirrors and rearview. Paranoia thickened the air inside her car, forcing her to cut the air up.

"You need to hurry up and get here. Don't worry about stopping for food. We can order something," Mia said.

"Okay. Can you stay on the phone with me?"

"Of course, but don't pull off until you feel like you can drive."

Teyona stayed parked until her heart settled and her hands stopped shaking. Calm enough to drive, she cautiously pulled away from the curb and headed toward Mia's house. What just happened had her so shaken up that she had no choice but to come clean to Mia about the notes she'd been receiving. She could no longer keep them a secret. If someone was out to get her, she wanted at least one person to be aware.

Mia didn't know why she kept peeking out of her blinds. It wasn't like the person leaving Teyona strange notes could enter the community. Still, she was on edge. Teyona had been at her home for over an hour and let her in on the chilling notes. Her mind was boggled. To her knowledge, Teyona bothered no one. Whoever was doing this was playing a cruel game, and Mia wanted them to quit.

"You sure you don't want to tell Daddy?" Mia questioned again.

Teyona shook her head. "No. It's not like he'll care anyway. He'll probably say I'm making it all up."

"Awww, Tey. Don't think that. Someone stalking you is serious. He wouldn't brush that off."

"Okay," she mumbled.

She wasn't in the mood to argue. Teyona had endured Matthew's harsh treatment for years. Her entire life, she had dealt with him ignoring her, acting as if she didn't matter, and simply diminishing any trust in him. What would be different now?

"Do you want to stay here for the night?" Mia asked.

"If you don't mind. I'm too shaken up to go back home now." Teyona tucked herself deeper into the couch's cushion, pulling her legs underneath her. Mia hated this. Seeing her baby sister so distraught broke her heart.

"You know I don't mind. There's plenty of space here. Whenever you're ready to go home, me and Jarel will follow you and check things out. Is that okay?"

Teyona nodded. "Yes. You sure me being here won't mess up any plans you and Jarel have?"

"It won't mess up anything. I'll just let him know what's going on and that he can't spend the night. He'll understand."

"I like him for you."

Mia smiled. "I like him for me, too."

Then her mood soured, thinking about how her father was trying to ruin them. Not wanting Teyona to see her distressed about the future, she fixed her face. Teyona had enough on her plate, and Mia wasn't about to add to it.

"I'm so busy with school, I don't think I'd have time for a boyfriend," Teyona commented.

Her words made Mia sick to her stomach. It was the same thing she used to say. The mindset of not making time for those who mattered was why she had been heartbroken before Jarel showed up. She didn't want Teyona to think that way, but she understood it. Completing college was much different than working. There was still time for her to adjust her mentality.

"You will if you want to. How did things go with you and the mayor's son? What's his name again?" Mia asked.

Teyona smiled. After the day she had, it felt good to do so.

"DeShaun. It wasn't a date, but it was one of the best nights I've had in a while. Too bad he doesn't live here."

"There's nothing wrong with long distance for now. Have you spoken to him since?"

Teyona shook her head. "Nope."

His parting words lingered in her mind just as much as their passionate kiss. She wanted him to turn her however bad he wanted her to be that night. If circumstances were different and he hadn't looked at their evening as her doing Matthew a favor, Teyona was sure the night would've ended differently.

"Oh," Mia chirped. "Well, sometimes you have to shoot your shot. Message him."

Teyona chuckled. "Seriously, Mia?"

"Yes," she replied, then laughed. "You already told me about scrolling his Twitter page, trying to learn more about him. What will messaging him hurt?"

Shrugging, Teyona said, "Nothing, I guess."

"Exactly. So, get to messaging him."

Mia's excitement fueled Teyona's interest. She had no plans to ever reach out to DeShaun. It was one of those instances when she just wanted to enjoy it and him for what they were, not what more they could've been.

Going to the Instagram app, she typed his name into the search bar. It navigated to his page, and she scrolled to see if he had uploaded any new pictures. Once she saw he hadn't, she tapped the message icon. Her eyes widened.

"What?" Mia questioned, leaning her way to glance at the screen.

Sitting right there in the message thread was an unread, requested message from DeShaun. Teyona's cheeks lifted as she smiled at the words he sent. He got straight to the point, and that turned her like for him up another notch.

DeShaunHill: *You've been on my mind. I hope you're having a good week, Nurse Grant.*

Mia grinned. "Well, isn't he quite the charmer."

"Right," Teyona said with a chuckle. "I love that."

Tapping reply, she thought about what to respond back. Teyona rarely checked her Instagram during the week, but she was glad Mia made her get on it today. Shooting her shot hadn't been needed because DeShaun shot his first. By the looks of it, he had hit all net. He was the remedy Teyona needed to get her mind off her life's woes, if even for only a moment.

TWELVE

Hazel rested against her kitchen counter with contemplation swarming her thoughts. She traced her finger along the edge of her cell phone, wondering whether she was making the right decision. Staring at the contact's name on her screen, Hazel wondered if the attached number still belonged to her aunt Nicole. She hadn't called her in so long, she wasn't sure, but she hoped so. While trying to figure out the mystery of what her parents' past consisted of and who, she figured her aunt had to know something. Their life was like a puzzle, missing pieces she couldn't quite put together on her own.

Nervously, she bit into her bottom lip, wondering if Nicole would even be willing to discuss such sticky details. The uncertainty gnawed at her, but she needed answers. Kids were never supposed to be placed in the middle of their parents' bullshit. But Hazel was in a bind, and it was too late to see her way out. Curiosity of the unknown had gotten the best of her.

After a few more moments of hesitation, Hazel tapped the blue phone icon and held her breath. The phone rang once, then twice before Nicole's voice filled the line.

"Hello?" she said sweetly, making Hazel smile. She missed hearing her voice so much.

"Hi, Auntie. It's Hazel, your niece."

Nicole laughed. "I know who the hell you are, girl. You don't think I have your number saved?"

Hazel chuckled at her aunt's witty response. "I wasn't sure this was even your number still. How have you been?"

"I've been doing just fine. In this kitchen, cooking Lenny some food. How are you? I haven't talked to you in so long."

Hazel exhaled. "I know. I have to do a better job of reaching out. Tell Uncle Lenny I said hi."

"I will. He's back there in the yard. So, what's going on? Is everything alright?" Nicole asked.

Though she no longer played a huge role in her sister's life, the love never wavered. She loved her nieces no matter what and hoped nothing bad had happened.

"Yes, everything is okay." *For now,* she wanted to say but didn't.

"How's your mother?"

Hazel cleared her throat. "She's actually the reason I'm calling."

Nicole stopped chopping an onion, washed her hands, and sat at the table. She had just spoken to Kimberly last week, and things were fine. Now, her niece was calling, and it didn't sound like anything good would be coming from this conversation. Nicole was bracing herself for the worst. She had all these years since Kimberly's accident.

"What's going on?" Nicole asked sternly.

Hazel took a deep breath, gathering the courage to ask the questions that had been haunting her since she discovered the credit card in Matthew's office.

"I…I need to ask you a few questions about my parents," she began, her voice trembling slightly.

Nicole swallowed hard. "Okay. What about them, Hazel?"

Hazel could sense the cautiousness in her tone, so she came right out and asked.

"Has there been any infidelity between them?"

Her question caused Nicole to release a heavy sigh. The seven seconds between her question and reply let Hazel know she wasn't about to tell the complete truth or possibly not the truth at all.

"Why are you asking *me* this? You need to discuss this with them," Nicole said, her tone guarded.

Her answer alone proved there had been some infidelity. Had there not been, she would've defended them both, no matter how much she didn't care for Matthew. If Nicole lived in town, she would've paid her aunt a visit and asked her questions in person just so she could see her reaction, but this phone call would have to do for now.

"I feel like you were close to them before things got weird. I need to know more about their past. Who they were before... before everything."

Nicole knew what she meant by everything. Kimberly's accident changed their entire lives. It wasn't her place to divulge that information, though. As much as she would love to, Nicole couldn't do it. Her loyalty was to her sister.

"Hazel, some things are better left unsaid and in the past," she said softly, her reluctance evident.

"Please, Aunt Nicole. Just give me something to work with," she pleaded, her voice laced with desperation.

If Nicole gave her something to go with, the credit card she had found with the woman's name would have made a little more sense. She would then have an excuse to keep executing her search.

"I'm sorry, niece. It's not my place to discuss your parents' business with you," she said sadly.

Hazel sighed. "Okay. I get it. It's not for you to tell me. Once I find out what I'm looking for, I'll let you know."

"Searching for something not meant to be found usually brings heartache, so I hope you're prepared for that."

Nicole's warning was clear as the sky. Hazel should've taken heed to her words, but she was already in too deep. Whatever she was bound to discover couldn't hurt worse than what she already knew.

"I am," Hazel concluded.

Nicole sighed. "I'll hold you to that. Was that all you wanted? Don't be just calling me to use me for information."

Back was her joking tone, which reminded Hazel of their memories. Nicole had always been deemed the fun auntie who let her nieces get away with whatever they wanted. She spoiled them rotten and was crushed when they drifted apart.

"It was," Hazel replied, laughing. "But we don't have to hang up. What've you been up to? I need to make a trip to the West Coast. The beach is calling my name."

"Come on through and get some of this California sunshine. You know our home is open to you and your sisters whenever."

Hazel was happy to hear that. She wouldn't mind taking a vacation after she tied up all her loose ends. Until then, she was on a mission. She felt like she was racing against time and something she had no clue about, but the race was on.

After hanging up with her aunt, she searched the web again for the mystery woman behind the credit card. Grabbing her MacBook, she sat crisscrossed on her couch and popped her knuckles. She typed the woman's name into Google, and a plethora of hits came up. Hazel clicked on almost every link, reading the description of who the so-called person may have been. When twenty minutes passed, she sucked her teeth and frustratingly glared at the screen. Then, it hit her.

"Oh, my gosh. What if this is a fake name?" she groaned, slamming the screen closed.

Setting her MacBook to the side, she hurriedly called Mia. She couldn't wait around to figure things out on her own; she needed some reinforcement and hoped her sister could help.

"Yes, Haze? I'm at work," Mia answered, walking down the hallways of the hospital to a patient's room.

"Hey. What time do you get off? I need to run something by you."

Her words were spoken much too quickly for Mia's liking as if she were in a panic, and that didn't sit well with her. After what Teyona had told her, Mia had been on edge and on high alert ever since.

"Why do you sound like that? What's the matter?" Mia asked, pausing her duties.

Hazel shook her head. "Everything. Just call me when you get off so I can come over."

"Fine," Mia sighed. "Between you and Teyona, I don't know who has me more worried."

"What's wrong with her?" Hazel asked lowly, almost afraid to hear what Mia would say.

"I'll let her tell you. But I have to go. I'll call you when I'm off."

Hazel hated that Mia had brought up something and didn't explain it. Now, her mind was on Teyona. With everything going on in her life, she hadn't been checking on her like a big sister should. In fact, she hadn't returned her call from days prior. She felt bad and was almost disgusted with herself for letting the drama of her parents consume her life the way it had been. She had gone from not caring about anything they had going on to wanting to know every detail of their past.

"It's for a good reason. Hell, I'm being blackmailed," she mumbled just as her phone vibrated.

She knew who was calling from the unknown number and became filled with dread. Cautiously, as if he had eyes on her, Hazel slowly picked up the phone and answered it.

"Who is this?" she questioned.

"It's time to collect," the mystery blackmailer said.

Hazel swallowed hard. "What do you want?"

"Twenty thousand dollars. You have five days to get it to me, or everything I know about your parents will be leaked."

Bile filled Hazel's throat, slicking her once-dry mouth.

"Are you serious?! I don't just have twenty thousand dollars sitting around!"

She was enraged and terrified that he had more treacherous details than he showed her.

"You're the daughter of the CEO of a pharmaceutical company. You may not have the money, but someone does. Figure it out. You'll hear from me in five days."

Hazel went to respond, but the line died. She hurriedly dialed it back but was met with an automated voice stating the number had been disconnected. Angry tears pricked her eyes as she slammed her phone into the couch. Five days wasn't nearly enough time to get the amount of money he was asking for. Not legally, anyway.

Glancing around her loft, she stared at the beautiful murals, canvases, and artwork filling the space. Most were her personal collection, while others were up for sale. She knew her paintings were one of a kind but didn't know how much value they truly held, especially the ones she spent weeks creating. An idea she had been trying to ignore entered her brain, and she squeezed her eyes shut. Putting her most expensive and enthralling work on an auction site was a last resort, and she was down to it.

"No. There has to be another way," she murmured.

Still, she wondered how much she could receive. There was money in her savings, but not nearly enough to cover his demand. Opening her MacBook, she typed in the website name and entered her credentials. She hadn't thought about Brush Bidder in months. Though she needed money and was trying to purchase a studio, the last thing she wanted to do was bid her most valuable pieces off. Her chest tightened just thinking about it. Months ago, she had uploaded images and details of her paintings but never hit submit for them to go live.

As she scrolled through her account, her eyes watered. This wasn't her first time being in a desperate position, but back then, it wasn't as harsh. The circumstances weren't as life-threatening. Now, her back was really against the wall.

Hazel looked at the paintings she uploaded with a heavy heart. The vibrant strokes and intricate details of her masterpieces seemed to lose their vitality, each swirl of color mimicking the looming threat over her head. Hazel had poured her soul into these paintings, each reflecting her deepest emotions. Yet now, they felt tainted, stained by the sinister force of a man who had invaded her life—which happened to be all because of her father. Hazel wasn't going to blame her mother for what was going on. She knew this had Matthew's name written all over it.

With a heavy sigh, she scrolled to the end of her listings. Selling her beloved artwork or facing the unknown consequences was a cruel ultimatum. She felt like she was sacrificing the essence of who she was and a piece of herself for the sake of her family, and it pained her. Not only would her parents receive backlash for whatever secrets were revealed, but she and her sisters would, too. Anyone connected to the Grant name would feel the heat.

Tears welled in Hazel's eyes as she increased the pricing on a few paintings. Each click of the submit button carried the weight of her despair, echoing through her loft like a lament of lost innocence. Her gift had nothing to do with her parents' sins, yet she was paying the cost. Every submission felt like a betrayal of her art, integrity, and everything she held dear. The predicament she was in was crushing her spirit minute by minute.

"I can't believe I'm doing this," she whispered, barely a hoarse murmur.

A part of her was torn away, piece by agonizing piece, as the listings uploaded. The database sent out notifications to potential buyers when an artist uploaded new work, and she was hoping no one was interested. Yes, she needed the money, but she needed her paintings, too.

Once they were all uploaded, Hazel sobbed as tears dripped from her cheeks onto the keyboard. Pushing the MacBook away, she curled onto the couch. It was a vulnerable moment she never thought she would be in. Unwillingly selling her artwork was more than a loss of material possessions; it was a loss of herself and her dreams and a stab in the heart as to why she started drawing. She felt hollow inside, and someone was going to pay for the pain she was experiencing. If she had to hurt, so did everyone else.

"You think twenty thousand was too low?" the man asked the woman sitting across from him.

She smiled and shook her head. "No. It's the perfect amount. It's not too low, so she can just send it off, but not too high that we don't get it."

He nodded. "Makes sense. You think she'll get it to us?"

"She has no choice. Unless she wants her beloved parents to go down for murder and be blasted everywhere, she'll do what's smart."

"I can't believe I'm doing this," the man groaned, shaking his head.

"Believe it. You're in too deep now."

"We could've gone about this another way."

She sucked her teeth. "Yeah? And what way was that? You came to me, remember? I didn't ask to be a part of this, but now I am, and we're going to do things my way. My hands were clean."

"I only came to you because you said you had some information I may have needed," he hissed, annoyed that he placed himself in this position.

"And I did. Now, we get to play hardball. This is payback, so tuck your feelings and be prepared to get our money in five days."

The man's nostrils flared. "Is money the only thing you care about?"

"It's not, but why not get more? Twenty thousand is just the start. Imagine how much more we can get."

He shook his head. "This is ridiculous. I should've just left well enough alone."

"No!" she said, slamming her hand on the table before calming down. "They will pay for what they've done. I don't give a fuck if we hurt everyone they love in the process. You wanted answers, so this is how we will get them. Do I make myself clear?"

The man snorted a chuckle. "You don't run me. I can walk away from this."

Smiling wickedly, she slid a gun and a recorder on the table between them. "You're a liability now. So, no, you can't walk away. Now, get your fucking head in the game and be prepared to retrieve our money. We're too close to toss in the towel."

Clenching his jaw and fists, the man watched with malice in his eyes as the woman stood and exited the room. She meant business, and it was best that he fell in line. Things had gone too far, but the treacherous deeds had already been done. It was too late to turn back now, especially with his life and reputation on the line.

THIRTEEN

As sunlight filtered through the curtains, Kimberly stood inside her walk-in closet, deliberating over what to wear for the day. It wasn't often she got out of the house, but she felt the need to. She hummed softly as she reached for a light yellow-hued blouse and her favorite pair of hip-hugging jeans. They resembled a semblance of comfort amidst the chaos that was brewing.

She clasped a silver necklace around her neck, slid on multiple white-gold Cartier bracelets, inserted her diamond-studded earrings, and spritzed herself with perfume. Giving her curls a shake, she exited her bathroom, ready to head out for the day. Kimberly slid her feet into a pair of Chanel sandals and grabbed her purse. Top of Form

Heading downstairs, the thought of making a quick bite to eat entered her mind, but she brushed it off. Had Matthew not fired their around-the-clock chef, she could've asked him to prepare her something. With their wealth, Kimberly saw no reason to have to do certain things if she didn't want to. Plus, she had gotten used to the luxury of not having to cook.

It wasn't because she didn't want to, but because she physically couldn't. For so long, her disorder prevented her from doing daily tasks such as cooking, so she left it to the staff. Even driving wasn't permissible. There had been a limit to the way she lived her life, and Kimberly hated it. At thirty-four, when she was first diagnosed, she never thought her life would become one of codependency and limitations.

Though her recovery took much longer due to her husband's spitefulness, she didn't take it for granted. Every moment of her life, from the minute she began to progress, was cherished and lived. No longer did she care about the opinions of others, especially Matthew's.

Deciding to grab a green juice to hold her over, Kimberly entered the kitchen. It was once a place she adored. Cooking meals for her family and seeing their faces light up with enjoyment made her day. Being a mother and wife had always been her pride and joy, but she didn't know how to get back to that place after her accident. For years, she felt like she was on the outside looking in on a life she couldn't remember creating. That was the past, however.

Just as the refrigerator door closed, Kimberly's phone vibrated inside her purse. She scrambled to retrieve it, catching the call before it was sent to her voicemail. Kimberly grinned, seeing her sister was calling. If only she had known the reason Nicole was reaching out, she wouldn't have been so eager to answer.

"Hey," Kimberly greeted, expecting casual chatter about her day and what she had going on.

"What have you been up to?"

The question was something she would usually ask, but Nicole's tone was anything but casual, and it caught Kimberly off guard.

"Excuse me?" she questioned, placing her juice on the counter. "What's the matter with you?"

"Why did I just receive a call from your daughter seeking answers about you and your husband's past?"

Kimberly's heart skipped a beat as she squeezed her eyes shut and tightened her hand around the phone. She had three daughters who had been of age to question the sometimes silent turmoil within their home. It was more deafening than the arguments they had to endure.

"Which daughter?" Kimberly huffed.

"It was Hazel. Something is going on, and I want to know what the hell you've been up to?" Nicole insisted.

"Why does it have to be me? We just spoke the other day, so where is all this coming from?"

Nicole shrugged on the other end. "I'm not sure, but I'm in the middle of it again. She asked if there'd been any infidelity between you two."

Kimberly's gasp echoed throughout the quiet home, and the phone almost slipped from her grasp.

"What?" she muttered, her voice a mixture of confusion and hurt.

She was struggling to process this. The news Nicole relayed was like a punch to the gut, leaving her reeling in disbelief. Never had her girls questioned the stability of their marriage. At least not to her or anyone else that she knew of. Kimberly's mind drifted to her and Hazel's most recent conversation, and she wondered if that sparked her curiosity.

"Yes," Nicole said sharply. "Whatever the hell is going on over there has her curious, and I'm not getting involved."

"Did you tell her anything?"

"Of course, I didn't. You know me better than that," Nicole spat.

Kimberly sighed. "I'm sorry. I do. It's just…I wasn't expecting to get this type of call."

"Imagine how I feel. After all these years…"

Nicole's words lingered in the air like a fog, threatening Kimberly's senses. Her chest heaved as she squeezed her eyes tightly. Her past, the one she tried burying, was coming back to haunt her, and she was sick. Her head spun with a whirlwind of emotions, wondering what had sparked Hazel's inquisitiveness. Top of Form

Kimberly took a seat at the dining table, similarly to the way Nicole had. The heaviness of the subject was weighing them down. She listened to her sister's background. The distinct sound of traffic filtered through the receiver, reminding her of the distance between them.

"You're in the car," Kimberly said.

"Yes. I had to go for a drive to clear my head so Lenny wouldn't question me. I'm tired of the secrets, Kim," Nicole replied, sighing.

"I don't know what to tell her."

Her voice was heavy with worry.

"Maybe it's time to tell the truth," Nicole suggested.

"No," Kimberly said with a fierceness she hadn't possessed in a long time. "Absolutely not. My family is already on thin ice. This will destroy us."

"It already has, Kim. Be honest with yourself for once and take accountability for your actions," Nicole hissed. "My nieces shouldn't still be subjected to this bullshit."

Kimberly snickered. "Is that how you feel?"

"Yes! For years, I watched you deteriorate into a person I didn't know. I had to help aid you back to the woman we thought you'd be again, only for everything to change. You got better, but nothing else did. When are you going to finally face the truth?"

Nicole's words jarred her. They were a reality slap to the face that she needed long before now. Facing the truth would require her to open too many closed wounds. Kimberly couldn't afford that. Not now.

"I can't," she said weakly. "I've left those memories behind me. I thought we could keep everything in the past and away from them. How is this happening right now?"

"You know the saying. What's done in the dark will always come to light. You can't keep flipping the switch off, Kim. It's drained and will eventually die."

Her metaphoric words chilled Kimberly's insides. Anguish washed over her as she thought about how things were about to play out. Hazel wasn't the one to back down when she had her mind set on something. Never did Kimberly think there would be questions about infidelity, nor did she expect Hazel to go to her sister, of all people. The lines of communication were open between them but clearly not open enough.

"I can't handle this right now." Kimberly sighed on the verge of tears. "How do I look my daughter in the eyes and tell her that her parents' marriage fell apart because of the mistakes we made?"

"Was it really a mistake, Kim?" Nicole questioned. "I mean, really?"

Kimberly inhaled and bit into her bottom lip. "Please don't ask me that."

"Listen, no more questions. I can't even begin to imagine how you feel right now, so I won't try. Hazel isn't a child anymore, and neither is Mia and Teyona. They're close, so eventually, they're going to ask each other questions. They deserve to know the truth, no matter how painful it may be."

The silence that followed Nicole's words led her to believe Kimberly's decision. She wasn't prepared to tell them anything and wouldn't. Nicole didn't have to know that, though. She lived hundreds of miles away.

"If any of them come to me with questions, I'll tell them the truth," she said, hoping to pacify her sister's worries.

"You promise me?" Nicole asked.

"Yes, I promise."

I can tell them what they need to know, not what I know is the truth, she surmised, satisfied with her terms.

"Okay." Nicole sighed with relief. "Everything is going to work out. You're not in this alone. You never have been. We'll get through this just how we've gotten through everything else."

Kimberly hoped her faith was as powerful as her sister's words because she knew nothing, not even her strained marriage, would work out once the truth was revealed. She could only hope her relationship with her daughters could withstand the storm because it was coming.

Mia wrapped her arms around Jarel's neck, not wanting to leave him. She had gotten off work and met him at his house, only to be told he had to go out of town for a meeting. Though it hadn't been long since she met his cousins, Mia felt closer to him than ever. Not knowing his true intentions, she was slowly falling in love with the man he portrayed to be.

"I don't want you to go," Mia whined, inhaling his masculine scent.

Jarel squeezed her waist. "I can tell," he said, chuckling. "I'll be back before you know it."

"Two days, right?" she asked, holding up her index and middle finger.

He mimicked her digits, making Mia grin.

"Two days, baby. I'll call you every morning and text you during our breaks."

"And call me at night before we go to bed, too," Mia added.

Jarel kissed her lips. "Yes, I'll call you at night, too, so I can listen to you play in my pussy."

His husky words had Mia rubbing the front of his jeans. The fabric bulged immediately, even though they just finished a steamy sex session forty minutes prior. Jarel may have been faking his role in her life, but the sex between them was real. He knew his cousin Sharon wouldn't understand, so he didn't bother explaining when she badgered him about it. In his mind, men could have sex and not get emotionally attached.

Gripping her ass in the work pants she wore, Jarel gave it a squeeze. "Don't start up nothing you can't finish."

Mia giggled and removed her hand. "I always finish. Save that for me," she said, kissing his lips.

"I got you. Come on. I'ma walk out with you."

"What time does your plane leave? I can drop you off," Mia suggested as he grabbed his carry-on suitcase.

"You don't have to. I know how you get in traffic, especially once you're off work," he replied, chuckling again.

"I'm glad you know. Text me when you make it," she said as they approached her car.

Jarel opened her door and gave her a long hug as if he were going away for weeks. It was what she needed, and he had to reassure her. Mia ate it up, but he lowkey loved the affection. As soon as the thought entered his mind, he pulled back and kissed her cheek.

"I'll let you know when I get there. Drive safely."

"Okay, baby. I…" Mia almost slipped up and said those three words but caught herself. "I'll text you once I make it home."

He gave her a head nod and waited until she pulled out of the parking lot before going to his car. For the first time this week, Jarel was being truthful. He did have a work conference out of town and was grateful for it. The space between them was needed; he needed to get his affairs in order. A few days without being in Mia's presence would do just the trick, or so he hoped.

Mia made it home in forty-five minutes and released the biggest sigh once she pulled into her garage. As soon as she parked, the security gate was calling to let her know Hazel had arrived. She had forgotten all about calling her when she got off work. Whatever her sister needed seemed important, so she prepared herself for the evening ahead.

"Now, what if I had been in a life-or-death situation?" Hazel asked as she followed her into the house.

"Well, I hope you would've called the police and not just me." Mia chuckled. "Did you bring some wine? I know whatever you are about to say is going to involve me having at least two glasses."

"Actually," Hazel enunciated, "I brought tequila and orange juice."

Mia's head snapped her way. The last time they drank tequila, Hazel told her she was being blackmailed. She could only imagine what news she had for her now.

"It's that serious?" Mia questioned.

"Yep," Hazel said, opening the bottle. "Go get comfortable because it's about to be a long night."

Exhaling, Mia slipped off her heels. She wondered why her sister brought her MacBook with her but didn't question it. Heading to her bedroom, she took a quick shower and slipped on a comfy lounge set with her fluffy slippers. When she made it back downstairs, Hazel had a mixed drink prepared for her and had taken residency on her couch.

"Thank you," she said, sipping the concoction. "Now, tell me what happened."

"Your parents are cheaters."

Mia choked on her drink. Her eyes widened as she patted her chest. "What the fuck, Haze. You can't just come out and tell me something like that."

Hazel shrugged. "It's the truth. I mean, I don't know which one of them is a cheater, but I'm leaning more towards that man you call a father."

"And how are you so sure about that?" Mia asked.

"That's just my assumption for now. I visited Mama the other day, and when I was leaving, I went to Daddy's office."

Mia waited until she took a sip of her drink before continuing. "You were looking for something?"

"Not necessarily, but I came across a credit card with a woman's name on it."

"That's why you asked me the name of his assistant," Mia acknowledged, and Hazel nodded.

"Yes. I didn't want to jump to conclusions."

Mia snorted. "I wouldn't put it past him if he were cheating. I'm not feeling him at the moment."

Her admission surprised Hazel. The way Mia lifted one of her shoulders, as if Matthew's behavior didn't faze her, wasn't the sister she knew. She expected her to go to bat for him. Now, it had Hazel curious.

"Wait. What happened between y'all?"

"We got into it because he wants me to work full-time at the office, and I told him no. He tried throwing in my face that everything I have is because of who he is and what he's given me like he was the one sitting through college or busting his ass to accomplish *my* goals," Mia said with a roll of her eyes.

"Mm," Hazel grunted. "And you wonder why I pay his ass dust. He's miserable."

"He is, and I guess I'm just now seeing it for myself. Then, he had the nerve to say Jarel and I aren't going to last. He's part of the reason I don't want to go full-time. That place will drain you if you let it. My contribution to the company as what it is right now is enough. So, it's forget him for now. That's why I don't care that we're stealing from him. He can't just treat people any ol' kind of way."

On one hand, Hazel felt bad for Mia. She detected the hurt in her sister's voice, not realizing their dad had only ever looked out for himself, no matter who he hurt in the process. The other part of her was glad Mia had finally seen his true colors. She needed her to keep on not giving a fuck about Matthew.

"It took you long enough to open your eyes to his bullshit. I don't know if it was because you were afraid of him or what, but I'm glad you found the light," Hazel said.

"He threatened to cut me off if I decided not to work for the company full-time," Mia shared.

"Cut you off how?"

Mia shrugged. "I'm not sure, but I lowkey want to find out," she replied with a snicker. "Call him on his bluff."

"Okay, Billie Badass," Hazel said, chuckling. "I like that in you. So, um…there's more I need to tell you."

Rubbing her temples, Mia exhaled. "What?"

Hazel hated that she had lied before because the money she told Mia she owed someone she actually needed now. Hopefully, her sister had a solution; otherwise, whoever was blackmailing her would be blasting their family.

"So, that day you came over after meeting Karter…"

"After Karter pulled up to my job," Mia corrected her.

Hazel waved her off. "Yeah, that day. Anyway. Before you got to my place, this random man had just left, claiming Mom had something he wanted. He had some photos of our parents that he threatened to leak if I didn't get him what he wanted."

Mia put her glass down. "Are you serious?"

"Yes. I wouldn't play about something like this."

"But why not tell me then? What the fuck, Haze. You said you just owed someone some money, and the extra pills I was getting for you were okay."

"I told you that because I didn't want you to worry, but then he called. He demanded I give him twenty thousand dollars in five days, or he's going to ruin our family."

Placing both hands on her head, Mia let out a frustrated scream before standing up from the couch.

"You know what? Nope. I can't deal with this right now. What the fuck have you gotten yourself into? Who is this man?"

"I don't know his name or anything about him."

"We can go to the police," Mia suggested.

"With what evidence? All I have is my word. That's not enough."

Mia paced her hardwood floor, shaking her head. She couldn't believe this.

"So, so…you're just supposed to cough over twenty-fucking-thousand dollars because he claims to have pictures that could ruin our family. Does that sound legit to you?"

"Not only does it sound legit, but the pictures were… They were of Mom and Dad placing a body in the trunk of a car."

Mia's hand flew up to her mouth. "Shut up," she whispered. "They killed someone?"

"That's what he's saying."

"No," Mia said, shaking her head. "No, no, no. Our parents aren't murderers. What the fuck!"

She was panicking, and Hazel didn't need that—not right now. They needed to find a solution quickly.

"Look, you probably don't want to believe any of this, but maybe there's some truth to what he's saying. And let's not forget the credit card with the woman's name on it. I called Aunt Nicole to ask her questions, and she sounded like she knew something."

"What do you mean?"

"She basically said if our parents had any issues in their relationship, it wasn't her business to share and that I needed to ask them."

Mia frowned. "If there was nothing to tell, why would she say ask them?"

"Exactly. That's why whoever this man is and what he's asking for seems legit to me. I just...I want to know what the fuck they were up to in the past. You and I both know it's no secret the weird stuff that was going on in the house before and after Mom's injury. You can act like you don't remember, but we both know the truth."

Sighing heavily, Mia sat on the couch. Propping her elbows on her thighs, she squeezed her eyes shut. She wouldn't consider their childhood traumatizing, but it definitely wasn't one she wanted to discuss. There were certain things she didn't want to relive.

"This is all too much. First, someone is leaving Teyona creepy letters on her windshield, and she thought someone was following her. Now, someone is blackmailing you."

Hazel drew her head back. "What do you mean someone is leaving her letters? When did this start?"

"I'm not sure when it started, but it happened again earlier this week."

"Did she tell you what kind of car they were in? I can have Karter keep an eye out."

Mia nodded. "Yes. It was a black Ford Fusion, but she said they pulled into a driveway. I thought maybe she was just being paranoid."

"Why didn't you tell me?" Hazel asked.

"She told me not to say anything to you yet."

Hazel sucked her teeth. "What the hell. Why not?"

"I don't know, but do you think it might be the same person?"

"Possibly. It's not a far stretch to think so. Maybe he was trying to get our attention."

"But why?" Mia questioned lowly. "What the hell does he want that Mom has?"

Not having the answers either, Hazel didn't immediately respond. But she knew whatever it was had to be something serious if he was going out of his way to cause all this drama and create such fear.

"I don't know, but if we don't have his money in the allotted time, he's leaking the photos. Honestly, I don't give a fuck about Matthew. I would've ignored the blackmailer's demands if Matthew had been the only one in those pictures, but Mom was in them, too. I don't play about her."

Mia wasn't as close to Kimberly as she was to her father, but she didn't love her any less. She didn't want to see anything bad happen to either of them. Leaking those images wouldn't just ruin them but her and her sisters, too.

"Who has twenty thousand just lying around to hand out?" Mia questioned.

"Not me. I wish I did. I had to open my account back up and put some of my paintings up for auction."

Mia gasped. "No, Hazel. Why would you do that? You were saving those for when you opened your studio."

Hazel shrugged. "I had no choice, Mia. I'm obviously in a fucking bind here."

Standing to her feet, Mia marched inside the kitchen. Snatching Hazel's MacBook out of her bag, she returned to the living room.

"Here," she said, shoving it onto her lap, damn near knocking her drink out of her hand. "Remove them."

Hazel rolled her eyes. "No, it's fine. I can draw more."

"No. Stop being stubborn. We'll figure out another way to get the money. I don't care if we have to steal it from the company. You're not selling your paintings."

Looking up at her, Hazel rocked the biggest grin. "What'd you just say?"

"I said you're not—"

"No, before that. You said you don't care if we have to steal it from the company," Hazel repeated, grabbing her laptop.

Mia rubbed the back of her neck. "Oh. I mean, I guess we could borrow the money. I was just saying."

"Yeah, borrow all the money our scandalous father should've been giving me anyway. Stealing from him doesn't sound like a bad idea. Aren't you on one of the bank accounts?"

"Yes, for emergency purposes," Mia answered.

"Well, my dearest sister…this is a fucking emergency. What's twenty thousand to the CEO of a pharmaceutical company, huh? He won't even know it's gone."

Hazel couldn't wipe the grin off her face if she wanted to. She logged into her Brush Bidder account and went to take her listings down. Her eyes stretched with excitement, seeing that one had been purchased. And not just any painting, but the one with the highest price tag. It was unexpected funds, not having faith that anything would sell, and now she was having second thoughts about removing them.

"Why're you looking like that?" Mia questioned.

"My highest painting sold."

Mia began clapping and poured each of them a shot. "That's great, sis! Congratulations. Are you going to leave them up? You don't have to."

She thought about it for a brief second. It had only been some hours since they went live, and she'd already made a nice profit. In her mind, it was sort of a confirmation of more that was to come. Hovering over her account information, Hazel logged out, leaving the paintings up.

She took the shot from Mia's outstretched hand. "I'm leaving them. I just got super inspired, though I'd been a crying mess earlier," she said, chuckling. "It is what it is. Plus, there's more money coming in soon. Between the pills and borrowing from the company bank account, I'm not worried about a thing."

Mia couldn't one hundred percent agree with her jolly sentiments right now. Until everything blew over, she was going to stay on alert. She did know one thing, though. Matthew was on her shit list at the time. Hitting him where she knew it would hurt would bring Mia as much joy as he had in his office that day. Payback was a motherfucker.

FOURTEEN

It was Monday, and Kimberly couldn't help but wonder if she would see her daughters' faces today. She held her breath every week, not knowing if it would be the last dinner they shared, but they continued to show up. She knew it was for her and not Matthew, but now she felt guilty. Half of the time, none of them wanted to be there.

The phone call from Nicole made her reconsider so many things. She wouldn't even have been mad if they had decided not to show up. What she was afraid of was one of them bringing up their past. Though Hazel had gone to her sister with questions, she knew it wouldn't be her, but then again, she couldn't be too sure.

Making her way through their home, Kimberly reminisced about the memories that didn't include pain—the times when she was happy to come home to her loving husband and didn't have to worry about where he'd been or who he'd been with. She wasn't sure if the money or the company created a wedge between them, but Kimberly regretted both. Sadly, she could no longer vent to anyone about it.

"Hi, Kayla," she said, speaking to their in-home chef.

Kayla smiled brightly as she closed the oven. "Hi, Mrs. Kim. How are you?"

"I'm doing well. Would you be willing to take on some morning shifts or meal-prep breakfast for me?"

"Of course. Were there specific days you'd like breakfast or a menu you had in mind?"

Kimberly chuckled. "I hadn't thought that far yet."

"That's alright. How about I come over in the morning and prepare a meal, and we can go over some options? How does that sound?"

"That sounds fine to me. Thank you for being so accommodating."

Kayla smiled. "It's no problem at all. I love your family. Please let Mr. Grant know that dinner will be ready shortly."

"Sure thing."

Walking out of the kitchen, Kimberly planned to head back upstairs until her daughters arrived, but she decided to take a trip down the hall. She rarely ventured to the side of their home where Matthew's office was, but she wanted to today. There'd been a point in their marriage where she would come into his office while he conducted work calls and seductively teased him. Or listen intently to how he wanted to grow the company to new heights and secure its legacy for generations to come. The love they shared and the promises they professed seemed like it never happened.

As she approached his closed office door, she could hear he was on the phone. His voice was strained as if he were arguing with someone, and she couldn't help but wonder who. She inched closer to the door with light steps, turned her head, and listened.

"That's bullshit, and you know it," Matthew hissed, pacing his office floor.

Kimberly hated that she couldn't hear the other person.

"Yeah, well, that's too fucking bad. You knew this years ago and should've stayed in your place."

There was a pause.

"Yes! Stayed in your place. All of this bullshit I have to endure is because you couldn't keep your mouth shut. I should've silenced you for good like I did— You know what? Don't call me again until you have your mind right. Did you forget who the fuck I am?" Matthew snarled.

Kimberly snickered and clasped a hand over her mouth. "The audacity," she whispered to herself.

"That's what I thought. Goodbye," he said, hanging up.

She waited until she heard him shuffling things around to make her presence known with a knock.

"Who is it?" Matthew shouted.

Kimberly didn't say anything. She loved toying with him since he claimed to hate hearing her voice. Matthew grunted as he marched over to the door, swinging it open. His cold gaze landed on Kimberly, who gave him a taunting smile.

"What do you want?" he asked gruffly. "And use your words today."

She smirked. "You're never going to change."

"What're you complaining about now?"

"Oh, nothing. Dinner will be ready soon. While you wash your hands, be sure to wash away that attitude. It may take a while, so I'd get to it."

Matthew dry chuckled. "Ha, ha. I wouldn't have an attitude if I didn't have to live in this house with such a miserable woman."

Had this been years ago, Kimberly would've broken at his harsh words. They no longer bothered her. The love between them had long ago vanished.

"You don't have to live here. In fact, I'd prefer that you didn't. We could've divorced years ago, Matthew."

He turned his nose up. "And you take my money and run off into the sunset? Over my dead body."

Kimberly giggled. "You do know a thing or two about those, huh?"

Matthew looked her up and down with envy and disgust. The prenup signed before their marriage had them contractually bonded for life. He wouldn't dare walk away. His ego wouldn't allow him to. Instead of responding, he closed the door in her face, making Kimberly laugh louder.

"Asshole," she hissed, walking off.

The hatred between them could make one assume they had never been deeply in love. It was disheartening to witness, especially from the ones close to them. Or more like the ones who *used to be* close to them. Everyone seemed to keep their distance now, more so because of Matthew. It was the reason Nicole had distanced herself, including Mrs. Maric, Kimberly's old friend. It was a cycle. One by one, people in their lives exited.

Kimberly made it to her room to freshen up before the girls arrived. Teyona was the first to show up, followed by Mia and Hazel. They took their seats at the table, and Kimberly entered with a smile.

"Hey, girls," she said, giving each of them a hug.

She loved on Hazel a few seconds longer, and she noticed.

"You must've missed me," Hazel said, eyeing her.

"I always miss you. Mia, how have you been?"

"I've been good, Mama," Mia said, texting Jarel.

Her mother noticed her distraction and smiled. Kimberly then focused on Teyona, her baby. She signed, asking if she was doing well. Smiling, Teyona nodded and signed back that she was okay and starving. Then, she stood to see if Kayla needed some help. With Mia in her phone and Teyona away from the table, Hazel took the opportunity to break the ice.

Getting Kimberly's attention, she signed, asking if there was something she was keeping from them. Kimberly tried to keep her expression neutral but failed. Her question had come out of left field, but she was glad Nicole had given her a heads-up. Signing back, she asked, *Something like what?*

"Something you think we should know," Hazel spoke, getting Mia's attention.

"Huh?" Mia questioned, glancing between the two.

Kimberly shook her head. "Nothing. We'll talk later," she told Hazel just as Teyona returned to her seat.

Kayla wasn't far behind her, and Matthew entered once she placed the drinks on the table. Seeing his daughters sitting on one side of the table when they would usually be spaced out let him know exactly what kind of evening it was going to be. Instead of addressing it, he took his seat and acknowledged them at once.

"Girls," he said, spreading the cloth napkin over his lap. "It's good to see everyone on one accord."

Hazel sucked her teeth but didn't say anything. There was so much she wanted to say, but she remained quiet as dinner was served. Today's menu consisted of lasagna, house salad, and garlic bread. For dessert, Kayla had prepared banana pudding. Everyone was quiet as a mouse, consumed with their own thoughts. Matthew broke the silence like he always did.

"The tenth annual global health gala is coming up," he acknowledged. "Mia, it'll be a good idea for you to go and network."

Looking up from her almost empty plate, Mia gave him a fake smile. "Sure, of course. Nothing like networking for the family."

Matthew squinted his eyes at her from across the table. "Are you being sarcastic?"

Hazel chuckled while Mia feigned innocence.

"What? No. I do think it'll be a good idea if I go, especially since I'll be more hands-on with the company."

That was news to Kimberly. "Really? You're quitting the hospital?"

Matthew looked on with a smug expression, waiting to hear her answer. He knew she would come around and take his offer.

"Not soon," Mia answered, wiping the smirk off her father's face. "I still haven't decided when, but it's a possibility. Maybe within the next few months."

"Oh," Kimberly said. "I guess that'll be good. You can be more hands-on with the internship program. As long as you're doing this for you."

Mia smiled her mother's way, loving how she cared about her well-being more than what she brought to the table for the company. She only replied with the answer she knew Matthew wanted to hear and was playing nice because of what she and Hazel had been up to all week. Withdrawing twenty thousand dollars from one of the company accounts over a span of a few days had her nervous, yet not giving a fuck. In actuality, she had just saved her father's ass, and he was acting as if she owed him something.

"She's doing this for the family. We're a legacy, and it's critical to have as many of our faces with the last name Grant present as possible," Matthew stated.

Kimberly rolled her eyes, mimicking Hazel.

"I'd like to go to the gala," Teyona said.

Mia perked up. She had attended so many with her father over the years that she wished she had someone else to accompany her.

"You should, sis. It'll be a great opportunity to cross paths with some influential people and get a feel for the medical field outside of work."

"That's what I was thinking," Teyona said, waiting for Matthew to chime in. When he went right back to eating, Teyona snapped. "Did you hear me?"

The bite in her tone made Matthew dart his eyes her way before his head swiveled from right to left.

"You're talking to me?" he asked.

"Yes. I said I'd like to go to the gala, as well."

"Then go. What're you telling me for?"

Teyona looked at him incredulously and chuckled. "Mom, I don't see how you've put up with him all these years."

"How she puts up with me?" Matthew spat, tossing his fork down. "I'm the one who's had to deal with three bratty-ass daughters and a supposed-to-be wife who doesn't appreciate me. You better watch what you say to me," he said, pointing his finger at Teyona.

Normally, she'd keep quiet, but she was fed up with him treating her like an outcast.

"And you should watch what you say to me. You talk to us, especially me, as if we're not your kids. Do you know how hurtful that is?"

He waved her off. "Oh, please. I don't want to hear anything about being hurt. You want to go to the gotdamn gala? Fine. Tell your sister to get you a ticket."

Mia glanced her way. "I got you."

"Thanks, but you shouldn't have to. You're going to die a bitter, miserable old man, and I hope you know that," Teyona spat with pure hatred.

Matthew's eyes widened at her harsh words before he chuckled. "Is that what you think of me?"

"I have a few more choice words in mind, but I don't want to ruin dinner. So, I'll keep them to myself."

"Yeah," he scoffed, drilling Kimberly with his cold gaze. "You better because I have some words of my own that'll ruin this circus of a family for good."

He went back to eating, letting his mysterious slew of words linger in the air. Hazel made eye contact with her mother, wishing she could see those thoughts roaming through her head. If she wasn't sure before that they had a dark past, today had cleared up any uncertainty.

When dinner ended, Matthew retreated to his office as always. He had nothing left to say to his family. Hazel pulled her mother aside while Mia and Teyona conversed by the front door.

"Hey, did you ever ask Mom about those journals?" Teyona asked, digging around inside her purse for her phone.

Mia cleared her throat, wondering where Hazel and her mother had snuck off. "Um, no. Not yet. Why?"

"I was just wondering. I looked up Mrs. Marie's journal business, and they're meant to help with grief. She said Mom played a huge part in her starting her business, so I was just curious. No biggie."

Now, Mia was even more intrigued.

"I'll have to check them out. Where are you headed?"

"Home. I have so much studying to do, and the only thing on my mind is napping," she whined.

"It'll all be over soon and worth it. Have you heard from DeShaun?"

Teyona blushed. "Yes. We have a date this weekend, and I can't wait."

"Safe to say he's applying pressure, huh?" Mia giggled.

"Absolutely. He said he wants to spend as much time with me as possible before school starts back up and his basketball schedule gets hectic."

"Awww. A man who makes time for you is something special."

"You would know. Jarel has you glowing," Teyona complimented.

Mia shied away from her sister's examination but had to agree. His time spent out of town truly did make her heart grow fonder. She was falling and was happy that Teyona was getting to experience the same feeling.

"He does, but this is about you. Be safe," Mia said sternly. "You're still sharing your location with me, right?"

Teyona nodded. "Yes. I trust him, so there's nothing to worry about."

"It's not him I'm concerned about. You have a stalker," she said, bending her fingers as if she were putting the word in quotations. "As much as I'd love for you to stay in the house, I know that's impossible."

"It is. Plus, I haven't received a letter or anything since the last one. Maybe it was just someone playing a prank."

Mia didn't think so, but she didn't want to make Teyona more paranoid than she already was. "Sure. We'll go with that for now. Text me when you get home."

"I will," Teyona said, hugging her.

Mia stepped out onto the porch and waved as Teyona drove out of the driveway. Going back inside the house, she went to search for her mother and sister, but before she could locate them, she received a phone call from Jarel. Though she was happy to see him calling, now wasn't the best timing. Mia answered anyway, giving Hazel enough time to berate her mother by herself.

On the opposite wing of the home, Kimberly stood with a nervous expression. Hazel asked her the same question she asked Nicole and was waiting for a reply.

"I don't understand where this is coming from," Kimberly said.

"I'm just curious, Mom. It's a yes or no answer."

Sighing, Kimberly shook her head. "It's not that easy of an answer, sweetie. Our business isn't yours."

"It is when it's detrimental to my livelihood," Hazel said with a growl in her tone. She dialed it down when she noticed Kimberly rapidly blinking her eyes. "Sorry. I didn't mean to snap at you."

"What's going on? Is someone trying to hurt you?"

"What? No. Why would you say that?" Hazel asked, appalled that of all questions, she asked that specific one.

"Never mind," Kimberly said, becoming flustered. "Things are okay with you and Karter, right?"

Hazel sighed. "Yes, Mom, we're fine. I only called Aunt Nicole because I figured she'd be open to discussing this with me. It's like you guys are hiding something."

"Just because we don't tell you every detail of our lives before we had you girls and after you entered this world doesn't mean we're hiding anything. Yes, our marriage is rocky, but we've never inserted you girls in it or made you feel like you had to choose sides."

"I chose a side the night he pushed you down the steps."

Hazel's words were colder than the ones she spoke at eight years old.

Kimberly squeezed her eyes shut, not wanting to relive that moment. It used to haunt her, and the nightmares appeared when she least expected them. Parts of her brain during recovery gave her glimpses of how she injured herself and how she became diagnosed with aphasia. Nicole was the first person to bring it to her attention.

Kimberly found it odd that Matthew forbade anyone from coming to the home when she started feeling better, especially when she regained her capability to talk. The only thing her health aide nurse told her when she asked what happened to her was that she fell down the steps. She had no reason not to believe her, but then she asked Matthew what happened, and his response led her to think no one had been telling her the truth or they didn't know it.

"You don't remember what you guys were doing before the fall?" Nicole asked, speaking her words slowly but naturally.

Kimberly was freshly diagnosed with what Nicole now knew as expressive aphasia. She could understand another person's speech but had difficulty speaking fluently herself. Nicole felt it was the perfect time to get some answers. The way Matthew hovered around them had been pissing her off. He had just left the home to handle some business, leaving the sisters alone.

Nicole rephrased her words when Kimberly looked at her, unable to answer.

"Were you two arguing before you fell?"

"We argue," Kimberly said, not fully understanding her question.

Grabbing some paper, Nicole wrote her question down. The doctor and nurses told her that sometimes reading the words instead of hearing them would help her understand. Once she read the words and nodded, Nicole's heart broke. She knew her sister could be misconstruing what happened or not fully remembering, but she wasn't going for it.

Taking her hands inside hers, Nicole spoke to her with tears in her eyes. "Your fall wasn't an accident, Kim. He needs to tell you the truth."

Those words seemed to register in Kimberly's brain.

When Matthew returned home for the evening, Nicole headed back to her hotel and mugged him on her way out the door. Figuring she and her husband must've gotten into it, he paid her no mind.

"Have a good night, sister-in-law," he called after her before heading up the steps to their bedroom.

Matthew entered, seeing Kimberly awake with an anxious expression on her face. Walking over to the bed, he kissed her cheek and lovingly rubbed a hand down her neck.

"How're you feeling?"

Swallowing her nerves, Kimberly picked up the notepad that Nicole left behind. She went to write out her question but had trouble finding the words. So, she used her voice. Matthew knew to be patient with her, but he wasn't prepared for her question.

"What happened to me?" Kimberly asked, staring at him with a look he had only witnessed once before.

"You have a brain injury."

Kimberly processed his words and shook her head.

"The truth," she said slowly.

Matthew pulled his hand from her neck and backed away from the bed. His glower frightened Kimberly, but she didn't move.

"The truth?" he spat. "With the state you're in, you can't handle the truth. Listening to your sister is going to get your feelings hurt. I'm the one here nursing you back to health, making sure our daughters are taken care of, and running a million-dollar company. That's some truth

for your ass, Mrs. Grant. Don't bring it up again. As a matter of fact, let your sister know she is no longer welcome in my home if she can't mind her business."

He left her no time to reply as he walked into their bathroom and closed the door. Matthew's words had come out way too quickly for Kimberly to grasp them all, but she understood him. His reaction had her questioning everything she thought she once knew.

"Listen to me, Hazel," Kimberly said. "Whatever you're looking to find out, stop. Okay?"

"But, Mom," Hazel fussed.

"No," Kimberly hissed. "Stop it. You're only going to dig up old wounds and information that is no concern of yours. If you love and care about me and your sisters, just let it go."

Hazel gritted her teeth.

"Please, Hazel," she practically begged.

"Fine. Whatever. I don't want you feeling bad if something happens to me."

"Don't try to make me feel bad because you're being nosey. Nothing is going to happen to you. Now, leave it alone."

Kimberly kissed her daughter's cheek and headed out of the room they were in. Mia acted like she was just heading down the hallway, but she had heard every word.

"You're going to your room?" Mia asked.

"Yes. You and your sisters be sure to take some leftovers when you leave."

Mia told her okay and entered the room. Hazel stood in the same place, refusing to believe her mother just checked her like that.

"What the hell was that?" Mia whispered, peeking her head outside of the door before closing it.

With an attitude, Hazel shrugged. "Not what I wanted to hear, but whatever."

"She said you were being nosey. Hell, we just paid someone twenty damn bands to keep their secrets hidden."

"And he'll probably want more. If he asks, I'm going to let him leak the images. I don't care anymore. This shit has me losing sleep and missing my man."

"Wait. Where's Karter?" Mia questioned.

"He's still in the picture, but I've been neglecting him. I can't tell his ass what's going on. He'll end up in jail."

Mia snickered. "True. Well, what next? I'm too invested. Plus, Dad is out of his mind if he thinks I'm coming to work for him full-time."

"Did you see that smug look on his face when you said you were?" Hazel laughed.

"Girl, he was ecstatic. I hate the way he treats Tey. He acts as if she's the child he didn't want Mom to have or something."

Hazel hated the way those words settled in her gut. "Maybe he didn't, and that's why he treats her that way."

Mia looked at her with sad eyes. "I hope not. Speaking of Tey, she asked me about Mom's journals again. Do you remember her writing in any when we were kids?"

Taking some moments to think about her past, Hazel hummed. "Kind of, but not really. I try to block out stuff from our childhood. You're older, so you should remember."

"She did, but I wanted to ask you. If Mom is hiding anything, I bet it's in those," Mia suspected.

"Yeah. Now, we just need to find them. Where would I be if I were a journal with things written inside that I didn't want anyone to know?" Hazel mused.

Kimberly's request to leave well enough alone had fallen on deaf ears. They were now on a mission and wouldn't stop until all the dots connected.

FIFTEEN

As Mia's back arched, her mind was void of any worry or stress. The air inside her bedroom was heavy with desire, each stroke from Jarel igniting something deeper within her. Her fingers traced the contours of his sculpted back before her nails dug into it. He was hitting her spot just right.

"Oh, Jarel," she moaned, pulling him closer.

Their lips met in a fervent kiss, tongues intertwining, leaving them panting once he pulled away. Jarel stared at her face. It was semi-dark inside the room. The moon cast its silvery glow through the curtains, giving him the perfect view of the sex faces she made. His nostrils flared, and his palm began to itch. Mia's eyes peeled open, and a lazy grin covered her face as he clasped his hand around her neck.

"Mmm," she moaned, loving his aggression.

Jarel hated how much wetter her pussy got. He squeezed harder, mimicking her slick walls around his dick. Mia's eyes rolled to the back of her head as she came undone.

"Fuck," Jarel hissed as he erupted inside of her.

He shuddered as she spasmed around his length, basking in their post-orgasm feelings. Pulling out of her, Jarel heaved, his chest rising and falling as he rolled over. Their breaths mingled in the air like whispers of a shared secret. They were being reckless, especially him.

Amidst the haze of their lovemaking, a somber shadow lingered in the corners of Mia's mind.

"That was good," she whispered, running a hand down his slick chest before slowly climbing from the bed.

Mia headed to the bathroom to use the toilet, clean herself up, and grab a warm, soapy towel for Jarel. He lay there with his eyes open, wondering what the hell he was doing. Things between them had gone past the point of no return, and he was struggling to reel it in. Making things complicated was exactly what he didn't want, but he had brought it upon himself.

Feeling Mia's presence, his eyes lowered to where she was between his legs, lovingly cleaning his now flaccid member. The pleased smile on her face as she did so made his dick jump, and she giggled.

"You want more?" Mia asked, looking up at him.

Jarel bit into his bottom lip and shook his head. "I'm good, baby. Your touch just does something to me."

She blushed before sauntering back into the bathroom. Returning, she cuddled up beside him in bed and rested her head on his chest. Absentmindedly, Mia drew circles with her finger along his abs. Jarel's hand stroked her back, offering an act of intimacy that Mia cherished, and she expressed it.

"No matter what type of day I have, I can always count on you to make it better," she divulged.

Jarel squeezed his eyes shut. Her confession made him feel like shit. On one hand, he cared about her; on the other hand, he knew he shouldn't. Everything he was doing was forbidden and downright disrespectful. Leading her on was his biggest regret.

"That's what your man is supposed to do," he replied.

"And you do it well."

She sighed like she wanted to say more, and Jarel took advantage of this vulnerable moment. His fingers massaged her scalp through her silk bonnet, and Mia moaned with satisfaction.

"What's on your mind?" he asked.

Mia remained quiet for a moment. There was so much she wanted to tell him. The things she and her family were going through made her feel anchored. She had vented to her friend Angel, giving her bits and pieces without revealing too much, but she needed another outlet.

"So much," she said, sighing again, then popped her head up to look him in the face. "Can I trust you?"

Her question was heavy, loaded with the type of worry Jarel felt the need to soothe. She was exposed right now, and whatever she was about to tell him, he wanted every detail.

"You know you can tell me anything on your mind," he replied, kissing her forehead.

"I know, but this has to stay between us. Okay?"

Jarel nodded.

Mia traced his face for any signs of dishonesty. He must have hid them well because she reclaimed her spot on his chest and began pouring her heart out.

"There are some things going on with my family. Apparently, there has been for a while, and everything is coming out."

"Everything like what?" he questioned, wishing his phone was near.

"My parents' past. It's sketchy, and I'm afraid to know what it entails, but I'm invested. Also, I've done some things recently that

I'm not proud of, but I can't see my sisters struggle. I'd do anything for them."

He clenched his jaw and tried not to tense up. "And I'm sure they would do the same for you."

"Even if it involved being put in a position to lose their license because you're stealing drugs you're supposed to prescribe to patients?"

Mia's revelation would've knocked Jarel on his ass had he been standing up. He absorbed the words she said, and his chest tightened. His body heated in anger, but he had to remain calm. Getting disgruntled now would ruin his chances of hearing more. He had been waiting for her to confess what he'd been suspicious of for months.

Mia sighed. "I know you're probably disappointed in me."

"I'm not. I'm sure whatever the reason is a good one. Otherwise, you wouldn't be doing it."

"It is. My sister…she's in a bind. It started off easy, you know. It was just pills and then money. Someone is blackmailing her, and I had to help her out. My dad doesn't make it any better. He throws everything he's done for me in my face and is threatening to cut me off from the company."

She scoffed, and Jarel gritted his teeth.

"Cut you off for what?"

"Because I refuse to let him run my life. He wants me to take on more duties at the company, but I don't want to. I see what it does to people, what it does to relationships, and I can't afford to lose you," she said, hugging him tighter around the waist.

I was never really yours.

Those words echoed loudly in Jarel's head. She was revealing so much, and he wondered why now.

"I'm not going anywhere," he lied reassuringly.

"Good." She sighed again, but this time, it was one of relief. "You've been so patient with me, even with everything you and your family have going on. I hope my sisters appreciate me like I know yours does with you."

His body steeled as it always did whenever she brought up his sister and family. Mia felt comfortable enough to do so, and Jarel had allowed her. It was a part of the game, but he was tired of playing.

While Mia opened the floodgates of her heart, spilling secrets that drowned him in agony, Jarel was thinking of his next move. He couldn't move recklessly with the information he had just been given, nor could he move off emotions. She knew too much, and now, so did he. Not only was her heart on the line, but his life, as well.

A piece of him regretted ever getting involved with Mia. But, like her, he would do whatever for his family, and she was about to witness just how far he was willing to go.

Jarel sat by his sister's bedside, the sterile scent of the hospital clinging to the air around him. The soft hum of medical equipment provided a constant backdrop to the otherwise silent room. Evelyn lay motionless, her chest rising and falling rhythmically with the assistance of the ventilator. Tubes and wires snaked from her body to various monitors and machines, a stark reminder of her fragile state.

His heart ached as he looked upon her pale, still face. Evelyn had always been his rock, his confidante, his closest friend. Seeing her like this, so vulnerable and lifeless, tore at his soul in ways he couldn't articulate. Knowing that someone he had grown feelings for was the cause behind her current state plagued him with guilt. He reached out and gently grasped her cold hand, willing some warmth and comfort to seep into her fragile form.

The events leading up to this moment replayed in Jarel's mind like a relentless loop. He'd been so caught off guard and still had been for months. Nothing made sense. He remembered the panic he felt when he found her that day. Then, the blaring sirens, the flashing lights, the frantic voices, and the overwhelming sense of helplessness as he watched paramedics work tirelessly to save his sister's life.

Now, here they were, suspended in a state of limbo, caught between hope and despair. The doctors had said it was a miracle Evelyn was still alive, but they couldn't guarantee what her future held. They spoke of possibilities and probabilities, of potential outcomes and long roads ahead, but their words offered little solace to Jarel. He was keeping the faith, though. He had no choice.

He couldn't shake the guilt gnawing at him from the inside out. Guilt for not being able to protect Evelyn, guilt for the way he was moving while she tittered the line between life and death. Jarel wished he could trade places with her to bear her pain and suffering so she could wake up and be whole again. A piece of him had been missing for months, and it lay right there in that bed.

Tears welled up in Jarel's eyes, blurring his vision as he struggled to maintain composure. He blinked them away, willing himself to stay strong. Evelyn needed him now more than ever and his unwavering support and love to guide her back from the brink of darkness.

He leaned in closer, his voice barely above a whisper as he spoke to her.

"I'm so sorry, Eve," he whimpered.

Jarel blamed himself for her condition. In the quiet confines of the hospital room, he poured out his heart. He promised Evelyn that he would never give up on her, that he would be by her side every step of the way, no matter what the future held.

An hour passed by in the blink of an eye. The steady rhythm of Evelyn's breathing was the only constant in the otherwise still room. As the minutes ticked by, exhaustion threatened to consume him. He had been on the go for days, which felt like months now. There was so much more ground to cover, and he wasn't giving up.

The shadow of a new visitor broke his gaze. Jarel sat up straight in the chair as Ricky and Sharon entered the room. He knew why they were there and wasn't ready to deal with them.

"What's up?" Ricky asked as they slapped hands. "How long have you been up here?"

"Not long," Jarel answered. Hours felt like minutes, so he wasn't completely lying.

Sharon didn't acknowledge him. Instead, she stepped around the opposite side of the bed to tend to Evelyn. She gently smoothed down pieces of her hair, adjusted her covers, and held her hand. Most of their family had stopped coming to see her. They claimed they were too hurt to see Evelyn this way, but Sharon knew better.

She had heard the gossip and rumors but ignored them until she had to check folks. It was better they stayed away anyway. Their negativity had no space inside Evelyn's room. Jarel was already bringing his, and Sharon was beyond upset but couldn't make him leave. She clung to the hope that somewhere deep within Evelyn's unconscious mind, she could hear them. Their words needed to urge her to fight.

"So, has she said anything else?" Ricky questioned.

That got Sharon's attention. She looked at Jarel, hoping he had some news they could use.

"Yeah. She practically confessed to what I've thought all this time. Her sister is the drug dealer, but she steals them for her."

"Damn," Ricky grumbled. "That's some shit."

"Yeah. I feel bad, though."

Sharon let go of Evelyn's hand. "You feel bad? Are you serious right now?" she hissed.

"Yeah. She's not really the one responsible for all this shit, but she's in the mix."

Sucking her teeth, Sharon walked around the bed. "Let me tell you something. That bitch is responsible, and she and whoever else are going to take the fall. You need to get your head out of her ass and be prepared to send her ass to jail because that's where she's going."

"How is she going to go to jail with no proof?" Jarel questioned.

"You sound like you trying to protect her," Ricky commented.

Sharon cocked her head to the side. "Exactly. What do you mean there's no proof? You said she confessed. Did you not record it?"

Jarel cleared his throat. "Nah. I, uh, I didn't have my phone on me."

Sharon's eyes turned to slits as she snatched ahold of his shirt. Jarel hopped up from his seat, smacking her hand away.

"Don't put your fucking hands on me," he fumed.

"Yo! Calm down," Ricky said, coming in between the two.

"If I find out you're hiding something and trying to protect this bitch, I'm taking you down with her. Family or not," Sharon hissed.

Breathing hard, Jarel watched as she snatched her purse up and stormed out of the room. Frustrated, Jarel flopped back in his seat, running his hands over his face.

"Aye, man," Ricky said, getting his attention. "What you doing? This wasn't the plan. You falling in love with this woman or something?"

He hoped that wasn't the case because if so, they were fucked. Not having the heart to answer him, Jarel remained quiet. His motives had changed. Jarel didn't know when, but they had. He didn't want to see Mia go to jail, but someone had to pay. If not her, then her sister, and that was too bad because all Mia was trying to do was help.

SIXTEEN

Teyona's heart fluttered with nervous excitement as she examined her reflection in the full-length mirror. She'd been looking forward to her date night with DeShaun all week and hoped whatever he had planned was much better than the week she had. Between her studies and family drama, Teyona was ready to disconnect from the world and everything it had going on.

DeShaun was only in town for a few days. With the school year quickly approaching, he wanted to spend some time with his family and friends. Teyona found it so endearing that he deemed her important. Carving time out of his busy schedule to see her smile was the only thing on his agenda. Baby girl needed it. The anticipation to see him tingled in the air surrounding her, a mix of uncertainty and thrill, as she wondered what the evening held in store.

She ran a hand down her black jeans, which had slits in the knees and accentuated her curves just right. Her cream silk top was tied, stopping right underneath her breasts that were sitting lusciously. Teyona wanted to look good for DeShaun but not come off like she wanted to give the goodies up— even though it had crossed her mind ever since they kissed.

There had been an undeniable spark between them, and Teyona wanted to explore it more. Through texts and FaceTime calls between her classes and his day-to-day schedule, she concluded he was just her type—chill yet still a big deal. DeShaun's charisma and charm were as evident off the court as they were on it. Teyona found herself drawn to his easygoing demeanor and infectious laughter, and she couldn't deny the attraction that simmered beneath the surface if she wanted to.

Her cell phone rang just as she swiped her last coat of gloss to her beat face. The incoming call from Cymone was just what she needed before she left.

"Okay, body!" Cymone sang, clapping her hands.

Teyona chuckled. "You see me? Your girl is getting her weight up."

"As you should. We're at the age where that grown woman weight is coming in, and it's sitting right on you."

"Thank you, girl. What you got going on?"

"Nothing at all. I was calling to see if you were ready for your date. Where y'all going?"

"Out to eat, and I don't know where else. I'm down for whatever, though."

Teyona didn't care what he had planned, as long as it was safe and a good time.

Cymone grinned. "I like that energy. Well, have fun. Text me once you make it home…if you go home."

"Girl," Teyona said, laughing. "I will be returning to my humble abode."

"Bring some dick back with you. Love you. Bye!"

"Love you, too, crazy," Teyona said and hung up.

Fifteen minutes later, DeShaun called, letting her know he was outside. After making sure she had everything for the night, Teyona grabbed her Louis Vuitton wallet on chain métis, slipped on her black stilettos, and headed out the door. Out of habit, her eyes scanned the parking lot for anything suspicious. She glanced toward her car, checking to see if someone had left her another note. When she didn't see one, she breathed a sigh of relief.

"Maybe they're done playing," she mumbled as she approached the vehicle.

DeShaun hopped out of the black Lamborghini Urus and strolled her way. Teyona's breath got caught in her throat as she took him in. He wasn't wearing anything flashy, but the crisp black tee, distressed black jeans, letterman's jacket, and Jordans on his feet had Teyona ready to go back in the house and take him with her. She let her eyes roam over his tall frame, loving the fresh six-stitch braids in his head.

"Damn, you look good," DeShaun praised, pulling her into a hug.

Without protest, Teyona fell into his arms, feeling her cheeks flush. His intoxicating scent of citrus, woods, and tonka bean had her eyes fluttering. Not to mention how solid his frame was against her now sensitive nipples. He had easily caused an array of butterflies to infiltrate her belly.

"Hey. Thank you," she said, blushing. "You smell good."

"Thank you, gorgeous," he replied, taking her in.

When he licked his lips but didn't open the door, Teyona became confused.

"What?"

"As fine as you look with them heels on, I'ma need you to run back in the crib and grab some tennis shoes."

Teyona's eyes dropped to her feet, her long silk press effortlessly framing her face. "Oh, okay. We're not going out to eat?"

"Yeah, and then sliding to this new arcade with a few of my people. That's cool with you?"

She nodded. "Yeah, that's fine. Let me go grab a change of shoes."

"A'ight. I'll be right here."

Teyona smirked, wondering where the hell else he thought he was going. His eyes stayed glued to her ass until she disappeared back into the house. She emerged two minutes later with a pair of tennis shoes to match her purse. DeShaun opened the passenger door for her to climb in, and she admired the fresh scent. It smelled like him.

Once she was buckled up, he pulled off and smirked. "What's good, Nurse Grant? How yo' day been?"

DeShaun's voice was buttery smooth, melting the nerves settled in her chest. Teyona could listen to him talk forever.

"It was relaxing. Got some cleaning done around the house. How was yours?"

"Straight. I ain't do too much. Chilled with a few of my family members. Feel like I been waiting all day to get some time with you."

Teyona chuckled. "Dramatic, aren't we?"

He smirked. "A lil' bit. Shit, I'm feeling you. Hope you like this restaurant. If not, we can go somewhere else."

His admission made her heart flutter. She was feeling him, too, and was glad he didn't mind expressing that. Like it had been since they met, conversation flowed easily between them as he navigated his SUV through the city. When they arrived at the restaurant, Teyona was surprised by his upscale choice. She wanted to ask if he was trying to impress her but didn't want her question to come off the wrong way.

She appreciated his efforts and even more admired him for going the extra mile, but he didn't have to. Mason's Steakhouse wasn't a spot you could just walk in and wait to be seated. You had to have reservations and be referred by someone to even get your name on the list. With him being the mayor's son, she was sure it wasn't hard for him.

"You come here a lot?" Teyona asked as he pulled up to the valet.

"Nah. I only been a few times. Why?"

He was hoping she wasn't about to ruin their night before it could even begin.

"I was just wondering. You know…I would've been fine with going somewhere not as stuffy."

"Stuffy?" DeShaun questioned, a chuckle falling from his mouth.

Teyona giggled. "Yes. I can't lie; the food is good here, but it's so bougie. They be giving out small-ass portions of sides. You have to have at least three drinks to even feel something, and the lighting is so dark it feels like you're in a basement."

His loud chortle filled the car. "Gotdamn. Tell a nigga how you really feel. So, what? You wanna eat somewhere else? I thought you would like this spot."

"I do, and I'm *so* sorry for making you think otherwise," she said sincerely. "We can eat here, but you have to take me to another spot on our second date."

DeShaun licked his lips, loving how she was already planning their future endeavors.

"Bet. With your pretty ass. Up here talking crazy like they ain't got the best steak in the city."

Teyona couldn't do anything but laugh as he climbed out of the truck. She was grateful she had been able to express herself without him getting in his feelings. That alone let her know that he was a rare breed and that their night was about to get even better.

They entered the restaurant and were greeted immediately with smiles. Upon DeShaun's request, they were seated at a table for two with much better lighting than the rest of the establishment.

The atmosphere was cozy and relaxed, and soft music played over the speakers, allowing the duo to get to know each other better.

"So, you telling me you can't play spades?" DeShaun asked with a look of disbelief.

"Why is that so hard to believe?" Teyona laughed, sipping on drink number two.

He shook his head. "That's a game all Black people should know how to play."

"Well, unless someone writes an instruction manual, I'm never going to learn."

"You bogus man," he said, chuckling. "I fuck with you, though. I need to see you in the stands at a few of my games."

His gentle smile and serious eyes should've let Teyona know he wasn't asking for her presence but demanding it. She licked her rum-coated lips and smirked.

"Do you?"

"Yeah. I'd like that."

"Me rocking a shirt with your name and number would look fly, huh?"

He grinned, and Teyona found it so cute. His dimples made her weak.

"Fly as hell, baby. I know you're busy with school and everything, but I'm just putting that out there," DeShaun said.

His words were spoken with confidence, sure that he would see Teyona's pretty face in the stands cheering him on.

"And will I be the only woman in the stands rocking your name?"

Her head cocked some to the side, and DeShaun chuckled. She wanted it to be known that she wasn't for any mess.

"I can't one hundred percent guarantee you'll be the only one, but you'll be the only one that matters to me."

Teyona smirked. *Smooth ass.*

"Hmm. I'll have to check my schedule. I'd love to come and support you. Don't be looking crazy when I'm screaming your name all loud," she said with a chuckle.

"You screaming my name is the least of my worries."

Teyona picked up on the sexual innuendo immediately but decided not to respond. Instead, she finished off her drink. DeShaun was her temporary distraction from the real world, and she didn't want to complicate things between them. She could tell her feelings were growing for him, and his were for her, too. If their impromptu friendship lasted through the summer and blossomed to more by his first game, Teyona would revisit this conversation. For now, she enjoyed the dessert he ordered for them, unknowingly missing the calls from Hazel.

"She ain't answer?" Karter asked, looking up from his phone.

Hazel flopped down on the couch with a huff and shook her head. "No. I just want to make sure she's good."

"It's the weekend. She probably in the house. She'll call you back."

Hazel hoped so. Normally, Teyona would be the one blowing up Hazel's phone, but now it was the other way around. Something in her gut told her to call and check on her, and she didn't ignore it.

Hazel had been on the go all day shipping off paintings, prints, and other products selling on her website and through Brush Bidder. She couldn't even enjoy the excitement, knowing the meaning behind her accomplishments. Basking in the moment only lasted so long until she was reminded of her reality. When her phone lit up with a text message, she thought it was Teyona getting back to her. When she saw it was a customer asking about some pills, she sucked her teeth.

"I'm tired of this," she mumbled, never thinking she would utter those words.

Karter glanced her way. "What you mean?"

"Selling these pills and living in constant worry."

"That's what comes with this lifestyle, ma. What you got to be worried about besides getting this money?"

Hazel had only told Karter half of the story about why she asked Mia to increase the supply of pills they were selling. She was moving sneakily but out of concern for not just herself but him and her family. As much as she hated what they were dealing with, she didn't think it was smart to involve Karter.

"There's more to life than making money. Someone is blackmailing me and my family."

Frowning, Karter scooted to the edge of the couch and peered at her. "What did you just say?"

"This man is blackmailing me and my family. He came here a few weeks ago with pictures of my parents and demanded I give him some money or he would reveal everything."

"Some nigga came to the place we lay our heads, and you're just now telling me?"

Hazel gulped and nodded. She could feel the heat radiating off his body, which was why she didn't want to say anything. Karter's murderous look wasn't good for anyone.

"Am I your man?" he asked, and Hazel's brows dipped.

"Yes."

"But you couldn't come to me about some nigga rolling down on you, pressing you for some money? Does that sound like some shit I'd let slide, Haze?"

His questions were rhetorical, but she answered anyway.

"No. But I didn't want to get you involved in our mess."

"Our?"

She nodded. "Yes, me and Mia. Everything we're doing is messy as hell and only getting messier. I love you too much to keep putting you in compromising positions."

Karter stared at her long and hard before mumbling, "Obviously, not enough."

When he stood up, Hazel hopped up behind him.

"I know you're not leaving?" she questioned.

"Yeah. What? You wanna sit here and talk now? We're a team. I don't give a fuck about compromising positions when it comes to your safety. You been in this bitch moving weird, and now I know why. What would've happened had that nigga and whoever else he hangs with ran down on me? I wouldn't have had a clue who he was or what was going on because my girlfriend failed to tell me," he said, shaking his head with disappointment.

"You can't blame me for another person's actions! Don't do that," Hazel grilled him.

"I'm not blaming you for anyone's actions but your own. You left me in the blind about some shit that could've gotten us both knocked, yet I'm supposed to stand here and be understanding. Yea, a'ight," Karter scoffed, sliding his Air Forces on.

"Baby, come on," Hazel said, grabbing his arm.

"Move, Haze. I need to clear my head. It's obvious you don't trust me or don't think I'm capable enough to protect you, so I need to evaluate some shit."

Her jaw dropped. "You mean think about if this relationship is for you. That's what you mean?"

She wanted clarification but surely didn't expect him to agree with her.

"Yeah, that's exactly what I mean. Lock up. Shit or not. Sounds like you coo' with muthafuckas running up in here."

Tears of understanding pricked her eyes, but she dared not let one fall. His words stung, but Hazel didn't have the bandwidth to hit him with a reply. She locked the door after his departure and stared at it for a few seconds before reclaiming her seat on the couch. As badly as she wanted to argue with him and fight for her relationship that was now on thin ice, Hazel said nothing. There was no use now.

Knowing that she didn't confide in him, Karter felt like less of a man. Had she revealed everything, Hazel was sure their argument would've been much more heated. She did trust him and knew he would lay his life on the line for her. No one had her back like Karter did, but Hazel was her sister's keeper.

In her feelings, Hazel sat on the couch, wondering when Karter would return. It had been only thirty minutes, and knowing him, he was probably driving around smoking, trying to make sense of what she'd told him. They rarely argued, which Hazel appreciated so much. Hearing disputes from her parents growing up and now as an adult triggered her. She and Karter got money together, loved on one another, and made plans to start a family. Now Hazel wasn't so sure where they stood.

Though he pissed her off, Hazel sent him a text letting him know she loved him. She was never too stubborn to admit when she was wrong, but she wanted to apologize to his face. Knowing she wouldn't be getting any sleep anytime soon, she stood up and stretched. Usually, she would paint when stressed, but all she wanted to do was curl up on the couch and watch movies while waiting for Karter.

Going to the kitchen, she sucked her teeth when she realized there were minimal snacks. Karter didn't live with her, but he might as well have, and they hadn't made their weekly grocery store run. It was about to be a long night, and Hazel needed something to munch on. Some days, she was a stress eater, and today was one of those days.

Slipping on her jean jacket and some Crocs, she grabbed her keys and purse before checking to make sure her gun was inside. A quick run to the gas station was all she needed to make, but her Glock was coming with her. It always had, but she made sure to have it with her at all times now.

The brisk night air hit her face as she eased out of her door and locked it. The cool breeze offered a small measure of solace. Keeping her head on a swivel, she hurried to her Jeep and hopped inside. Hazel's heart thudded as the engine rumbled to life with a soft roar. She cranked up the radio, trying to distract her brain from what Karter said. He was right. He should've been in the know no matter what was going on. Leaving people in the blind was how she and her sisters got into this situation in the first place.

The drive to the gas station was short, but every second felt like an eternity. Backing into a spot in front of the brightly lit convenience store she visited often, Hazel took a deep breath and exhaled, forcing herself to push aside the lingering hurt and anger.

The chime above the door signaled her entrance, and she took confident steps straight to the chip aisle. Her stomach rumbled, telling her she needed to eat more than junk food, but she ignored it. She had been more emotional than usual and figured she was PMSing, so she gave herself a pass.

Grabbing a bag of Flamin' Hot Lays, Cool Ranch Doritos, and a bag of Cheddar Ruffles for Karter, Hazel headed to the next aisle. She swiped up her favorite chocolates, including a bag of peanut M&Ms and a Twix for her man. If he decided to come home, she wanted to also apologize with gifts, not just words.

As she headed to the checkout counter, Hazel's gaze fell on a display of colorful flowers. Without hesitation, she picked a small bouquet of daisies, their cheerful petals a stark contrast to the storm raging inside her. Maybe a bit of beauty could help chase away the darkness, if only for a moment.

"Beautiful flowers for the pretty lady," the Hispanic man behind the counter said.

Hazel offered a weak smile. "Thank you."

He returned the gesture with a sympathetic nod and began ringing up her things. The flowers were on the house, but she didn't know it. Stepping outside, she clutched the bag and eyed the parking lot before making it to her Jeep.

Before she pulled off, she pulled out a Snickers bar and tore into it. She needed something to comfort her for the silent ride home. Music wouldn't do. With her doors locked, she started to pull off until she saw a familiar face emerge from one of the cars at the pump. Jarel was lost in his own world with his phone to his ear, seemingly in a heated conversation.

Hazel's mind immediately went to her sister. They had spoken minutes before she called Teyona, and Mia mentioned that Jarel had to work late. This didn't look like work to her, and she made a mental reminder to bring it up but in a way that wasn't harmful.

She knew inserting herself in her sister's business was wrong, but Hazel couldn't help herself. The swirling in her gut was telling her something wasn't right. To her surprise, Jarel walked out of the store just as she rolled her window down. Ducking, Hazel listened intently as he strolled past the driver's side.

"I said I'll be there in a minute, man. Yeah. She's at home. Bye," he grumbled before shoving the phone inside his pocket.

Hazel had to will herself to calm down. Her chest heaved as if she'd been caught.

She? He has to be talking about Mia.

Hazel watched as Jarel pumped his gas, and she buckled her seatbelt. The urge to follow him soared through her like no other. It might not have been a smart idea, but it was what she planned to do. She pulled out of the parking lot behind him, leaving some space in between. Thankfully, he didn't seem to be in a rush. When

Jarel passed the exit to Mia's home ten minutes into the drive, Hazel's skin prickled with heat.

"What the hell are you up to?" Hazel mumbled.

Following him was so out of her character, but it felt normal. She hadn't felt like herself in months. Grateful her Jeep could overlook the cars in between them, Hazel continued her pursuit. Five minutes later, Jarel turned into a subdivision Hazel didn't recognize. It was nicely built, though. It was a typical suburban neighborhood, quiet and unassuming, but Hazel's mind raced with suspicions.

He bypassed the apartment buildings and drove toward the townhomes. Her breathing grew harsher as he pulled into one of the driveways. Hazel was going to lose her shit if Jarel had a secret family.

She gritted her teeth and prepared to hop out and confront him but thought about how this would look. So, she waited. Her breath caught in her throat as Jarel parked and exited the car. He was so comfortable with his surroundings that he hadn't noticed he was being followed, nor did he glance in Hazel's direction. Still, she ducked just in case.

The sinking feeling in her gut had led her to this moment, and her mind raced with possibilities she didn't want to acknowledge. With squinted eyes, she peered through her window, watching as he ambled to the front door and knocked as if he were still upset. Hazel's pulse quickened as she reached for her phone. With shaky hands, she pulled up the camera and zoomed in. She stopped breathing when the front door opened and a figure emerged—the soft glow of the porch light illuminated a woman's silhouette.

Time stood still as Hazel sat in disbelief. With the way she was parked, she noticed a hint of a smile on the woman's face as she kissed Jarel's cheek. Her lips were much too close to his mouth. Hazel's eyes widened in shock. Before she could comprehend it all, Jarel stepped inside, and the door closed. Her stomach churned with a sickening mixture of betrayal and shock. There was no way Jarel was cheating on her sister. She blinked, hoping she was making an assumption. The woman could've been anyone.

Hazel repeated those words as she remained glued to her spot. She struggled to process what she had just seen but wasn't making any excuses. With the way things had been going in their lives, she wouldn't be surprised if this was one more slap to the face. A lump formed in her throat as she thought about what to tell Mia.

"I can't tell her this. It'll break her heart," Hazel groaned as her chest tightened with regret.

Sitting alone in her Jeep, Hazel felt profound sadness and betrayal, knowing her sister's world was about to come crashing down around her. She also felt a flicker of determination, a resolve to stand by Mia's side and support her through whatever came next. It was what she always did, no matter what.

Slowly, she pulled down the street with her thoughts racing. Her brain rummaged through the events of the last month, and she wanted to throw up. There was so much to intake, and she and her sisters were feeling the brunt of it all.

"Wait," she gasped, slamming on the brakes.

A bitter taste filled her mouth as she threw the gear in park and looked over her shoulder at the house. A wave of nausea washed over Hazel as she took in the car Jarel had just climbed out of. Quickly, her mind replayed the conversation she and Mia had that day at her house.

Hazel drew her head back. "What do you mean someone is leaving her letters? When did this start?"

"I'm not sure when it started, but it happened again earlier this week."

"Did she tell you what kind of car they were in? I can have Karter keep an eye out."

Mia nodded. "Yes. It was a black Ford Fusion, but she said they pulled into a driveway. I thought maybe she was just being paranoid."

Tears of anger pooled in her eyes; all she could think about was revenge. Hazel was staring at the same black Ford Fusion that had followed Teyona that day. Her little sister wasn't being paranoid like Mia thought. Jarel was in on whoever was trying to cause them harm, and Hazel wasn't going for it. She was conflicted, though. Telling Mia would shatter what she thought was her fairytale love story, but keeping it from her would hurt worse.

"I can't tell her yet. Not like this," Hazel mumbled.

She and Kimberly were more alike than she knew.

SEVENTEEN

The weekend for the 10th Annual Global Health Gala had finally arrived, and Mia was more excited than she had previously been. She was the more sociable one out of her sisters and looked forward to seeing some of the people she communicated with throughout the States. Mixing and mingling with them wasn't the sole purpose behind her joy. Not having to attend with Matthew was.

Mia walked into the hospital room and stopped herself from rolling her eyes. When she got the call from Daniel, her father's assistant, that Matthew was being rushed to the hospital, Mia was beyond concerned with worry. Now, she had no remorse as she watched him gripe and groan, still holding on to his bad attitude.

"This is complete bullshit," Matthew fussed. "One of the most important weekends for the company, and I'm laid up in the hospital."

It serves you right, Mia thought.

He was lying in bed with his leg elevated and wrapped in bandages. What was supposed to be a quick fundraising game of softball turned into disarray once Matthew injured his leg. The doctors said it was a torn ligament in his knee. It was mild but would still take at least three weeks to recover. With his age and stubbornness, probably more.

"Maybe this was a sign that you needed to sit down somewhere," Mia said.

He cut his eyes at her. "Don't start your mess, Mia. Why are you the only one up here? Where are your sisters?"

Mia knew asking about her mother hadn't crossed his mind. Even if it had, pride wouldn't let him express his thoughts aloud. Kimberly received the news from Mia and sent some encouraging words. That was all. Matthew could take that time lying in bed to think about all the vile things he had done in his life. Kimberly didn't want or need to be there for that.

"Well, Teyona is in school, and Hazel has a job."

Matthew grunted. Her response wasn't what he was trying to hear.

"If I get me some crutches, I could still make it to the gala."

Mia chuckled. "Daddy, no, you can't. It's okay to miss out on things. Isn't that what you have me for?"

His eyes lit up. "You've been acting like you can't stand me, so I don't know. *Is* that what I have you for?"

His condescending tone made her neck hot, but Mia played her role. Her stoic expression would never give way to how she was really feeling. She was learning that it was the only way to deal with her father. After all these years, she finally saw what Hazel and Teyona had been saying.

"Of course it is. I'll be sure to let everyone know how saddened you are about missing the gala, but your health comes first. It would look ridiculous for you to be limping around, going against everything Grant Pharmaceuticals stands for."

Beaming, Matthew nodded his head. "That's my girl. Always staying on top of business. Let Ben know his contribution to the health school has been beaten. I'll have Daniel write up a new check from us."

"I can do it. I'm sure he's swamped with work," Mia said.

"Okay, but make sure it's before tomorrow evening so you can announce it."

The smug look on his face was sickening. Matthew wanted to rub it in Ben's face that money was plentiful. That was fine because Mia would make sure she and Hazel got their cut, too.

"I will. Now, I'll have to find me a new date," she said, laying it on thick with her pouting face.

He grimaced as he adjusted in bed. "What about that boyfriend of yours? I'm sure you can take him in public, and he won't embarrass you."

This time, Mia did roll her eyes. "I can, but it's so last minute. It doesn't matter. I'll go by myself and have a good time."

"I thought your sister was going?"

It felt awkward hearing him ask about Teyona. Though she wanted to attend at first, Teyona changed her mind. Instead, she made plans to hang with DeShaun. A weekend with him sounded much better than trying to appease her dad and a bunch of folks she knew kissed his ass.

"Nope. Just me. I have some things I need to get done, but I'll call and check on you later."

Matthew grunted and waved her away. Mia shook her head and walked out of his room. The man was so grumpy and full of himself that it made no sense. If she were her mother, she wouldn't have come to check on him either. The loving daughter in Mia wouldn't allow her to do that, though. She held a soft spot for the man who raised her, but she was learning to place boundaries between them. Otherwise, she would remain at his beck and call, turning a cheek to his ugly ways.

When Mia made it to her car, she called Hazel. She had been ignoring her all week, and she didn't like that. Though she sent her a text letting her know things were good, Mia felt otherwise. It wasn't like them to go days without hearing each other's voice or seeing each other's faces.

"Hey," Hazel answered. "I'm painting, so I'll have to call you back."

"Oh," Mia quipped. "Well, okay. Glad to see you're in your zone. You sure you're good?"

Hazel cleared her throat. She and Karter had made up, but Hazel wasn't good. Jarel's deceitfulness was still heavy on her heart, and avoiding Mia was the only way she could refrain from sharing the bad news.

"Yeah, I'm good. Just happy to be back in my creative space," Hazel answered.

Mia smiled. "I'm happy to hear that, sis. Really. I didn't want anything. I'll call you later. Love you."

"Love you, too."

With her heart now content since she spoke with Hazel, Mia called the next person on her list. She knew Kimberly would give her some pushback for what she was about to ask her, but Mia didn't care. She was grateful for her father's unexpected injury and wanted to take advantage of it. Sometimes, life had a way of working out for the best, even amid its challenges.

The Rolls Royce Phantom glided to a stop in front of the venue, and the driver climbed out.

"I can't believe you talked me into coming to this," Kimberly whispered in a hiss.

Her grumbles only made Mia smile. Since her father couldn't attend the gala, Mia took Kimberly as her date for the evening. In her eyes, it was only right. She had been the main supporter and right-hand man in getting Grant Pharm. to where it is today. Plus, Mia wanted her mother to get out of the house and mingle.

"Well, we're here, so there's no turning back now. Aren't you excited to see some of your old friends?" Mia asked.

Kimberly was uncertain and slightly unsettled. She hadn't been to a gala or health event in years—not since a year or two after her diagnosis. The stares she received haunted her for weeks. Instead of people speaking to her in a normal tone, they shouted their words as if she were deaf. Kimberly felt humiliated and ashamed of who she had become and didn't want to subject herself to that kind of pain until she got better. By the time she did, Matthew and her marriage was so rocky that showing her face at these events was no longer a priority for her.

"Sure," Kimberly replied.

Going into her evening purse, she pulled out a compact mirror and checked her reflection. The makeup artist had done an amazing job on her face for the night. She wanted a glamorous, polished look that spoke boldly to the person she was today. The Kimberly they once knew was gone.

The bold berry color on her lips made them look plump, and the light shimmer on the inner corner of her eyes accentuated her light brown orbs. She exchanged her subtle jewelry for statement diamonds and sapphires, which adorned her decolletage and complemented the hue of her dress—and a dress it was.

Kimberly figured she'd go big or stay home. Her dress was a masterpiece of a design that her wardrobe stylist at Vanity picked out for her. It was a drastic difference from her conservative attire. The rich satin shade of midnight blue draped elegantly over her slender frame, announcing her curves. The bodice was intricately adorned with sequins and shimmery beadwork that caught Kimberly's eyes at first glance. It was the only dress she tried on.

She had thought about not drawing attention to herself, but it easily gravitated her way. Once they entered the grand ballroom, all eyes were on her. The floor-length gown garnered head turns as she moved with poise and grace. Though it hadn't been mentioned much in recent times, her name still held weight. Kimberly Grant was a vision of opulence, elegance, and refinement. Her plunging neckline added a touch of allure but remained tastefully sophisticated.

Mia beamed with pride as she watched her mother own the room. The sparkling hairpin she added to her chignon at the last minute gave her ensemble the perfect finishing touch.

"You look so beautiful, Mama. I'm happy to have you by my side tonight," Mia gushed, batting her wet eyes.

Kimberly squeezed her hand, warmed by her words. "Thank you, baby. I'm happy to be here with you."

"Mrs. Grant, what a pleasant surprise to see you and your lovely daughter this evening."

Chet Ryan, CEO of another million-dollar health company, greeted the duo with hugs. At one point in time, he had been against Grant Pharmaceuticals, claiming that a Black-owned company of its stature wouldn't last. Then, he asked for partnership once he saw how much of an impact it made. Shame on him, yet Kimberly remained graceful.

"Chet, it's been so long. How is Renae and the girls?"

"Way too long. They're doing good. You know she hates these things," he whispered with a chuckle. "Is your husband around? I need to catch up with my old friend."

Mia smirked. Matthew bad-talked this man like a dog. If that's what he considered an old friend, she didn't want any.

"Unfortunately, he won't be able to make it. He injured himself yesterday during the charity softball game."

Chet sighed, with his thin lips pressed together. "Aw, man. I hate to hear that. Speedy recovery for Matthew. Send him my love."

"Sure thing," Kimberly said sweetly.

Mia waited until he walked away and was out of earshot. "Now, why did he sit up here and act like he and Daddy are the best of pals?"

Kimberly snickered and swatted her arm. "Hush. You know everyone who attends these things fake the funk. Let's take some pictures."

They posed for a few pictures in front of the well-put-together backdrop before heading to their assigned table. Amidst the sea of guests, Kimberly couldn't ignore the whispers of admiration and awe. Her presence stood out like a beacon of elegance in a room full of admirers. Many had questions, while others were pleasantly happy to see her face.

Finally, they made it to their table, which sat off to the left of the main stage. After taking their seats, Mia took in the venue and had to give props to the decorators. Every year, they upped the grandeur. You could tell wealth was in the building, with the towering marble columns adorned with cascading vines and crystal chandeliers casting a soft, ethereal glow across the space. Even the air was different as she inhaled.

Soft music filled the space, mixing with the murmurs of conversation. Mia couldn't help but wonder what awards would be presented tonight. Each year, the attendees were given the opportunity to vote for their favorites in numerous categories. Grant Pharmaceuticals had an entire wall full of awards from this event and many others throughout the years. Matthew wanted them to be the best and always strived for it.

"Thank you," Mia said as the waitress assigned to their section placed glasses of water down.

"My pleasure. May I start you off with a glass of wine this evening?"

Mia nodded. "I'll take champagne, please."

"And for you?"

Kimberly glanced over the list. "Chardonnay, please."

The waitress nodded and walked away. Minutes later, chilled flutes filled with their preferred choices were placed in front of them. Mia sipped, feeling the urge to order a second serving already. Kimberly only ordered, just in case. She'd had a glass while getting her hair done and another on the way to the gala.

"Kimberly?"

Her name was said in a questioning tone as if the person couldn't believe it was her. The woman speaking rounded the table with bright eyes and shock.

"Marie," Kimberly uttered, standing to her feet.

The two women embraced and almost broke down in each other's arms. They were the best of friends until her injury, but things had changed. Kimberly broke away first, not wanting to ruin her makeup.

"My gosh," she choked out. "It's so good to see you."

"You too," Marie said, dabbing her face with a cloth napkin. "Mia, hi." She gave Mia a side hug. "I was not expecting to see you here. Is…is he here?"

Kimberly shook her head. "No, or I wouldn't be."

Marie's throat bobbed. "Of course. How have you been? I hate that we're no longer in contact, but it's for the better, right?"

She wanted Kimberly to give her a different answer than she had been receiving all these years. Marie always wanted to rekindle their friendship, but Matthew forbade it. He had made it seem like it was Kimberly's idea, and it hurt her to her core. After years of hushed rumors, Marie found out he had lied. He claimed she wasn't beneficial to Kimberly's progress and cut off all communication between them. He'd inflicted the type of pain Marie promised to never allow to happen again, but she was willing to start over. Now, she wondered if Kimberly felt the same.

"No, it never was. I'm *so* sorry for everything. Would you like to catch up outside of here?" Kimberly asked, her voice full of hope.

She missed her friend and her old life that brought the light out in her eyes, not dimmed them.

Marie eagerly nodded. "Yes, of course. Put my number in your phone." Kimberly reached to grab her phone, and Marie gently took hold of her hand. "And don't apologize. Nothing that happened to you was your fault. You're not to blame for anything that happened between us, either. Okay?"

Nodding, Kimberly swallowed her tears. Those words meant more to her than Marie would ever know. She saved her number under Dr. Marie, and they hugged again before she walked away to take her seat. Mia had tons of questions, but she didn't bother asking any. The smile on her mother's face was enough to know that tonight hadn't been just for her. Kimberly's presence was needed and missed immensely.

As the evening unfolded, Kimberly found herself away from her table and mingling with old colleagues. With the presence of her husband not looming over her, she felt the freest she'd ever been. She had introduced him to most of the people in attendance. Yes, he'd put in the work for the company to be where it was, but her dedication and service were why it lasted once he became the CEO at thirty-five.

Standing from her chair, Mia walked over to her mother, who was on the dance floor. Laughter fell from her lips as an old student of hers twirled her around. She was so proud to see some of the students she taught take the healthcare field by storm, leaving their mark in the industry.

"Mama, I'ma run to the restroom. Are you good?" Mia asked.

Kimberly's smile stretched across her face. "I'm more than good, baby. Handle your business."

Mia giggled as Kimberly shooed her away and continued dancing. As she navigated through the crowd while holding onto her black silk dress, Mia was stopped and greeted. She was the face to know and converse with since Matthew wasn't in attendance, but she couldn't now. Mother Nature was calling.

Approaching the lavishly decorated restroom area, she paused momentarily, adjusting the pearl necklace draping her neck. There was only a short wait, as too many flutes of wine had been consumed. She hummed to the beat of whatever song was playing through the speakers while making her way into an empty, spacious stall.

Thankfully, her dress wasn't difficult to slide down her frame as she handled her business. With a wipe and quick zip of her dress, she was out of the stall and standing at the clear sink. She washed her hands, made subtle adjustments to her hair, and touched up her makeup with a sponge brush from her purse.

Satisfied with her appearance, Mia smoothed down the fabric of her gown and gave herself a brief moment to breathe. These galas could be a bit overwhelming if you weren't used to them. The thing is, she was, but she felt pressured by Matthew not being there. Her emotions were the total opposite of Kimberly's. She had attended in his absence, yet his presence still lingered. Pushing out a breath, Mia shook it off and exited the restroom.

"Another glass of wine will calm me down," she said to herself.

With her clutch in hand, she opted to go to the bar instead. Her requested beverage was placed in her hand, and she headed back to their table. First, her eyes searched for her mother. No matter how much fun she was having, Mia had to check on her. When she no longer spotted her on the dance floor, she began to worry. Her head swiveled around the space as her chest constricted.

"What the hell," she hissed, spotting Kimberly.

She wasn't alone.

Ducked off in the corner away, Kimberly and a man Mia had never seen before were in a heated conversation. She could tell by the movement of her mother's hands and the snaking of her neck that this man had her fucked up. Mia was already making her way toward them, but she put a determined pep in her step when he gripped Kimberly's arm.

Kimberly looked as if she saw a ghost as Mia approached them. Shoving the man in his chest, he glared at her and sharply pointed his finger.

"This isn't over," he spat with a cold tone that rattled Mia.

This man, whoever he was, wasn't an old friend of her mother's. That was for sure.

"Hey!" Mia called after him.

He didn't bother to acknowledge her before blending seamlessly into the crowd and leaving without a trace.

"Um, who was that, and are you okay?" Mia questioned.

Kimberly was so shaken up that she couldn't speak. All she did was nod.

"Do you want to leave?"

Kimberly nodded again. Her responses reminded Mia of when she was relearning to speak. She was bereft of words, and so was her daughter. Mia didn't know what had just taken place, but she knew one thing—Kimberly had a treasure chest full of secrets, and she was determined to dig them out.

EIGHTEEN

Hazel hadn't smiled this big in months. Not even the piece she was working on provided this sense of gratification. She fanned the baggy shirt she was wearing as sweat coated her skin. Nervousness clung to her, but excitement with each word spoken through the receiver was building up.

"The art show isn't until the winter, but we want to secure the line-up. My team and I think you'll be a perfect addition," Janae said.

Hazel was hesitant to answer when the unknown number appeared on her phone's screen. She was sure it was the mystery blackmailer calling. The shock that shot through her when Janae introduced herself as the gallerist of Visionary Vault, Hazel could've passed out. The introduction was welcomed but not needed.

Hazel was highly familiar with who she was as the owner of such a profound Black-owned art gallery. Since college, she had watched her YouTube videos, vlogs, and any interviews Janae was featured in. She was the Who's Who in the art world and Atlanta.

Not only had she personally reached out to Hazel, but she wanted her work featured in one of the biggest art shows of the year.

"I'd be honored to participate," Hazel said humbly, although she wanted to scream.

"Perfect. I've had my eye on you for a while; I just hadn't had the time to reach out. Are you currently working on a piece?"

Hearing that she knew who she was and wanted to work with her had Hazel fanning her wet eyes. This was truly a dream come true. All of her prayers were being answered.

"I'm working on a few projects," she replied.

"I want you to create something fresh," Janae said. "A new canvas with something out of the box and thought-provoking. Give me emotions, intrigue, and a piece so profound that everyone will want to buy it."

Hazel nodded, eager to get to work. "Is there a specific theme I should aim towards, or just let my hand flow?"

"Each artist has a theme for the show. Yours is human connection. I want you to make this piece a part of you. Explore the relationships, bonds, and emotions between people and their environment. Think of the people in your life who mean the most to you."

Her mind was working overtime with fresh ideas already. The excitement Janae spoke with reminded Hazel of her purpose for drawing. It meant more to her than paint, ink, or lead on display.

"Human connections. I love that theme and already have a few ideas in mind," she said.

"That's what I love to hear. If you need to spark some inspiration or get feedback, I'm a text away. You can even come down to the Vault and escape. As creatives, we need a safe space. I'll have my assistant email you everything we'll need from you, and we'll go from there. Do you have any questions for me?"

Hazel smiled. "No questions at the moment. Thank you again for this opportunity. You've inspired me throughout my entire career to keep going and dig deeper. This means more to me than I can express through words."

"Express it through your art. I'm happy to be here and further push you along your journey. We'll chat soon, Hazel. Enjoy your evening."

"You, as well. Have a good night."

As soon as she heard the three beeps indicating the call had ended, Hazel dropped her phone onto the kitchen counter and exhaled. Then, her mouth spewed a shrill of pure excitement, disbelief, and joy. Had Karter not been tuned in the entire call, he would've thought someone was killing her.

Panting, Hazel rested her palms on her knees and cried from her gut. This moment was so surreal. Every sacrifice she had made—the feeling of not being worthy, selling her soul, being blackmailed, and telling herself that one day it would all pay off—was being released from her body. She'd held on to everything, storing it away. Because at the end of the day, she had to keep going. She didn't know what she was going towards besides her studio, but now she knew.

God hadn't forgotten about her.

"Thank you, God," she cried, lifting her hands. "Thank you!"

Her shouts had Karter emotional right along with her. Every day, he saw the work she put in. Hazel's vision boards around the loft, notes she showed him on her phone, their raspy conversations in the wee hours of the morning, sharing her dreams while lying on his chest...it all had come to fruition.

Grinning, he walked over to her with his arms wide open. Hazel fell into them, and he squeezed tightly.

"I'm so fucking proud of you, baby. You earned this shit. Straight up," Karter said.

Hazel's chest hiccupped as he praised her. His words always sent her head spinning and made her heart flutter, but they hit differently today. The cadence in his voice stirred an onset of new emotions.

"Thank you. I can't even believe that just happened. Like… what the fuck," she whispered, then yelled, "My art is going to be in the Visionary Vault!"

"Hell yeah, it is!" Karter shouted and clapped loudly.

He was her hype man, and Hazel couldn't help but laugh. As to himself as he was, for her, he was whomever Hazel needed him to be, and she loved that. Grabbing her face, Karter kissed her lips, and using his thumb, he wiped the moisture from underneath her eyes.

"I'm so happy," Hazel whimpered.

"I know you are. You gotta stop crying, though," he said, chuckling while wiping another tear that slid down her cheek.

Inhaling, Hazel blew out a deep breath. "Okay. I'm sorry again for not telling you everything that was going on."

"Where that come from?"

Karter had already forgiven her, and they talked it out. He didn't want her to keep bringing up the situation like she was trying to convince him that she was sorry. He believed her.

"I just need you to know it. I'm so thankful for you. You could've stayed out that night, but you came back home. You didn't leave me, and you've been by my side through everything. On the days when I wanted to give up, you pushed me, reminding me of my potential and how far I've come. I don't want you to ever feel like your presence in my life doesn't matter because it does."

"I don't feel that way. You know, you been holding a nigga down, too. Going against your family and all types of silly shit. We ain't gotta keep going over what happened. That shit is over with, and you have more important things to worry 'bout," Karter said.

"You're right. I'm not going to be able to sleep tonight. All I'm going to be thinking about is my piece and what it will be about."

Pulling her into his chest, Karter placed kisses along her neck. "I can think of a few ways to put you to sleep."

Squirming under his soft lips, Hazel craned her neck, giving him better access to one of her hot spots. Karter knew them all. Before she could get into the moment, her phone vibrated along the counter.

"Naw. Call whoever that is back," Karter said, pulling her hand away as she reached for it.

Hazel moaned, "It might be someone important."

He eased up, allowing her to grab it. Her heart began to race when she saw the unknown caller. It wasn't hard to guess who it was. She had been anticipating his call but hated it had to be today of all days. Hazel let it roll to voicemail, but he immediately called right back.

"Aye," Karter said through gritted teeth, "you want me to talk to this nigga? Whoever this is ain't about to have you afraid to answer your phone."

Hazel shook her head as her stomach twisted with anxiety. Karter answering and patronizing him would only make things worse. With her mood ruined, Hazel answered the call. She was hoping this would be the last she heard from him. He got the money. What else could he want?

"Hello."

"I don't like to be ignored."

His voice was calm, yet it still chilled Hazel's frame. Her arms pricked with goosebumps as she anticipated his next words.

"You see I answered," she snapped, finding her voice.

He chuckled. "As if you had a choice. I'm getting beside the point. You'll never guess who I ran into recently."

Hazel swallowed, not wanting to ask who. Honestly? She didn't care because she knew nothing about him, yet he seemed to know so much about her and her family. It was sickening.

"Ol' Kimberly still looks the same."

His tone was menacing. Her blood ran cold, hearing her mother's name fall from his lips.

"What did you do to her?" she hissed, gritting her teeth.

How did he manage to run into her mother, especially now? Panic surged within her as she struggled to keep her composure. She made her way into the living room, ready to take a trip to her parents' house.

"I haven't done anything to her yet. Unlike you, she seems to want to cooperate. So, here's what's going to happen."

"What do you want?" Her voice was stern, hating that he was demanding more from her.

"I want answers," he replied cryptically. "If your mother gives me what I want, I'll try to leave the past in the past."

His words didn't sound convincing at all.

"And if not?" Hazel found herself asking.

"If not, she may or may not face the consequences. Or would you prefer it to be your dad? The two of them…" he said, making a ticking noise with his mouth. "They are some ruthless human beings. Why they had children and made them suffer, I'll never know. Hopefully, Kimberly holds up her end of the stick."

With that, he hung up, leaving his threat hanging in the air like a heavy, ominous drape. If he pulled it back, it would reveal the worst. Hazel's mind raced as she tried to think of a way out of this nightmare, which had haunted her for weeks. There had to be a way to put an end to this blackmailer, and she hoped her mother did just that. After all, she was the one with the secrets and the reason this man contacted her in the first place.

"I hope you feel better. Don't worry about your shifts being covered. People have already volunteered to work them for you for the next three days. We'll see you back here next week," Mia's supervisor from the hospital said.

Releasing a desperate cough, she said, "Thank you so much. I hope I'm feeling better soon."

"Me too. See you next week."

When the call ended, Mia exhaled. She hadn't lied to get off work since she was in her early twenties. Back then, she was still trying to live the nightlife while balancing a career. Now, she had called in fake sick for another reason. Glancing up at the name on the building, a bubble of nerves filled her chest.

She knew her curiosity would get her in trouble one day, but she needed to find trouble—it had the answers she was looking for.

Stepping out of her car, Mia took in her surroundings. The air was eerily quiet as her thoughts ran wild. She pulled the door open to the main office and headed to the counter. A young man wearing a dark green collared shirt with the name *Store & Go* embedded on the left side greeted her with a smile.

"Good afternoon. How can I help you?" he asked.

"Hi. I came to retrieve a few things from my storage unit but can't seem to find my key. Is there any way I can get a replacement?"

"There is a twenty-five-dollar fee. What's your name?"

"Mia Grant."

He typed her credentials into the system, but nothing came up. Mia knew nothing would. She was playing the role of a regular customer but would use her last name to pull some weight if she had to.

"It doesn't look like you have a unit with us, Ms. Grant," he said.

"Perhaps it's under one of my parents' names. My father is on bed rest at the time and sent me to retrieve a few things."

He nodded. "We can search it that way. Let's start with your mother's name."

"Kimberly Grant."

Typing the name in, he pulled up nothing. "There is no unit under her name. Let's try your father's."

"Matthew Grant."

Immediately, he recognized the name, and his eyes stretched. "The owner?"

Mia smiled. "Yes."

"I'm so sorry about that, ma'am. You should've told me."

He chuckled nervously, typing in the name. He made a few clicks and scrolls with his mouse. When his brows dipped, Mia became worried.

"Is there something wrong?"

"No. It's just that this unit was somehow removed from the system. Nevertheless, I can get the key for you."

That revelation should not have come as a surprise, but it did. She was expecting the unit to be under Kimberly's name. Now, she wondered which one of them had actually opened it. Mia was soon going to find out.

"Okay. Thank you."

"Not a problem," he said.

Mia hated that she was putting this man's job on the line, but she had no choice. She needed answers.

She waited for ten minutes, and he returned with a spare key.

"Sorry about that. I had to cut a new one. There seems to have only been one copy made in recent years. There's no fee," he said, smiling.

"I appreciate you so much. I'll be sure to let my dad know how great of a job you're doing."

He beamed wide. "Thank you!"

Mia headed toward the door but then stopped and turned around. "Oh. I almost forgot. Which unit is it again?"

He glanced at his screen. "J152."

Mia thanked him again and exited the building. Hopping in her car, she proceeded to aisle J and drove slowly until she approached unit one-fifty-two. She didn't know what led her to check the storage units; it had been the last thing on her mind. She couldn't stop thinking about the journals Teyona and Ms. Marie mentioned. She had a strong feeling they were a significant part of the answers she was looking for.

While she was up late the night before, Mia thought about all the businesses her father owned outside of the pharmaceutical company. It hit her like a ton of bricks when she realized the only place to look was the storage units. Matthew's brother was the manager, and Mia was glad he wasn't at work today. Otherwise, she would've had to finesse a little more to get a key.

The bold letter and numbers of the unit stared at Mia as she used the key to unlock it. Lifting the gate, she blew out a deep breath. She wasn't prepared for the piles of boxes, but she appreciated how neatly they were placed. That alone stood out to her. Her dad wasn't a neat freak…Kimberly was.

"Hmm," Mia hummed, scenarios swirling in her mind. "So, Mom got the storage unit and put it in Dad's name. Or they already had one and had it removed from the system. But for what?"

The questions tormented Mia as she began to go through every box. Some were labeled, but she still went through them just in case. Other boxes weren't labeled at all, making her task that much more difficult. An hour into her quest, defeat threatened to settle in her aching bones as she popped her knuckles and stretched her neck and back. She was about to give up until she came across a gray container. It was the only one of its kind inside the storage unit.

That has to mean something, right?

Blowing out a breath and patting her perspired forehead, Mia pushed it across the concrete. Taking a seat on her makeshift chair of boxes, she popped the top. A grin covered her face as she spotted a stack of journals. She was hoping they had all of her answers. First to be removed was a black fedora hat. A baby blanket that she could vividly remember Teyona having sat underneath. Next was a photo album.

Mia got comfortable and began flipping through the pages. She smiled as images of Teyona as a newborn neatly decorated the first few pages. Her birthdate, time of arrival, and the hospital where she was born had all been neatly written.

"Aww," Mia cooed, looking at pictures from her sister's first birthday party.

Some pages in, there was a picture of Teyona in the same fedora hat she just set aside. As she continued looking through the photos, one thing was clear—this was an album for Teyona with barely any pictures that included Matthew. Mia didn't want to think too much into that observation, but how could she not? Almost one hundred photographs, and Matthew was present in maybe only two?

"Something isn't right," Mia mumbled, closing the book.

As she did, a lone picture fell out. Picking it up, she examined it and gasped. Quickly flipping it over, she read the back.

Uncle G and Teyona – Summer 2000

Squinting, Mia drew her head back.

"Teyona was only one," she mumbled, examining the picture.

Her sister's age didn't have her befuddled. It was the man in the photo—the same man she saw having a heated argument with

Kimberly at the gala. To Mia's knowledge, neither of her parents had a brother named G, so who was this man?

Placing everything back inside the container, Mia sealed it and tossed it into her backseat. She didn't care that she had left the storage a mess. With all the dust inside, she was sure no one had been inside it for quite some time.

Speeding out of the parking lot, she dialed Hazel's number. When she didn't answer, Mia hung up and decided to head to her sister's house. Finally, she was getting closer to whatever secret her parents were hiding.

Hazel's hardwood floor was scattered with journals, pictures, and handwritten notes between two lovers. Assumptions didn't need to be made anymore. Based on what they read in the pages of numerous journals, Kimberly had stepped out of her marriage. Not only did she have an affair, but she became pregnant. They had turned Hazel's living room into a chamber of revelations, where the past was speaking louder than the present. Yet, there was still so much to go.

"I can't believe Teyona isn't Dad's," Hazel murmured.

Like Mia, she was still in disbelief. It all made sense now: the way he treated her, how he never did much for her, and his attitude whenever her name was mentioned. Teyona wasn't his biological daughter, and he made it known. Yet, they were just now able to read between the lines.

"Me either. Mom knew all this time," Mia said.

"Her damn uncle is blackmailing me like I had something to do with Mom keeping Teyona away from them. Why go through all that when he could've just explained his motive?"

"It has to be something deeper. A missing part," Mia concluded.

When Mia arrived at Hazel's, she immediately showed her the picture of the man holding one-year-old Teyona. When Hazel confirmed he was the same man blackmailing her, it all began to make sense. Now, they needed to find out who and where Teyona's father was.

"There's a lot of missing parts," Hazel said, clearing her throat.

Mia glanced her way. "Why are you looking like that?"

"There's something I need to tell you."

Groaning, Mia leaned her head against the couch. "Just spit it out. Nothing can be worse than finding out our parents were cheating on one another."

Kimberly had gone into great detail about Matthew's affair and how she no longer felt love in their marriage or home. It was heartbreaking to read about their mother feeling alone in their home with a man she had practically known her entire life. They weren't condoning their mother's behavior; however, they understood her decisions.

Hazel hated to burst her bubble, but unfortunately, there was something worse.

"There might be," Hazel said. "Jarel—"

"Jarel, what?" Mia questioned, lifting her head.

The stare she gave Hazel tempted her to say forget it. Mia's heart slowed to a steady beat but felt heavier than ever. She couldn't handle any more bad news, especially not anything about her man.

Instead of verbally communicating what she had to say, Hazel pulled her phone out. She scrolled to the photos she had taken that evening when she followed Jarel and handed her phone to Mia.

"What am I supposed to be looking at?" Mia asked with a bite in her tone.

Hazel didn't take offense.

"The day we talked and you told me Jarel was working late, I saw him at the gas station. I overheard him talking to someone on the phone, and I decided to follow him."

"Hazel," Mia grumbled, handing her the phone back.

"No, no. Wait. Just hear me out. I swear I'm not trying to hurt your feelings, but you should know this."

Sighing, Mia clenched the phone in her hand. "Go ahead."

"So, I followed him. I don't know how he didn't see me, but I'm glad he didn't. He pulled up to this house, and I saw a woman open the door. At first, I thought it was a woman he was seeing, and my heart broke for you. But when I pulled off, I realized the car he was driving fit the same description as the one you said was following Teyona that day."

Mia blinked her watery eyes and glanced down at the phone. She swiped through the pictures again. When she saw the black Ford Fusion, she squeezed her eyes shut.

"Maybe it's a coincidence," she said softly, not wanting to believe what she was hearing or seeing.

"As bad as we both want it to be, it's not. Jarel is up to something, and I think it's all tied to who we now know as Teyona's uncle. Or maybe it's something different. I don't know who that lady is. Do you?"

Shrugging, Mia zoomed in on the picture. It was blurry and dark, but the woman didn't look like the cousin she had met.

"No. Maybe it's just a friend of his. I can ask."

"Okay...ask, but what about the car? You can't tell me that isn't weird. I wish Teyona would've gotten the license plate. He doesn't even drive that."

Mia knew he didn't, but she wasn't trying to accept that the man she fell in love with had stepped out on her. She felt like her mother after finding out Matthew had cheated.

"You know what. I'm not going to jump to conclusions. Like I said, I'll just ask him. I mean, I have proof."

"You can't show him the pictures, Mia. I followed him like a crazy person," Hazel insisted.

Mia gave her a deadpan stare. "Well…"

Hazel chuckled, trying to lighten the dark mood. "Right. That was crazy of me, but I followed my gut."

"Of course, and I thank you. How about we just go to the lady's house."

"See, now you're talking crazy. Hell, no. We don't know who she is or what she's got in there. The hell, Mia?"

Mia shrugged. "We want answers, right? I know I do. Hand me your MacBook."

Hazel stared at her, trying to see where her mind was at. Clearly, it wasn't in the right space. With a heavy sigh, she handed her the MacBook. Navigating Hazel's phone as if it were hers, Mia airdropped the clearest images of the house to the device. Pulling up Google Chrome, she did a reverse image search. After about five minutes of making sure the photo matched her research, she smiled.

"Found her."

"You want to go tonight?" Hazel questioned.

Mia shook her head. "No. I'm drained. Today was a sucker punch to the gut with everything we found out. I'll talk to him, and if I sense he's lying, we'll pull up over there and get our own answers."

Okay with that idea, Hazel nodded. "That's fine. Now, what about Teyona? Should we tell her or let Mom know we found out?"

"I don't think that's our place to tell her. As badly as I want to, Mom is responsible for that pain. We only found out because shit started getting weird around here."

"Too weird. I now know why he kept saying Mom had something he wanted," Hazel scoffed.

"It was his gotdamn niece," Mia grumbled.

Now, they needed to know where his brother was.

NINETEEN

Kimberly didn't know why she called her sister. Well, she knew why. Yet, she wished she hadn't now that they were on the phone. Nicole could never talk Kimberly out of something once her mind was set on it. She had been that way since they were kids. If there was a game Kimberly wanted to play but didn't know how to play, she watched and learned, even if it was dangerous. If there was a boy Nicole wanted to talk to but was too shy, Kimberly went to talk to him for her sister. She had no qualms about doing what was best for her or anyone she loved. This time, though, she had dropped the ball and was trying to right her wrongs. Finally.

"I just don't think this is a good idea, Kim," Nicole groaned.

"We're meeting in a public place. Everything will be fine."

Nicole huffed. "So you say. Graham walked up on you at the gala like he was about to whoop your ass."

Kimberly didn't mean to laugh, but the way Nicole said it had her cackling. The sisters shared a moment of laughter, though there was nothing comical about the situation. She had been so spooked seeing Graham at the gala that Kimberly wanted to take off running. She couldn't recall the last time she had seen him.

"Please, let's not talk about that. I couldn't even speak," Kimberly said, wiping her eyes from laughing so hard.

"What'd you end up telling Mia?"

"Nothing at all. That's why I'm going to meet him, so I can decide how to tell the girls. Especially Teyona. If anyone deserves to know the truth, she does."

Nicole was quiet for a few seconds. "Would you have told her if Graham didn't pop up asking questions?"

"Yes, eventually," Kimberly said, telling the truth.

She never wanted to keep who Teyona's real father was a secret; it just happened. It was as if he'd fallen off the face of the earth, and then she suffered from her fall, and nothing was the same since. Had she been given the chance to tell Teyona the truth, it would've been way before now. The way things were unfolding, Kimberly hoped and prayed she would forgive her. As far as Matthew, she couldn't care less about his feelings.

When Nicole said nothing else, Kimberly asked, "What? You don't believe me?"

"I do. I just wish you would've left him before all of this. I always said you were too good for him, but you were in love and already had Mia. Then Hazel came, and I was like, okay...two girls. Maybe this is it. Then, Teyona popped up out of nowhere."

The fact that Teyona was born six years after Hazel wasn't what made Nicole scratch her head back then. It was the conversations shared between the married couple, then relayed to her sister, that confused Nicole.

"Yeah...well. You knew how she got here after the fact," Kimberly said.

"Not until she was six, Kim. But the deed is done."

Kimberly grabbed her purse. "Yes, it is. I'll let you know how everything goes."

"Please do and be safe."

"I will."

When the sisters hung up, Kimberly exhaled. She kept everyone in the dark about her affair except Nicole. What started as friendly conversations between their classes turned into lunch dates, then phone conversations, and then dates in the office and out of town. It was brief yet impacted her entire life. The only thing Kimberly regretted was having married Matthew and letting him treat her daughter any kind of way. She would check him and stand up for Teyona, but Kimberly realized she could've done much more.

Making her way down the stairs, she was surprised to see Matthew sitting in the grand room. With his leg injury, he seemed to be moving along just fine. Kimberly didn't bother to speak, which was nothing new. They moved about the house like two strangers instead of husband and wife.

"Kimmy," Matthew called out.

She stopped in her tracks. He hadn't called her that nickname in years. Had this been a different time—one where her insides set ablaze when called the pet name, Kimberly would've loved it. Matthew using it now meant he wanted something.

Pivoting, she walked in his direction. Their eyes connected as she stood outside of the room. Regardless of how much she couldn't stand him, Kimberly would never deny his handsome looks. His rich, ebony skin, silky black hair with streaks of silver, and tall, lean frame used to be it for Kimberly. Even in his sixties, Matthew exuded pure confidence that men wish they had and an air of sex appeal that women clung to. There wasn't a thing you could say about her husband that could convince her that he wasn't the love of her life.

Those eyes of his told a different story.

They were brown, deep pools of wisdom and vitality, but Kimberly saw beyond that. There was a sense of emptiness portraying his darkness within. With a predatory gleam and crooked smile, Matthew always looked like he was plotting his next move. She noticed the subtle hint of amusement when he belittled someone or the satisfaction at the thought of causing harm or manipulating people. Matthew was cold and calculated––a man who could no longer sway her with his looks.

"Where's Nick?" she asked.

"I sent him home for the day."

She didn't know why he had sent his help home. If he needed something, he would be better off calling Nick back than asking her. Kimberly crossed her arms over her chest.

"Okay."

"Can you take a seat so we can talk?"

Her head cocked to the side. "Talk about what?"

"Why didn't you come visit me at the hospital?"

Kimberly laughed, hoping she maybe misheard him. "Excuse me?"

"Do you know how embarrassing it was to keep telling those nurses that my wife should be here soon or my wife is going to help me out at home?"

"Do you think I give a fuck?"

Kimberly's tone was chilling.

"You should! I needed your help."

"Maybe I'm missing something. Don't sit here with your propped-up leg and fake hurt because I didn't come to visit you. That's gaslighting one-oh-one. You do it so well that another woman would foolishly fall for it, but not me."

"So, you don't believe me?" Matthew asked, trying to pull her sympathy card, but there wasn't one.

"Not at all. Should I remind you how you treated me after my head injury? No, no. Would you like me to call out all the vile, hateful, disrespectful things you have said and done to me over the years? Because we can take it there."

Matthew deviously smirked, and Kimberly shifted her stance, ready to go to war. He had chosen the perfect day.

"Sure, Kimmy. Tell me what I've done," he said.

"Stop calling me that. I'd rather save my breath for the next man."

His smile dropped. The act he was putting on vanished so quickly that Kimberly wanted to laugh.

"That's how we got here in the first place. You opening your legs for the next broke-ass man," Matthew spat.

"Is that so? Because I can recall that mistress of yours playing on my phone, popping up on the campus where I worked, and letting it be known that she was going to take my spot. Oh, how quickly we forget our own sins."

Matthew chuckled. "I could never forget. They made me the man I am today."

"Some man," Kimberly scoffed. "The same man who shoved his wife down a flight of stairs because you weren't ready to face the truth behind your actions. Is that man in the room with us still, or did you make him disappear like you did Lawr—"

"Don't you dare speak that man's name in my house!" Matthew roared, standing to his feet.

A shot of pain ripped through him from the abrupt move, but he kept his game face on. Kimberly smirked. She knew just what nerve to push to take him over the edge.

"What a shame. After all these years, you still can't handle the truth and confess what you did."

"And you were the saint in all of this?!" Matthew spat, spittle flying from his mouth as his eyes glossed with a fiery hate.

"No, I wasn't, but let's not act like you weren't the reason for me to seek attention from another man. I told you I wanted another baby, thinking it'd help mend our almost-broken marriage. What did you do? Pour yourself into work and stay away from home. Not to mention, you kept messing around on me."

"What the hell did you expect me to do, Kim? I'm the CEO of—"

"A pharmaceutical company," she said, finishing his sentence. "That's an excuse. You're also a father, a son, an uncle, and most importantly, a fucking husband! This company got all of your time, and you lost your family."

"No, this company showed me that family isn't shit. That they'll stab you in the back when they don't get their way. We were fine with Mia and Hazel. I just made CEO, and you were advancing in teaching. We didn't need another child."

"That decision wasn't solely yours to make," Kimberly hissed.

"Yeah...well, I did. I made the decision for both of us."

Kimberly blinked slowly, taking in his words. "What're you saying?"

"I didn't find out Teyona wasn't mine once I found and read that journal you'd been writing in. I knew she wasn't mine the moment you got pregnant because I had a vasectomy the year prior. There was no chance I could've been her father."

Kimberly's mouth fell ajar, but no words or sound fell from her lips. As if a heavy veil had been dropped over the room, it was blanketed with silence. Matthew's confession made the tension between them unbearable. The pregnant pause gave just enough time for it to sink in. All this time, she thought Matthew only knew Teyona wasn't his because she was worried about her real father's whereabouts. It never once crossed her mind that he would do something as devious as undergoing surgery so they, as a married couple, could no longer have kids.

The furniture, once familiar and comforting, now felt like silent witnesses to a breach of trust. The sofa where they had shared countless moments of intimacy suddenly felt alien and out of place. Kimberly felt out of place. It felt like the walls were caving in on her as she thought back to the frightful night that ultimately changed her life.

Kimberly stood at the side of her oldest daughter's bed and kissed her forehead. She had already tucked in the youngest, Teyona, and she was knocked out.

"Mommy, will me and Hazel always have to dress alike?" Mia asked.

"No, not always. You don't like dressing alike?"

Young Mia shrugged. "It's okay to me. Haze doesn't like it, though. She's always fussing."

"Do not," Hazel said, walking into the bedroom from their bathroom.

Kimberly looked at her second-oldest daughter. "You can fuss about it. I do, too," she told her and winked.

Dressing them alike was cute when they were younger. At ages twelve and eight, the sisters wanted to express themselves freely. Kimberly agreed, but Matthew always wanted twins and felt they should at least keep the trend going until they were teenagers. Mia had one more year.

Hazel smiled up at her mother as she tucked her in the bed.

"Did you get all those little critters out of your nose?"

Hazel giggled. "Yes, Mommy. See."

She lifted her head, and Kimberly examined her nose. "Good job. Waffles for breakfast in the morning?"

"No, pancakes!" Mia shouted.

"Ssshhh. Tey is sleeping," Kimberly told her.

"Sorry," Mia whispered. "But I want pancakes."

Hazel rolled her eyes. "She was talking to me, and I want waffles with chocolate chips."

"Mommy can make both like always. Now, you girls better not start arguing when I leave. Your sister is sleeping, and she needs to stay that way."

They both grumbled out an okay.

"I love you both so much," she said, feeling emotional.

"We love you, too, Mommy," the girls replied in unison.

Kimberly couldn't help but grin. "Twins, after all. Goodnight."

She eased out of their room and shut the door. Exhaling, she ran a hand through her hair and walked down the hallway to her and Matthew's bedroom. She entered the room and shook her head at the perfectly made bed. Kimberly wasn't expecting her husband to be home. Once again, he had to work late.

His excuses went in one ear and out of the other, and they had been for years now. No man who owned the company worked until eight in the evening or later some nights. Kimberly didn't even plan to make a fuss tonight. She never did. Instead, she walked inside their massive bathroom, ran her a bubble bath, and relaxed.

An hour later, she was sitting up in bed with her favorite pair of pajamas on, her hair wrapped, a glass of wine on the nightstand, and her journal on her lap. Her heart was as heavy as her mind was as she scribbled words to no one in particular. There used to be someone she wrote them to, but she could no longer reach him.

"I don't understand where he went," Kimberly mumbled as she let her pen bleed.

After pouring her heart out over three pages, Kimberly decided to call it a night. Just as she closed her journal and stood from the bed to empty her bladder, Matthew entered their bedroom. Her eyes fleeted over his disheveled attire, and she clenched her jaw. If his loosened tie and wrinkled shirt weren't evidence that he'd been out cheating, his white collar was. He didn't even have enough respect to change his lipstick-stained shirt before coming home. Kimberly was disgusted.

"I hope you wore a condom," she spat, walking into the bathroom.

Matthew chuckled. "Like you, huh?"

Kimberly's entire frame froze at the counter. She couldn't show him that he had rattled her that quickly, so she kept her poker face.

"Are you accusing me of cheating on you?" she questioned, coming to the doorway to stare at him.

"I'm not in the mood to play mind games, Kimmy."

"You walk in our bedroom at almost midnight smelling like some cheap hoe, lipstick stains on your shirt and neck, and have the nerve to come at me crazy? You're the one playing mind games, Matthew," she spat, walking out of the bathroom.

"Okay, Kimmy," he huffed.

"No, it's not okay. We've been through this already. You remember what happened with the last mistress I caught you with," she grumbled lowly as if she didn't want anyone to know their secret.

Matthew smirked. "Yeah…we put her ass in a trunk."

"Because you can't keep your dick in your pants. I don't see anything comical about this."

"Life is funny sometimes, Kimmy. Lighten up, dear."

Matthew was pissing her smooth off, and she wanted to get as far away from him as possible. Thankful that he had nothing else to say, Kimberly grabbed her wine glass and headed toward their bedroom door. Suddenly, she wasn't tired at all. While she made her way to the kitchen to refill her glass, Matthew stripped from his shirt. Tossing it inside the hamper, he padded to the bathroom but stopped when he saw her journal on the nightstand.

He'd been waiting for her to leave it lying around accidentally, and it had been the night. With his chest heaving, Matthew didn't bother to see if she was making her way back upstairs. He grabbed the black journal and opened it to the entry she had just finished writing.

Something happened to Lawrence. I can feel it in my soul. That's how connected we are. I don't want to assume that Matthew somehow found out about us and harmed him, but it would make sense if he did. It's not like Lawrence to just go missing. He wouldn't just leave me and the girls behind, especially Teyona. She's starting to look more and more like him each day, and it saddens me that he doesn't get to see her.

Matthew slammed the journal shut and stormed out of the bedroom. He had no plans to argue with her tonight or even throw it in her face how he knew about her and her coworker sleeping around. The dirt he'd done over the years was unforgiving, and he knew it, but Matthew drew the line at Kimberly possibly having let his daughters meet this man.

"Kimberly!"

The bass in his voice echoed throughout the quiet house as he stomped down the hallway. Her journal was behind his back. The glass in Kimberly's hand slipped when she heard her name yelled. She had no time to worry about the red wine staining the carpet as she rushed toward the steps. Matthew greeted her at the top.

His eyes, which used to be filled with love when he saw her, were now narrowed and filled with a fierce rage. Kimberly's heart raced as she made it to the top step.

"Have you lost your mind? Our children are sleeping," she hissed, *worried about waking the girls.*

"I haven't lost it yet. You bitch and complain about my whereabouts and the times I come home late, but you're not innocent," he said, jabbing *her in the chest with his finger.*

Kimberly gasped and placed her hand over the tender spot. "Don't you dare shove your finger into my chest. Are you high?"

"I know all about your relationship with that professor."

"My relationship? I don't know what you're talking about."

"Here you go with these fucking mind games!"

He didn't care that he was yelling. Kimberly's cluelessness was making his blood boil.

"I'm not you!" she yelled back. "I don't have to play—".

Her words were cut short once he pulled the journal from behind his back. Matthew saw the moment her soul left her body. He wanted to smirk, but this wasn't about having a one-up on her. Not right now.

"Yeah. Keep talking. What is this then, huh?"

Kimberly's eyes watered, and he stepped closer to her face. She stepped back.

"You don't get to stand in my face and shed fucking tears!"

Her chest hiccupped. She couldn't believe she'd been so careless and left her journal for him to find. Not knowing what all he read, Kimberly tried to play into that.

"Give me my journal, please. You can't just invade my privacy."

"Fuck your privacy. You had my daughters around that man?" Matthew asked.

Her eyes widened. "What? No. I'd never. Just give me my journal back, and we can discuss everything like adults."

"Is that all you care about? Some stupid notebook pages!"

"Right now, yes."

Matthew's hand wrapped around her neck before she could finish her sentence. Squeezing tightly, he stared her in the eyes.

In an almost inaudible tone, he whispered in her ear, "I thought I got rid of him, yet you're still worried about where he is. Have you not learned your lesson yet?"

She wanted to cry hearing him confirm that he had done something to Lawrence, but she couldn't. Kimberly could hardly breathe as her fingers dug into his hands. She felt her foot on the edge of the step.

"Answer me," Matthew hissed.

She nodded her head, and he tightened his grip, keeping her at the edge.

"And you want to leave me? It's okay if you do. You've wanted a divorce for years now. I can't let you leave, Kimmy. But you can take a breather for yourself. Do you want that? A few hours to yourself to get your mind right?"

Kimberly didn't know what he was saying, so she nodded again. She felt his grip loosen, and her life flashed before her eyes as she went tumbling down the stairs.

"The only way out is death," Matthew mumbled coldly before springing into action when she hit the last step.

He wanted her dead for her deceit, but Kimberly survived. Now, he was paying for his gruesome sins. Telling her about his vasectomy at that moment wasn't on his mind. Matthew wanted her to take Teyona, not being his, to her grave.

She stood in disbelief and shook her head. "How could you do that?"

Her question was a whisper of hurt and disgust. She wasn't expecting to feel anything, considering she hadn't for years when it came to his words, but this gutted her. Matthew stood before her with a hint of defiance and guilt on his face.

"My future was on the line. I told you I didn't want any more kids."

"Do you hear how selfish you sound? *Your* future? What about *us*? That wasn't something you should've done without discussing it with me."

Matthew shrugged. There was nothing Kimberly could've said then or now that would've changed his mind. He saw how much a newborn slowed things down. When Mia and Hazel were born, he hardly got any work done. Even with help around the home, Kimberly wanted him there. She didn't want to experience any milestones with their children without him. Matthew couldn't afford that.

"There was nothing to discuss, Kim. I told you what I wanted, and you kept pushing for something different," he said unapologetically.

His eyes held no remorse as he sat back down on the couch.

"So, so…our marriage was a dictatorship? You call the shots, and I just roll with them?" Kimberly questioned, hurt beyond her core.

"Isn't that how it's always been?"

"No, you asshole. It hasn't been that way. Had you never pushed me—"

Matthew waved her off. "Stop with the dramatics. I didn't push you. You slipped. I guess that was karma's payback for having an outside child on me."

When he chuckled, Kimberly picked up the first thing she saw and hurled it at his head. The glass vase missed him by an inch, shattering against the wall.

"I want a divorce," Kimberly said sternly.

Matthew's heart locked in his chest. She had never uttered those words, knowing the consequences behind them.

"What happened to til' death do us part?"

"I won't wish death on you. I'm sure that mistress you never got rid of will take you out when the money stops flowing her way."

He smirked, running a hand over his beard. "You know…I never thought we'd get to this point. A divorce will be such a sticky situation. You and I both know how I feel about those. Ask that baby's father of yours. Oh, my mistake. You can't, can you?"

Kimberly bit into her bottom lip as Matthew laughed loudly.

"You're a waste of a human being and will pay for everything you've done to me and my children," Kimberly hissed.

"As if they'll give a rat's ass about you once they realize you were just as much of the cause of our damaged family as I was. It doesn't matter. I have my company, right? Since you claim I love it more than you, I'll forever remind you that I do."

A divorce wasn't happening if he had any say-so. Besides a contractual agreement that tied them until certain clauses were reached, they were connected by their pasts—secrets that haunted them in their sleep and while they were awake. If Kimberly wanted to leave, it would take much more than her saying it for it to happen.

He was all for reputation and image, but at this point, he didn't care how he would look if she divorced him. The only thing Matthew cared about was his money. There was no way in hell he was going to willingly give up almost everything he owned because Kimberly now wanted out.

No longer being able to look at his face, Kimberly stormed out of the house. She was seconds away from committing a murder, but that would only make her just like him. Now more than ever, she was convinced Matthew had killed Lawrence, Teyona's father. A man with his ego wouldn't allow another man who impregnated his wife to just walk away. She knew that for a fact.

What Kimberly didn't know was that Teyona had heard almost every grueling detail of their conversation. Her entrance into the home through the side door had gone undetected, just like her exit. What was supposed to be a friendly visit to her parents turned out to be her hearing the most gut-stabbing, heartbreaking confession of her life. Someone had to pay.

TWENTY

Dribbling the ball with purpose, DeShaun stopped at the arch of the court and sank a three-pointer. The move was so effortless he could do it in his sleep. With the season coming up in a few months, he was in the gym outside of practice, perfecting his craft. As a college senior, he had to go out with a bang.

"You hooping like you got something to prove," his teammate and friend, Marc, said.

DeShaun smirked. "Ain't shit. You know how I do."

Regardless of how he got into this position, he made it a point to push himself to his limits. He had been told all his life that the way he showed up in practice was how he would show up on game day. Taking a seat next to his bag on the bench, DeShaun guzzled down a bottle of water at record speed.

"Yeah, I do. What you got up for the rest of the day?" Marc asked.

"Heading to the crib to chill. I got company."

DeShaun replaced his tennis shoes with some slides and stretched his legs.

"Word?" Marc smirked, adjusting his locs that were in a ponytail.

"Yeah," DeShaun said with a chuckle. "You don't believe me?"

"Nah, nah. I do. I just never heard about you leaving a broad at the crib."

Marc was digging for information, and normally, DeShaun wouldn't have minded sharing. Teyona wasn't a normal girl, though. What they had brewing wasn't something he felt comfortable speaking about just yet. Not with her reasoning for being there. He respected her too much to tell his homeboy her business.

"Yeah…she different, though. Might let you meet her one day," DeShaun said with a smirk as he stood and grabbed his duffle bag, swinging the strap on his arm. "I'm out."

"A'ight, fool. Catch you later," Marc said as they slapped hands.

Walking out of the gym on campus, DeShaun tossed his bag in the backseat of his Urus and hopped in the driver's seat. Lil Baby's song "Sum 2 Prove" blasted through the speakers as he pulled out of the parking lot. After what he considered a light workout, DeShaun usually got a Chipotle bowl or a smoothie. Something healthy to replenish his system. With Teyona in town, he didn't want to get his usual and leave her hanging, so he hit her up.

Snuggled deep under his covers inside his bedroom, Teyona yawned and ran her hand over the cool sheets in search of her phone. She didn't know how long she had been knocked out. Thanks to DeShaun's blackout curtains and living by himself, she was getting some of the best rest she'd had in days. Not knowing where to go but needing to get away, she called him.

DeShaun put her on the first flight out of Atlanta to South Carolina so she wouldn't have to drive, and she had been at his place since. That was two days ago, and Teyona wasn't ready to leave. In fact, he told her to make herself at home for as long as she felt comfortable. Thankfully, her summer courses had ended the week before, so she had some free time—time to figure out her next moves.

"Hello," she answered groggily, finally locating her phone.

"Damn. My bad, baby. You were sleep?"

She yawned, stretching her body out. "Mhm. It's so dark in here all the time. I love it."

DeShaun chuckled. "I can see. You probably haven't gotten up to do anything."

"I went to use the bathroom, thank you," she said, laughing. "Are you on your way back?"

"Yeah. I'ma stop and grab something to eat. What you want? You need to eat something."

Yesterday, she had no appetite, and he understood that. Today, DeShaun would make her at least try to eat something, even if it was only some fruit.

"I know. What do you usually eat after practice? I can eat that."

He smirked. "Chipotle it is, then. Text me your order, or you wanna stay on the phone with me?"

"I'll text it to you. I'ma get myself together before you get here," she said, tossing the covers off her frame.

Clad in nothing but her panties and a tank top, Teyona was more comfortable than ever, and that included her being comfortable in her surroundings. DeShaun's place wasn't a pigsty, unlike the homes of some men she had encountered. Clothes and shoes were scattered about, but he wasn't messy, and Teyona appreciated that.

"A'ight. I'll see you in a minute," he said, and they hung up.

Releasing another yawn as she entered his bathroom and flicked the light on, Teyona examined her reflection. Her hair was all over her head, crust was evident in her eyes, and bags were underneath them from her lack of sleep. Though she didn't look as bad as she felt, Teyona wanted to look somewhat presentable for DeShaun.

Knowing she was about to eat, she waited to brush her teeth but did wash her face. Before turning on the shower, she texted him her order. Stripping, she tossed his shower cap over her head and climbed into his standing shower.

While standing under the running water, she thought of how DeShaun didn't think twice about telling her to come to him and welcomed her to his crib without worry. The comfort of his hug when he picked her up from the airport almost made Teyona break down, but she held it together. Now, she let the tears fall as she stood behind the glass door and lathered her washcloth. They blended with the water that was soothing her pain, and she let it all go down the drain.

Nothing could've prepared her for what she overheard from her parents. At first, she had no idea what they were talking about and why. She'd felt the tension between them for years but brushed it off. There wasn't much she wanted to say to Matthew anyway, with his standoffish attitude, and now she knew why.

He was a man who felt it was okay to step out on his wife, but when she did the same, it was an issue. The double standards were ridiculous, and Teyona's ears bled listening to them argue. Knowing he was the cause of her mother's injury and diagnosis of aphasia hurt her even more. Her childhood, adolescent, and young adult years weren't as rewarding without Kimberly being at her best. Teyona had missed out on so much, and though she hated Matthew for what he did, she didn't put all the blame on him.

Her mother played a hand in the woman she was today—why she wasn't as confident and second-guessed herself often. Teyona had gone around thinking she wasn't loved, when the truth was the man who she wanted the love from wasn't obligated to give it to her. Yes, Matthew had stayed in the marriage and took care of his household, including her, but that was as far as it went.

Over the last two days, Teyona had time to think about everything she heard. She knew there was more to the story and was trying to prepare herself to hear it all once she returned. There was no way Kimberly had gone twenty-four years with this secret and had nothing more to tell.

Freshly showered and with a somewhat clear mind, Teyona rubbed lotion into her legs. She heard the front door open, and her heart began to beat at a different pace. Her anticipation to see him was through the roof. Sliding on a pair of his slides, she ventured to the kitchen, where he stood at the sink washing his hands while talking on the phone.

"Nah. I'm in the crib for the day. I told Marc's ass that earlier. Yeah, I'll link up with y'all this weekend. Bet."

He ended his call and smirked at Teyona. "What's up, baby? How was your nap?"

She walked over to him, wrapping her arms around his waist. Standing on her tiptoes, Teyona kissed his lips, not caring that he was getting his slightly musky scent on her freshly washed body.

"It was good. How was practice?"

DeShaun had lost his train of thought for a second. "It wasn't a real practice. Just shooting some hoops with the fellas. I like you in my shirt."

He tugged on its hem, wondering what was underneath. The oversized t-shirt with his school's name on the front stopped mid-thigh.

"I like me in your shirt, too. I'ma have to take some home with me."

"Yeah, gon' head and do that. Let's go in here and eat."

He carried their bag into the living room and set up a few table trays. Knowing she wouldn't want to watch Sports Center, he handed her the Roku remote. Teyona hardly had time to watch TV, so she wasn't sure what was new. Keeping up with celebrities wasn't her thing when she was living a reality show herself. So, she turned on a crime documentary while they ate. He'd gotten a burrito while she had a bowl.

DeShaun had been so engrossed in the episode that he didn't realize thirty minutes had gone by until Teyona stood up to throw her trash away. He had only made it through three-fourths of his burrito and hadn't picked it up since the show started getting good.

"Look at you," Teyona said, laughing.

He smirked. "Man. You should've never put me on this show. I'm gonna be binge-watching it when you leave."

"Don't be laid up watching it with someone else either," she warned.

"Never that."

She threw her trash away and went to brush her teeth. When she was coming out of the bathroom, he was walking inside his room.

"I'ma hop in the shower right quick. You wanna do something today?"

Teyona shook her head. "Not really. If you had plans, I don't mind just chilling here."

"You are my plans."

His answer made her heart flutter and pussy clench.

"Oh. Okay then. I guess I'll let you get in the shower then."

"You guess, huh? You got in there without me before I got here."

She giggled. "I didn't know I was supposed to wait for you."

"I'm just teasing, baby. I'll be out in a minute."

Teyona exhaled when he stepped inside the bathroom and closed the door. She wasn't prepared to see him in all of his naked glory. While he held her the night before, she most definitely felt the monster between his legs and was two seconds away from hopping on it. She kept her composure, though. There would be plenty of time to get tangled between the sheets.

DeShaun stepped out twenty-three minutes later, the steam from the bathroom filling the air along with his fresh scent. Teyona kept her eyes glued to her phone, ignoring her sisters' calls and texts. The only person who knew her whereabouts was Cymone. She briefly told her what happened on the ride to the airport, but she needed to see her in person to break it down.

When he slid into the bed beside her, Teyona lowered her phone and smiled. DeShaun was so handsome. She pressed her finger inside the indention in his cheek and scooted closer to him.

"You smell good," she cooed.

He grinned with his eyes closed, her body heat and voice lulling him to sleep. Her presence alone made his day.

"Thank you. You smell like me."

"I do. Thank you for letting me hide away here. I know I probably messed up your flow."

DeShaun opened his eyes and looked at her. "Nah, you ain't mess up anything. I wouldn't have told you to come out here if I didn't want you here."

Teyona registered his words, but she was having a hard time believing them. Not because she didn't think he was being truthful, but the trauma of growing up and not feeling wanted was bleeding into her adulthood, making a fucking mess. Therapy was working, but after what she found out, Teyona knew Mrs. Morris would have to extend her sessions. She was regressing slowly but surely, temporarily reverting back to the stages she had progressed from.

Sighing, Teyona let her guard down some more. "Okay. I just had to let you know."

"It's all good. Do you wanna talk about it? How you really feeling?"

Her eyes watered, and DeShaun pulled her on top of him without thinking. He sat them up on his bed and rubbed her back as she cried into his shoulder. She didn't mean to break down, but she couldn't help it. That one question broke the dam.

"That's it, baby. Let it all out. You don't gotta keep hurt bottled up," he said soothingly.

After a few minutes passed and she pulled herself together, Teyona lifted her head. He wiped her tear-stained face and kissed her lips.

"That felt good, didn't it?" he asked, knowing what a good cry could do for the soul.

Teyona nodded. "Yes, but I need you to make me feel better." She was hurting and, more than anything, needed him to take the pain away.

Eager to be at her service, DeShaun obliged. Slow kisses started on her face, trailed her neck and collarbone, then down to her shoulders. As his warm hands gripped her waist, he realized she only had on panties underneath his shirt. That realization made him want to please her more.

The silence between them wasn't awkward, and DeShaun could tell Teyona was comfortable. He knew that from more than just her being in this position. She had no problem helping herself to his products, genuinely smiling when he tried cheering her up, but most of all, she trusted him. In one of her most vulnerable moments, Teyona came to him, and he didn't want to let her down.

Laying her on her back, DeShaun lifted the shirt above her breasts and suckled her nipples. Teyona's back arched as she moaned softly with pleasure. His lips trailed lower, licking her stomach before sliding her panties off. Her legs fell to the side, making space for him.

"You're already so wet," DeShaun complemented, rubbing two fingers through the mess she had made. The mess was because of him.

Teyona's stomach caved when they slid inside of her.

"Oh," she moaned.

He stroked them in and out of her slick walls, preparing her for what else he had in store. Using his thumbs, DeShaun spread her lips apart and dragged his tongue up and down her slit. He used one hand to push her thigh back before latching onto her clit. Teyona inhaled sharply before the sweetest, longest moan fell from her lips.

"Mmm," DeShaun groaned.

Face deep, he flicked, sucked, and licked all over her womanly parts, getting her off just how she needed. He wanted her to melt in his mouth, releasing all the built-up tension for him to drink down. She tasted so good that DeShaun couldn't think straight. He knew her visit was impromptu, but now, he didn't mind if she stayed longer than she thought she was welcome. While he ate her up, he was thinking of a master plan—one that involved keeping her in his life so he could show her what real love felt like and mend her broken heart.

Mia hated confrontation. More than arguing, she despised being lied to. She hoped Jarel would tell her the truth about what he had been up to, because with the way she was feeling, Mia was liable to snap. All week, she did her best to act normal around him, even while noticing things about him that she hadn't before.

The way Jarel sometimes looked at her with disgust confused her. Mia wasn't desperate, and she'd questioned him more than once if with her was where he wanted to be. Of course, Jarel reassured her that it was, but now she knew he hadn't been truthful.

Entering his house, she figured he must've forgotten that he told her to come over. Thankfully, the door was unlocked. It gave her a chance to eavesdrop on the phone call he was on. Mia walked lightly through the dimly lit living room with her heart pounding. Her anger had simmered since Hazel delivered the bad news, but it still swirled in her belly alongside devastation. The duo was causing a ruckus she wished would go away.

Her phone burned inside her pocket like someone who'd come into some unexpected money. The photos—evidence if need be—had been scrutinized all week. Had she not wanted to speak with him first, Mia would've pulled up over the woman's house and gotten her answers. She told herself this matter required patience. She couldn't let her curiosity win right now.

She approached the bedroom that he had turned into an office. The door was cracked, and Mia's chest heaved as she got closer. She squinted as if that would help her listen better. Jarel was on the phone with someone, and it didn't sound friendly. In fact, it sounded as if he were on the verge of tears.

"We can't take her off life support. I don't care what anyone is saying. They don't have the last say-so," Jarel fretted.

Mia held her breath while whomever he was speaking to replied.

"No, that's my decision to decide. Leave her on there. You don't get to call the fucking shots because you're her family. I'm her—"

The person on the other end cut him off, and Jarel exhaled. Feeling another presence close, he turned around. Mia acted as if she were about to knock.

"Yeah, whatever. Bye." Jarel hung up and waved her inside the room.

His body language immediately told her not to hug him, but she did anyway. She wanted to approach the situation carefully so he would feel open to telling the truth. As she got closer, Mia could smell the liquor on his breath. She wasn't sure what kind he'd indulged in, but it was emitting off of him like he had sprayed it on.

"Is everything alright?" she asked softly.

Jarel didn't answer for a few seconds, but when he did, Mia closed her eyes at his reply.

"I fucked up," he grumbled.

Mia wanted him to continue. She knew a drunk mind revealed sober thoughts.

"Everything is messed up because I had to know the truth," he said, pulling out of her embrace.

He looked down at her with glossy, unreadable eyes. She could tell he had so much to say but didn't know where to start.

"The truth about what?" Mia asked.

"Everything."

She had rehearsed the words she wanted to say a thousand times in her mind, but those weren't the ones that came out of her mouth next.

"Are you cheating on me?"

His bewildered expression before calming down told Mia everything she needed to know. Still, she kept her cool. She wanted to hear his lies, watch him make up lies from the jumbled thoughts in his mind.

"Why would you think that?"

"I was just asking. You're talking about telling the truth, and I haven't been feeling the love lately. You've been going out of town more. It's just all so sneaky."

Jarel frowned. "I'm being sneaky because I have to work?"

"You weren't at work the other weekend. My sister said she saw you at the gas station."

"Mia, come on. You believe everything your sister tells you?"

"Yes. Why shouldn't I?"

He didn't answer her question. Jarel only stared at her before heading for the door.

"Let's go in the kitchen. I need another drink."

She wanted to tell him no, he didn't, but instead, she kept her comment to herself. They made it to the kitchen, and Jarel poured himself a double shot of Hennessy. Without flinching, he tossed it back as if it were water.

"You want one?" he asked.

"Sure," she answered, then thought, *Might as well be tipsy for whatever he's about to tell me.*

Jarel grabbed her a shot glass and filled it to the brim. Grimacing, Mia tossed it back. A chill ran through her body as she shivered from the alcohol. The effects seemed to hit her immediately as she patted her chest. They remained quiet for a while until Jarel broke the uneasy silence.

"I knew what you were doing before you told me that night," he said, not going into further detail.

Mia remained quiet, so he continued.

"I didn't have facts, but I had an idea that you were stealing from your father."

Mia's heart raced as she clenched her jaw. *Is he a fucking cop?*

"Okay," she said.

"You told me your reasoning, but it doesn't make what y'all are doing right."

"I know that. You've done some things here lately that aren't right, either. I have proof."

The thought of what she knew he had been doing made Jarel's nostrils flare. He didn't want to lay his dirty laundry out right now. There would be a time for that.

"I'm sure you do. I know what I've been doing is wrong, but I'm not cheating on you. There's so much I want to tell you, but it'll only get you caught in the mix. The only person responsible for everything is your father."

Mia's brows dipped. "My father?"

"Yes. He's the reason so many lives have been ruined, and I want revenge."

He said the statement so casually that Mia was taken aback. *Okay. This took a turn I wasn't expecting. Let me play into it.*

She knew she had to play the role if she wanted to get more information out of him. Hazel told her that moving off emotions wouldn't be the best choice, so she tucked them away. Ironically, she and Jarel had the same sentiments about her father, which wasn't surprising. He had crossed a lot of people in his life, including her.

"He is. I can help you get revenge."

Jarel's eyes sparkled with relief.

"You'd do that for me?" he asked, his voice layered with apprehension.

"Yes. He's hurt me, my sisters, my mom, and so many people. You'd think a man of his stature would move with morals and compassion."

He snorted. "Right. I hate that you were caught in the middle of everything. You and Hazel. She shouldn't be out here selling drugs to people, not knowing the harm they can cause. It's fucked up."

Mia regretted sharing her secrets with him. Jarel wasn't throwing it in her face, but she could tell it would only be a matter of time before he did.

"Yeah. So, what did you have in mind? He's been on my shit list for months now, and I'm just waiting for the perfect opportunity to hit him where it hurts."

Jarel smiled. It wasn't a genuine smile, and it made Mia's skin crawl. All this time, he had ulterior motives, but she had a few of her own, too. She promised Hazel she wouldn't stop by the woman's home to get answers, but she was breaking that promise tonight.

"I know he has, just from what you told me. Time to get this man back, baby."

"Just promise me one thing…" Mia paused. "No matter what happens, keep loving me."

Jarel gulped and quickly poured himself another shot.

"Of course. You know I love you. Nothing is coming in between that," he replied, then tossed his shot back as if he were rinsing his mouth of the lies.

She had been waiting to hear those words. Unfortunately, Jarel had said them much too late. Love couldn't save him.

Mia checked the picture on her phone's screen and eyed the house. She had the correct address, and now she needed to check her nerves. Once Jarel drank himself into a deep slumber, Mia left his house and drove to the home Hazel followed him to. The subdivision was so quiet and cozy that Mia was sure the families could hear her thoughts.

Staring out of her windshield, she noticed how dark the sky had gotten since she arrived five minutes earlier. Hoping it didn't rain, she took a deep breath and climbed out of her SUV. She wasn't exactly sure what she was going to say to this woman, but not saying anything wasn't going to happen. Mia had been quiet for far too long.

Her knuckles rapped against the coral-colored door, which was immediately pulled open. The woman standing before her was strikingly gorgeous, with fierce copper eyes, honey-hued skin, and a scowl on her face. She was older, maybe in her late fifties, but she was fit. Mia could tell she worked out by the visible abs in her athletic gear. When Mia noticed the gun in her hand, she took a step back.

"You shouldn't be here," the woman said. "Whatever answers you're looking for about your father, I don't have them. Unless you're here to drop off my credit card."

"My father? I didn't come here to talk about him. Who are you to him?"

The woman chuckled. "Who I am doesn't matter."

"It does because my man came to your home the other day, and I want to know why," Mia spat.

The woman chuckled again. "Oh, you're here about Jarel. Cute. You must know something. Otherwise, you wouldn't have boldly popped up to my home. So, let me ease your worries. I'm someone's mistress, but not his. He's way too young and dumb. What you do need to know is that he has it out for you and that drug-dealing sister of yours, so watch your back. You unintentionally hurt someone close to him, and he can't let what you did go that easily. It's payback—not just for you, but for your father, too. Now, if you'd excuse me, I need to get back to curling my hair. Don't show up here again, or you'll be getting sent back to your family in a body bag like they tried to do me."

The door slammed in Mia's face, and her jaw dropped. Stumbling backward, she jogged to her car, her heart about to jump out of her chest. She burned rubber down the street, replaying the words in her head. The woman rattled them off so quickly that Mia's head was still spinning.

The mention of Mia bringing her credit card made her think of the one Hazel found on Matthew's desk. It had to be the same woman. There was no getting around that. She did notice that she didn't seem to care for Jarel. That much was clear. Her warning was loud and clear, though.

I need to watch my back.

Mia needed to see Hazel. Their scamming ways had caught up to them and in the worst way. Threats were hitting them from all sides, and Mia was still confused about how Jarel was involved. She couldn't have hurt him more than he had hurt her, but that was yet to be determined. Mia felt like Steve from *Blue's Clues* collecting evidence, but she was down for the adventure. She would turn into whoever she needed to be for her sisters. Anyone threatening their lives was a threat to her. Jarel was included in that, no matter how much she loved him.

Love could obviously get you killed.

Word to her mother's journals.

TWENTY-ONE

Kimberly entered the restaurant with confidence in her stride. Searching the floor, she spotted Graham in the back of the room, away from all the other tables. They both preferred it that way. As she got closer, Kimberly couldn't help but notice how much he and Lawrence favored each other. That's why she thought she had seen a ghost when she saw him at the gala.

"You're late," Graham grumbled.

Kimberly smiled. "I'm here. Let's focus on that, shall we?"

"Don't come in here with your fake polite bullshit, Kim. I'm not here for it."

"I'm not being fake," she hissed, her smile dropping, "Do you really want to get off on the wrong foot?"

"I should be asking you that. You're the one who had to reschedule and have been keeping secrets. Play nice, or things will end badly for you. I can promise you that."

Kimberly's throat bobbed as she swallowed her words. Graham certainly wasn't playing nice, and she didn't expect him to, but sheesh. Taking her seat, she stared him in the face.

"Okay. Should I start first, or do you want to tell me how you found me?" she asked.

"It wasn't hard. Y'all make shit too easy."

"Y'all. As in Matthew and I?"

"No. Your daughters. I feel kind of bad that I got them involved in you and your murderous husband's bullshit, but I had no choice."

Kimberly struggled to keep her composure. Knowing he had been in contact with her daughters made her chest ache.

"Did you harm them?"

"Probably mentally, but that's it. Got me a little insurance money just in case." Graham chuckled.

"Where have you been? Why wait all these years to pop up and cause chaos in my life?" Kimberly asked.

"I was in prison. You know we don't have a close family, so I'd been out of the loop for years."

While he was locked up, Graham was going through his own emotions. It was hard enough trying to remain sane, so thinking about his brother missing was something he tried keeping off his mind. That was until people got in his head, and he started thinking of the people who may have wanted to hurt Lawrence.

He didn't know all of his brother's enemies but made a list of people anyway. With little family around, Graham got in touch with a friend and told him what he thought. It had been a few years since he'd been locked up, and everyone seemed to brush his advances off. *He's been missing going on three years, bruh. Do you really think he's out there?* one friend questioned. Graham wasn't sure, but it didn't hurt to want someone to continue looking.

That never happened. Neither did him being released early so he could do his own digging around. Years went by, and instead of becoming frustrated due to limited resources behind bars, Graham kept his thoughts to himself. There was one person he planned to get in contact with when he was released, and she was now sitting in front of him.

"How long were you in?"

Graham clenched his jaw. "Twenty."

"Oh. Um, wow. That was a long time." She wanted to ask why but left it alone. They weren't there to reminisce about him.

"Yeah. Too fucking long. People seemed to have forgotten who I was. They stopped searching for my brother, but I never stopped thinking about him while locked down. Him or my niece."

Kimberly sipped from the straw in her glass of water. "Yeah, well, you didn't have to go about seeing her the way you are now."

"What way is that, Kim? The one where it'll keep me alive and out of jail? 'Cause that's what I'm doing. Sort of." He chuckled, thinking about how he held Hazel at gunpoint and demanded twenty bands from her.

"What is that you want, Graham? I have enough on my plate, and adding you to it is going to stress me out."

Graham smirked. "You've changed over the years, but I can see why my brother loved you. You were all his ass talked about. The man wouldn't stop running his mouth. Then, you brought my niece to meet me, and I didn't even know you were pregnant, let alone married. That caught me off guard, but we rolled with it. Then, my brother went missing."

Kimberly's chest heaved as he quickly recalled their past lives.

"I'm so sorry about what happened to him," she said, truthfully sorry.

"You see, Kim...I'd believe you were sorry if I didn't think you knew exactly what happened to him."

Her eyes widened. "I don't. I swear I don't. I have my suspicions and always have, but that's not something I'd keep from you or anyone."

"Yeah? Not even for that rich husband of yours?"

"Fuck him," Kimberly spat with much disdain in her voice.

Graham drew his head back. "Well, damn." He chuckled. "Tell me how you really feel."

"That's how I've been feeling about him since he tried to kill me. So, no, not even for my rich husband would I keep something like that hidden."

"I didn't think he had anything to do with Lawrence's disappearance until someone reached out to me."

Kimberly leaned across the table. "What? Who would reach out to you with something like that?"

"His mistress."

She wanted to smack the smirk off his face.

"Let me guess, you're crawling in between her thighs, too."

"I don't lie in bed with demons, and she's one for sure."

Kimberly rolled her eyes. "I can't believe you linked up with her. How did that happen, and why? I'm sure she's in it for herself—she always has been."

"She reached out to me on Facebook. I'd just gotten out of prison and shared a picture of me and Lawrence. I said something along the lines of not letting his name be forgotten and that I would do my best to figure out what happened to him. Everyone brushed his absence and disappearance off like he meant nothing, so I was interested when she messaged me. She said she had some information about him that she thought I would like to know."

"Of course she did," Kimberly huffed.

Matthew's mistress, Paula, had been a pain in Kimberly's ass for over a century. At this point, she could consider herself Matthew's second wife. Kimberly didn't care for the title anymore. How someone chose to stick around and deal with a married, cheating man who was also a narcissist, she didn't understand. Then again, maybe Kimberly did. She hadn't left him either, so they were more alike than she wanted to believe.

"It wasn't much, but she gave me just enough to look into your family. Your daughters are some true criminals. I guess they got it honestly," he concluded.

Kimberly didn't want to know what he was talking about.

"What did that woman tell you to make you start looking into us?" she asked, ready to know Graham's motives.

"She told me how you knocked her upside the head, and she somehow woke up in a trunk."

Kimberly snickered. "That was her fault. I knocked her ass out for talking crazy to me and sleeping with my husband. That was years ago; she's still holding on to that?"

"I guess so. She had pictures from that night."

Kimberly's face paled. "What? What do you mean she had pictures?"

"She said she felt like she knew Matthew was going to hurt her one day, so she had somebody watching her moves. Someone was snapping pictures when y'all popped up to her place that night. Somehow, they knew Matthew wouldn't kill her. I'm not sure how they knew that, but they didn't go to the police, and she popped back up a few days later. Matthew has been paying her off since."

A lot of things had been shocking to hear lately, but this didn't come as much of a surprise. The pictures? Yes. Matthew paying her off to keep her mouth closed? Not shocking at all. His love for Paula ran deep. Plus, she knew too much. Their pillow talk sessions after being inside her had Matthew confessing his sins like she was a priest. At this point, she wasn't just being paid off; he was taking care of her for life as if she had declared vows.

"Hmm," Kimberly hummed. "So, because she thought she was about to die, she assumed he had something to do with Lawrence's disappearance?"

"Yeah, and more than that. You know how some men get. You cheated on him, had a baby, and were planning to leave him. Matthew shared all of that with her. It's hard to say what I would've done if I were in his shoes, but it wouldn't have been anything he did. A man of his caliber and reputation wasn't letting you or her walk away."

It was clear Graham had no idea what had happened to Kimberly. Paula failed to mention that small detail about her, but it didn't matter because he was right. She was planning to leave him. Had she kept her heart off the pages of her notebook, things could've possibly turned out much different.

"I wish he would've. I regret ever getting myself involved with Lawrence. He was way too good of a man to be harmed."

Graham's eyes darkened. "Yet, you got him hurt. If you loved him like you claim you did, there's no way you'd still be sitting here with that man's last name. What about Teyona? You were never going to tell her, huh?"

"Leaving him has nothing to do with my love for your brother. I never stopped loving him. I was going to tell her when the timing was right," Kimberly pleaded.

"Yeah…I don't believe that, but believe me when I say this. You asked me what it was that I wanted, and I want to know where my brother's body is. I also want to see my niece. Either you find something out and arrange for me to see her, or I'm going to take matters into my own hands and figure some shit out on my own."

Kimberly cocked her head to the side. "Are you threatening me?"

"I am, and I don't give a fuck whose mother you are. I didn't spend time in prison for as long as I did for no reason. It's all I know, so going back won't hurt a thing," he said, standing from the table and leaning close to her ear. "I'll be in touch. Don't make me come looking for you. I'm good at finding people who don't want to be found."

His words left a cold front in the atmosphere, making Kimberly regret ever meeting him. Graham was serious, and her time was ticking. Kimberly didn't know the first place to begin searching for evidence about where Lawrence could be. Asking Matthew would be of no use. They hadn't spoken to one another in over a week.

Kimberly thought about going to the police, but that would only incriminate herself. She knew just as much as Paula did, but she had the title of being his wife. So, it would look worse. As hard as she tried to keep her daughters out of their mess, it looked like she was going to have to tell them the truth. They needed to hear it from her, not piece it together from words, pictures, and assumptions.

The first stop Teyona made when she returned home was Hazel's place. She didn't want to leave DeShaun, but she had to come back to reality. Real-life shit was going on in her world, and she didn't want to taint their peace. He had been such a gentleman, catering to her body, heart, mind, and soul while there.

What started as a daunting favor turned into something much more than they either expected but gladly accepted. Teyona promised to squeeze the games she could into her schedule and planned on rocking his name. First, she had to tie up a bunch of loose ends.

"You made it?" Cymone asked.

She stayed on the phone with her the entire ride from the airport.

"Yeah, I just pulled into the parking lot. I'll text or call you when I get home."

"Okay. Be safe."

Teyona told her she would and shifted her gear into park. Out of habit, her eyes roamed the parking lot, and she spotted Mia's Range Rover. She could only avoid them for so long, so she got out of her car and made her way to the door. Hazel wasn't expecting any company, but when she heard Teyona announce herself, she tucked her gun and pulled the door open.

"Hi," Teyona mumbled, walking inside.

Hazel pulled her into a tight hug. "Don't ever just fall off of the face of the earth like that, Tey," she lovingly scolded like only she could.

"You're lucky I had your location," Mia said, smiling softly.

She pulled Teyona into her warm embrace, kissing all over her face and making Teyona groan.

"Ugh! Stop it."

"I missed you," Mia said, putting her body at arm's length.

Mia immediately detected the sadness in her sister's eyes. Then, it hit her. *She knows.* The silence was enough to convey her message.

"No need for the sad looks. Yes, I know Matthew isn't my dad. It hurts, but how I found out has me in a place of not caring. My emotions are all over the place."

Hazel gulped. "Well, okay then. No need to ease into this gently at all. We were trying to think of a way to tell you, sis."

"Can we all sit down? I feel lightheaded."

"I hope you're not pregnant," Hazel said, her words making Mia laugh.

"I'm on birth control. I just need to eat something."

They all ventured to the couch. Teyona opted to sit in the chair.

"So, how was South Carolina?" Hazel asked.

"I wanted to stay. Let's not talk about that right now, though. How'd you find out he wasn't my dad?"

Hazel looked at Mia. It was her discovery to reveal.

"I read it in one of Mom's old journals. That container over there is full of things that only pertain to your childhood and your real dad. Some other things that happened led us to that conclusion, but those were the most prevalent."

Teyona eyed the container. She didn't have the mental capacity to search through it right then, but she planned to. Anything to help her learn about her real dad was needed since everyone wanted to keep that fact away from her.

"How did you find out?" Hazel questioned.

"I overheard them arguing," Teyona replied. "It was worse than anything we heard growing up. Dad…I mean, Matthew… confessed to being the reason Mom was diagnosed with aphasia. Did y'all know that?"

Mia rubbed the back of her neck while Hazel gritted her teeth.

"Just tell me! You two have been keeping secrets from me for years. I'm a big girl. I can handle the truth," Teyona begged.

Mia spoke first. "I knew but didn't want to believe it."

Hazel rolled her eyes, still annoyed that Mia fed into Matthew's bullshit for so long.

"I always knew. We saw him do it."

Teyona gasped. "No."

"Yep. They were arguing one night, and I made Mia get out of bed so we could listen. We opened the door and watched. He was choking her before pushing her. It wasn't forceful, but enough to make her lose her balance since she was already standing on the edge of the top step."

The tears she thought she'd rid herself of emerged in her eyes, and Teyona hurriedly wiped them away.

"That is…fucked up. How could he do that to her just because she had a baby outside their marriage? He was cheating, too."

"It's sinister, and he has to pay," Hazel spat.

"He's not the only one who needs to pay up for what he's done," Mia said, causing Teyona's eyes to roam her way. "Jarel was the one following you that day."

Her mouth dropped. "*Your* Jarel?"

"He's not hers anymore," Hazel said, and Mia cut her eyes at her. "What? Well, he isn't."

"Okay, but you don't have to say it like that. Anyway, Hazel followed him to Dad's mistress house one day and—"

"Wait." Teyona chuckled. "You did what?"

The trio couldn't help but burst out laughing.

"I know," Hazel said. "I was on some crazy mess, but it worked out in the end. We didn't know who the woman was at first. I found a credit card in his office with her name on it and started digging around. I couldn't find much, but then I spotted Jarel out one night when he told Mia he would be working late and decided to follow him. Long story short, Mia pulled up on the lady and figured out who she was. She told us to watch our backs when it comes to Jarel because we hurt someone close to him."

Teyona rubbed her temples. "Are we…are we living in a twilight zone?"

"Gotta be. Things only get worse. Do you have somewhere to be today?" Hazel asked, standing from the couch.

"No. This was my first stop. Something told me that y'all already knew about Matthew, so I came here. Mia, do you think Jarel was the one putting notes on my car?"

Mia's mouth fell open. She had forgotten all about that.

"Honestly, Tey, it could've been him or your uncle."

"My uncle?"

Hazel handed her a shot glass of tequila.

"Yep. Drink up, sis. We have so much more to tell you."

For the next two hours, the sisters discussed every instance they felt was tied to what had been going on. Hazel even went as far as to pull out a whiteboard to connect names. Matthew was at the center , and a bunch of arrows branched off his name. The only two people with question marks by their names were Jarel and Lawrence.

"Dad's mistress said we hurt someone close to him. I don't even know people close to him except his cousins," Mia said with a heavy sigh.

"Are those even his damn cousins for real?" Hazel questioned.

Mia laughed, not being sure of anything anymore. Doing a quick Facebook search could possibly answer her questions, but Mia didn't have it in her to play detective. She didn't feel like exerting any more energy on Jarel or his family right now. Tomorrow, she would start fresh.

"This is all so crazy. So, what are we going to do? Dad can't get away with what he did to Mom."

"Right, and Jarel can't hurt you and think he's going to get away with it. He said he wasn't cheating, but the man is lying about something. Then, he had the nerve to say he wants revenge, and I'm out here hurting people. If anything, I'm helping people who society has fucked over. Myself included. We have to get rid of him."

Teyona licked her lips. "Um, Haze...you're sounding like our parents."

"I mean, the apple doesn't fall far from the tree," she said and shrugged.

"You want to kill—"

"No," Hazel hissed. "You can get people out of the way without ending their life. He's not going to continue to play a hand in ruining ours, is all I know."

Mia remained quiet. She was coming up with plans in her head and finally thought of one she figured might work.

"I got it," she mumbled and sat up on the couch.

"Got what?" Teyona asked.

"How we're going to take both of them down."

Hazel smirked. "I'm listening."

"Me, too. Do you think it'll work?" Teyona asked.

Nodding, Mia smiled. "I can almost guarantee it will. Y'all trust me?"

They nodded without thinking. That was all the confirmation Mia needed. No matter how shaky things were or how hurt she was, it was time to put the work in. Operation "Take Jarel and Matthew Out" was in full effect.

TWENTY-TWO

Mia stood inside her father's home office with tears dripping down her cheeks. She could've gone to school to be an actress with the way she was putting on an act. Her claims of being the dramatic daughter were somewhat true in this instance. Matthew was eating up every bit of the scene before him, but Mia knew it was because Grant Pharmaceutical's name was involved.

Mia didn't want to hear the "I told you so" about Jarel, so she hoped he didn't play on that. She should've known he wouldn't when he got directly to the point about what she had just said.

"So…you're telling me the guy you've been dating is blackmailing you and Hazel and threatening my company?"

Mia nodded and sniffled. "Yes."

"Stop with all the damn crying, Mia! Woman up and tell me again what's going on."

On a whim, Mia came up with the idea to make it seem like Jarel was going to go to the police and air out the shady business dealings he so-called found out about Grant Pharm. Mia and Hazel were liabilities because she was stealing drugs for her.

"He's threatening to go to the news stations and police about things he found out about you and the company. I don't know what it is, but it's bad. And, um, Hazel and I are going down, too. I was stealing pills out of the pharmacy for her when she hurt her wrist last year, but then she started selling them. I didn't know until it was too late. Apparently, she sold some to one of his family members, and they got sick. He's wanting to sue us and do some other things."

Matthew chuckled in disbelief as he stared at his oldest daughter. He deemed her the smartest child, but right now, she looked like the dumbest fool in his eyes.

"Okay...let me get this straight. He got close to you so he could try to take *my* company down? Is that what you're telling me?"

Mia hated to admit it, but that's exactly what Jarel had done. She nodded her head. "Yes."

"And all of this came about how?"

"Because I asked him if he was cheating on me, and we got into an argument. He just started airing everything out," Mia partially lied.

She wished he had spewed everything she still had questions about, but she was being patient. Everything would come to a head soon. She could see the wheels turning in her father's head as he pondered what to do next.

"So, because you couldn't let the man live his life in peace, you cause all of this drama? I'm so disappointed. Not only were you and that criminal of a sister of yours stealing from me, but you also got your heart broken while doing it. What did I tell you would happen, Mia? Huh? The shit between you two wasn't going to last. That's okay, though, baby girl, because neither is he."

Mia wanted to reach across his desk and slap him. She couldn't believe he was placing the blame on her and being so heartless about it. His words stung. For once, she thought he would show some sympathy regarding her love life and not treat her like she was an employee or disposable. Mia now had an idea of how her mother must've felt.

"I'm sorry, Daddy," she said, keeping her game face on and sticking to the plan. "What can I do to make things right? He can't expose us like that. We have to make him pay."

Matthew smirked. "Oh, he's going to pay, all right. That's the mindset you should've had to begin with, and none of this would've happened. You're going to run this company one day, and you have to keep folks in line—even the outsiders who test your hand. You show them who's in charge. You got that?"

Mia nodded.

"Good. Now, here's what I want you to do," Matthew said.

Mia listened intently for the next ten minutes to the plan she ultimately put in motion. She was beaming inside, knowing Matthew had fed right into her scheme. He needed a taste of his own medicine for once. When she stood to leave, Mia caught a glimpse of the credit card Hazel had mentioned.

"New assistant?" Mia asked, lifting the paper that the card was attached to.

Paula Moss. Hmm, now I know your name, old lady.

Matthew hurriedly grabbed it. "No. Mind your business and get going on what I need you to do."

"Sure thing, Dad. Thank you for being understanding. I love you."

"Yeah, yeah. I love you, too. Now get out."

Mia smirked and walked out of his office. He wasn't going to love her for long.

Heading to the kitchen for a snack, Mia was surprised to see her mother. Monday night dinners had stopped weeks ago, and no one seemed to question why or put up a fuss. As always, the unspoken words between them spoke loudly. Everyone knew what was going on but remained quiet. Not anymore.

"Hey, Mama. How's G?" Mia boldly asked.

Kimberly choked on the glass of water she was drinking. Her eyes stretched as she looked at Mia's calm expression.

"How's who?" Kimberly asked.

"We know who he is. We were just waiting for you to tell Teyona," Mia said, stepping closer. She wrapped her arms around her and hugged Kimberly with all her might. "I'm so sorry for everything you had to endure. No woman should ever have to go through that pain."

Kimberly was stunned. "H-How did you find out?"

"The storage unit. I can't explain everything right now, but you need to call Teyona. We all need to sit down and talk, but her first. She's hurt."

Wetness blurred Kimberly's vision. The crack in her heart that was holding it together split.

"I promise I'll talk to her. Are you safe? How is Hazel?"

"We're safe, and I want you to be, too. I don't have everything sorted out yet, but when I do, you'll hear from me. Promise there will be no more secrets."

Kimberly didn't want to make any promises. Her entire life was based on secrets. It was all she knew, but it no longer had to be that way.

Sighing, she said, "I promise. I'll be sure to pick up when you call, too."

"Okay. I love you. I have to run."

Mia gave her a quick kiss on the cheek and left the house. Kimberly couldn't move. She did feel a weight lifted off her shoulders, knowing she didn't have to break the news. She just had to explain everything if they were willing to listen. Pulling her phone from her pocket, Kimberly dialed her sister's number.

"Hello," Nicole answered.

"The girls found out about the storage unit. I thought you put it under your name."

Nicole sucked her teeth. "No, I put it under Matthew's like you asked me to. You said he never goes there to check the place."

"In his name?" Kimberly hissed. "Gotdammit, Nicky. You know I couldn't quite comprehend everything back then."

"Oh, you're pissed," Nicole said, laughing at hearing her nickname. "What's the big deal? You said you were going to tell them anyway."

"I was, but I didn't want them to find out that way. I've traumatized them. I just know it."

"No worse than what they've already endured, sis. That's not me trying to be an asshole, just a realist. How's everything else coming along for Graham? Is he still fine?" Nicole whispered.

Kimberly laughed. "I'm not telling you. You're a married woman."

"Hell, so were you, and you see how that turned out."

"You're going to stop taking jabs at me. Plus, I'm still married," she said, rolling her eyes.

"Not for long, sis. Not for long."

Patience wasn't Mia's strongest characteristic, but she had been working on it. It had been a little over a week since Matthew gave her orders to set up a meeting between him and Jarel. At first, she thought he just wanted to talk to him and possibly pay him off, but now Mia knew better.

His request to meet at the storage units at eleven in the evening wasn't meant for talking. Mia drove to the far backside of the property toward a singular storage unit bigger than the rest. The trees surrounding it gave it an eerie feeling. Once she got out and took in her surroundings, it resembled a warehouse.

A few minutes later, Jarel's car pulled up, and Mia checked her attitude and facial expressions. It was hard to maintain her niceness when all she wanted to do was put her hands on him. He was dressed in jeans, a black hoodie, and sneakers. With a swiftness, he walked up to her. Mia's body stiffened as he hugged her.

"What's up? He here yet?" he asked.

"Not yet. He'll be here. Let's go inside."

Jarel followed her into the building, and she flicked the lights on. It was a mess of dust, boxes, a trailer, and a long freezer in the corner.

"We couldn't have just met him at the house?" Jarel questioned.

"No. This is where he wanted to meet. Are you sure this is going to work?"

Mia was acting again, and Jarel fed right into it.

"Yes. I'ma ask a few questions, get my answers, and then demand that he make some changes. If he gets out of line, I got something for him," he said, patting the pocket of his hoodie where his gun was hidden.

She wanted to protest and tell him that wasn't necessary but didn't. She had to act as if she was on his side.

"Good. I have mine, too, just in case. I'll follow your lead. Just don't...don't hurt him too badly," Mia pleaded, producing fake tears that never fell from her eyes.

Jarel kissed her cheek. "I got you."

Tires could be heard on the gravel outside as a vehicle approached. Mia said a quick prayer and held her breath as Matthew entered the building. He was dressed like he was going to a meeting, and that almost made Mia laugh, but she held it together.

Who wears a suit to handle this type of business? she thought.

"Mia. My lovely daughter, how are you?" Matthew asked.

She intertwined Jarel's fingers with hers. "Let's skip the pleasantries. My man has something he wants to say."

Matthew laughed. "Your man, huh? Alright, let's hear what you have to say. My time is valuable."

"You're supposed to be a man who cares about the people in his community, yet you're flooding it with prescription drugs that kill people," Jarel grumbled.

Matthew chuckled. "Okay, I see. You're one of those people who blame everything on the system. Let me guess, a loved one of yours suffered from a drug they got from my company?"

"Damn right, they did," Jarel spat. "Abnazol isn't helping anyone. It's hurting them."

"Take your beef up with the FDA," Matthew responded calmly.

Jarel snatched his hand out of Mia's grasp. "Nah, I'm taking it up with you."

"By requesting this meeting? Then what? Nothing is going to change. I hate men like you. You don't understand a man's job but want to jeopardize it. That's little boy shit, and you thought it was okay to drag my daughter into this and turn her against me?"

"You can't get away with ruining people's lives. Your daughter doesn't even like you," Jarel sneered.

Matthew smirked. "Is that so? Come here, Mia. I know you think you love this man, but trust me, he's no good for you or this family."

When Mia's feet didn't move, Matthew squinted his eyes. This wasn't the plan he told her or the one she agreed with. Mia was supposed to walk over to him.

"Mia," he said sternly.

"I can't, Daddy. You've caused too much harm to him and his family. He just wants you to stand up for what is right. You have a lot of power in the health industry," Mia said.

"And I'm supposed to stop making money off it because one person had a bad side effect? That has nothing to do with me. Now, what I can do is give you a bit of money and have you leave my family alone. I don't know what evidence you claim you have on me, but that's not something I take lightly."

Matthew wasn't backing down, and neither was Jarel.

"You're not sympathetic at all. I see why your wife cheated on you and had another man's child," Jarel spat.

Mia gasped as Matthew pulled his gun out. Without thinking, he sent two shots into Jarel's chest. Slowly, he walked up to him as he stumbled backward into some boxes. Mia's eyes watered as he fell, coughed out blood, and pressed firmly into his chest.

"Talking like that will get you killed, boy. Another man's business is never up for discussion. You see," he said, bending down to stare him in the eyes, "I tried to be reasonable and pay you off, but you just had to take it there. Now, I'm going to watch you bleed out like the upstanding man of this community that I am. How's that for some sympathy?"

Standing up, Matthew brushed his pants off and tucked his gun. He pulled it out so quickly that Mia didn't see the shots coming. She swallowed her sobs as she kneeled near Jarel's side.

He looked up at her with pleading eyes. His mouth moved to tell her he was sorry, but nothing came out. She watched as he took his last breath before succumbing to his gunshot wounds. Mia dropped her head and cried hard. She was upset with him for what he'd done, but she didn't want to see him die.

"Mia, get it together. This is what comes with the Grant name. Don't touch him," Matthew scolded.

"You didn't say you were going to kill him," she cried, her tears finally falling.

"What did you think I was going to do? He was trying to ruin my name."

Mia hopped up from her crouching position. "No, he wasn't. He just wanted you to hear him out, but like the callous man you are, you had to take things to the next level. You couldn't stand hearing the truth."

"You better watch it," Matthew spat, pointing his finger.

"No! I've been watching what I say and how I move on your behalf for years. And for what? You're a horrible person!"

Matthew's eyes widened. Mia had never raised her voice at him or spoken to him so disrespectfully.

"Are you mad because I killed your little boyfriend? That's too damn bad! I'm your father, and you will talk to me like you have some sense."

"Fuck you," she spat harshly. "You pushed Mom down the steps, treated her like she meant nothing for years, and was so cruel to Teyona. Jarel was right. I see why Mom cheated on you with Lawrence. He was a better man than you'll ever be."

Anger like he never felt before coursed through Matthew, but he did his best to constrain it. Mia was his daughter, his firstborn. He couldn't hurt her, but he would make sure she felt it.

"If you weren't my child, I'd put you right next to him. Keep your distance, Mia. You're officially cut off from this family. And if you decide to run your mouth about what happened here tonight, just know it'll get worse for you."

Mia laughed. "No, father dearest…it's going to get worse for you."

Suddenly, police sirens echoed in the distance. They were quickly approaching, and Matthew had nowhere to run.

Matthew glared at her. "You tried to set me up?"

"No, I did set you up, and you're going to prison."

"With what proof?" He laughed. "We can frame this as this deranged, scorned lover kills her boyfriend in a cheating scandal gone wrong."

Mia walked over to the window, picked up a small black device, and lifted it into the air.

"I knew you'd try to pull that card, so I recorded everything. Actually, it's live. Everything that went on tonight is being listened to by the police. I'm not as dumb as you think I am."

She smirked as the doors busted open. With their guns drawn, the police advanced Matthew and immediately placed him in handcuffs. His Miranda rights were read to him, but he wasn't listening. His blood was flowing through his ears with pure rage. Biting into his bottom lip, he nodded at Mia and smirked.

"This isn't over, Mia. I promise you!"

Mia waved bye and pulled out her phone. She opened her camera app and followed behind them out of the door. Red and blue lights illuminated the dark area, and over twenty cars filled the parking lot. Parked next to Mia's Range Rover was Hazel's Jeep.

Matthew looked as if someone had smeared poop across his face when he noticed Hazel, Kimberly, Graham, Nicole, and Teyona standing out in front. They were there to see him do the walk of shame, and Matthew didn't care, but Teyona's appearance made him want to commit another murder.

With a grim expression on her baby face, Teyona stood with her arms crossed, and the black Fedora from Kimberly's container rested atop her head. She cocked her head to the side when he noticed what she was wearing. Matthew vividly remembered spotting Lawrence in the same hat the first time he caught him and Kimberly together. She sensed it and told him not to wear it again, so Lawrence gave it to her. Now, it belonged to Teyona, who wore it proudly in his honor.

Matthew laughed. "Is this what family is for? After all that I've done for you women! You all will pay!"

Hazel wiggled her fingers, telling him bye. "Oh, we're going to get paid. Believe that."

Kimberly pulled Mia into her chest. "Are you okay, honey?"

Mia cried and shook her head. She was never going to be able to get the image of Jarel's lifeless body out of her mind.

"It'll all be okay. You just wait and see."

She hoped her mother was right because, right now, Mia couldn't see things being okay for a long time. Putting Matthew in prison was a start, though, and she'd take it.

TWENTY-THREE

Paula dialed Graham's number for the fourth time, growing increasingly frustrated. She hadn't heard from him in days and needed an update on what was going on. The last he told her was that Kimberly would get back with him.

She wanted her revenge, as well. Being a side chick to a married man for over thirty years wasn't something she was proud of, but Paula had convinced herself she was okay with it, even though her ego wasn't. She didn't have to deal with kids, though she wanted some. She could fully submit or ignore his demanding ways because she wasn't his wife. Their terms were circumstantial and involved money. Without it, Paula was losing her mind.

"You are not my woman," Graham grilled her as soon as he picked up. "Don't ever call my phone back-to-back like that."

"I need to know what's going on!"

"Jarel is dead, and Matthew is in jail. We have nothing further to discuss. Lose my number," he said and hung up.

Hurriedly, Paula snatched up the remote and turned on the news. The breaking news headline made Paula fall onto the couch. *Matthew Grant of Grant Pharmaceuticals Arrested for Murder.*

Graham called the headline months ago when he held Hazel at gunpoint, and now it was true.

Paula began to sob into her hands. Not only was her man gone, but her money train, too. She was sick to her stomach knowing that, but her sudden queasiness also came from knowing the police might bring her in for questioning. Of all the years Matthew wanted her to go away and stay ducked off, Paula didn't listen. Now, she was ready to flee the state.

Shakily, she dialed the number for her son, who lived in Arizona.

"Hey, Mama. What's going on?" he answered.

"Hey, son. I was thinking…I need a change of scenery. Can I come vacation there for a few months?"

He laughed. "A few months? You finally trying to relocate, huh?"

"Yeah, I think so. That'll give me time to find a place."

"That's fine with me. Send me all the details, and I'll prepare the guestroom."

Paula hopped up from the couch and headed to her garage to grab her suitcases. As badly as it was going to hurt her to do, she had to cut ties and leave Matthew in the past. Not even she was as loyal as he thought.

Months Later

"About time you moved out of this house," Nicole said, watching the movers carry boxes out of the front door.

Kimberly sighed. "It's been time. I had to wait, though."

Nicole nodded, understanding. There were certain clauses in their prenup that Kimberly couldn't ignore. One was that if she decided to leave, she would get nothing in her walk. Another that she would've never in a million years thought would happen was her becoming sole owner of Grant Pharmaceuticals.

Matthew had shocked her with his news of having gone behind her back and gotten a vasectomy but somehow left out the part about her taking ownership of the company. In the event that Matthew died or went to prison, all rights would immediately be placed in Kimberly's name. If the stress of the trial didn't kill him, knowing his wife—whom he hated—now owned his beloved company would. The thing was, Kimberly didn't want it. Upon realizing she would be the owner, Kimberly handed it over to Mia. In her mind, it was the least she could do.

"I'm thinking about traveling for the next three months," Kimberly said.

"The girls going with you? Hell, am I going with you?" Nicole asked.

Kimberly laughed. "Sure, sister. You can tag along. It'll be my treat to Teyona if she wants to go. I told her she should take this semester off with everything that happened, but she refused."

"She's in her last year. I could've told you that girl wasn't taking a break. What about Hazel?"

Kimberly smiled, thinking of her headstrong child. "She has a huge painting opportunity, so she already passed. Before you ask about Mia, she doesn't want to go. She said I need this time to myself—something about this house had me trapped for years, and I need to experience life."

"She's not lying. You were given a second chance at life and need to live it. That man, whose name I won't ever speak again, was holding you back," Nicole said.

Kimberly couldn't help but agree as she stared at their empty house. It'd been vacant for years; only now, the materialistic things were gone. She felt a sense of sadness but profound happiness as she locked the doors once the movers were done.

A new chapter of her life was on the horizon, and Kimberly only wished she could've shared it with her once true love. Since she couldn't, she would make the memories count for them both.

Mia powered down her desktop for the day and stood from her desk. Releasing a yawn, she gathered her belongings and headed out of her office. With a press of a button, the door locked, and she smiled up at the sign on the door: *CEO Mia Grant.*

It didn't take long for her to fall in position and start running things. What was once a daunting feeling of taking on so much responsibility, Mia stepped into it with her head held high. Her position at the hospital did become a thing of the past, but she still made plans to stop by and visit.

"See you next week, Ms. Grant," the receptionist said with a wave.

Smiling, she replied, "You can call me Mia."

With a new position came a new schedule. Even though she didn't have a man and was still mourning over Jarel's death, Mia wasn't about to work herself like a dog. She was at the main headquarters two days a week and sometimes three if needed. Unlike her father, who wanted it to be known he was running things, Mia didn't have to do all of that. Her respect was earned far before she became the CEO and would remain.

Hopping in her Range Rover, Mia headed to the one place she knew she shouldn't. Although she had learned patience, her curiosity still got the best of her. When she arrived at the hospital, she pulled a baseball cap over her short hair and slid on a pair of Dior shades. Going into her purse, she pulled out a piece of paper, looked at the room number written on it, and stuffed it back inside.

Mia was trying to keep a low profile for what she was about to do. Entering the elevator, she pressed number four and exhaled.

The elevator dinged at her stop, and she glanced at the receptionist's desk. Knowing she had to sign in, she scribbled a fake name.

"Hi. Who are you here to see?"

Mia smiled. "My cousin, Evelyn."

"Oh great. She's been getting a lot of visitors."

That took Mia by surprise, but she kept it pushing. According to Jarel, she was in a coma and on life support. *Maybe her condition has changed.* Mia's thoughts were right. Hearing voices as she approached the room, she ducked around the corner. Thankfully, the door was open, and the room was on the corner so she could eavesdrop.

"A'ight, sis, we gon' be back up here later to check on you. Hopefully, by the end of this week, you can leave this hospital and move away from this punk-ass city."

Mia squinted. She had heard that voice before. *Ricky?*

"I'm so ready to leave," Evelyn replied. "When you come back, can you bring me some real food?"

Ricky chuckled. "Yeah, I got you."

He left out, and Mia waited until she heard the main doors close to exhale. She was taking a chance, seeing as though her father had killed their family, but she felt burdened. Though she wasn't solely responsible for Evelyn's condition, she still felt the need to apologize. Not wanting to seem suspicious, she went to the restroom and stood around for a minute before coming back out. She gave herself a mental pep talk before knocking and entering the room.

Evelyn's head popped up from her phone's screen. "Oh, hi. Are you here to ask me more questions?"

"Not today. I'm sure you're tired of those," Mia said with a chuckle, hoping she would tell her who had been there asking her questions. She had an idea it was the police.

"I am. So, thank you."

"You're welcome. I wanted to stop by and offer my condolences. I'm so sorry about the death of your brother."

Evelyn's face was marred with confusion.

"My brother? Ricky just left."

"Oh," Mia quipped, thrown off. "I could've sworn Jarel said Ricky was your cousin."

Evelyn chuckled. "No. Ricky is my brother. My fiancé could get his words mixed up sometimes."

Mia choked and began coughing. "Excuse me. What'd you say Jarel was?"

"My fiancé. I'm sorry…who are you again? I never got your name," Evelyn said, now on high alert. She thought Mia was one of the detectives assigned to the case.

Shocked by what Evelyn said, Mia didn't bother explaining who she was and why she was there. Instead, Mia hightailed it to her SUV and climbed inside. Tears brimmed her eyes, but not out of sadness. She laughed from the depths of her gut at Jarel's audacity.

"His fiancée," Mia breathed. "How fucking stupid was I?"

She thought back to the dinner date when he introduced Ricky and Sharon. She knew they were siblings, but he never once said Evelyn was their sister. He couldn't because she was supposed to be his sister, not a woman he planned to marry.

Mia's heart broke for Evelyn. She had finally awakened from her coma and was hit with the news that Jarel had been killed. Losing him while he thought he'd lost her for good made her wish she never woke up.

Jarel hadn't been completely honest with Mia. He was falling for her but knew it was wrong. That's not how things were supposed to be, but it happened. When Jarel planned to find out who sold his fiancée the weight loss pills that caused inflammation in her brain, he never thought he would come in direct contact with the source.

In preparation for their wedding, Evelyn began taking the weight loss pill unbeknownst to Jarel. When he found her unresponsive one morning, she was rushed to the hospital and later fell into a coma. After a month of the doctors giving him no real answers, Jarel started searching on his own. He looked through her medicine cabinet, checked her drawers at work, and even went through her phone. It was then he found out who she'd been in contact with.

Hazel had been supplying her with the pill for months but couldn't meet her one evening. The day she sent her boyfriend, Karter, was the day Evelyn was rushed to the hospital. He had accidentally sold her the wrong pills, and none of them knew, not even Jarel. All he knew was that someone was going to pay.

Months Ago…

"Mia, can you please do me this one favor? I have an art gig and can't meet her. She's a loyal customer who I've missed," Hazel whined as she slipped on a pair of pants.

She had a meeting with an art agency but had customers waiting to be served. Not wanting to miss out on Evelyn's money, she asked Mia to meet her instead.

"I swear this is the last time, Haze. I'm not a drug dealer," Mia hissed.

Hazel laughed. "Technically, you are. Thank you, sis! I'm sending Eve's number over now."

Mia mumbled whatever and hung up. It had been two months since she started stealing from the pharmacy, and Hazel just kept pushing the limits. Having her meet customers on her off day was a sure sign that she was losing her mind. When Mia pulled up to where she was supposed to meet her, she stayed in her car and sent her a text.

Hey. I'm here in a black Range.

Sorry. I'm not going to be able to make it.

"*Are you serious?*" *Mia huffed.*

She rolled her eyes and glanced around the parking lot. This trip was a blank mission, but she could at least get some food. Little did Hazel or Mia know, but Evelyn hadn't been the one to text that she couldn't make it. It was Jarel. He needed to see the face of the person who was the cause of Evelyn's condition.

He sat inside a coffee shop with a clear view of the parking lot. His eyes were trained on the Range Rover as Mia hopped out. Jarel frowned at her polished appearance and glowing skin. He just knew there was no way this woman was a drug dealer. When she stepped inside the coffee shop, his mind went into overdrive, wondering how he could get close to her. Without thinking much about it, he approached the counter where she stood ordering a coffee and chocolate chip muffin.

"*Her things are on me,*" *he said, stepping up to pay with his card.*

Mia faced him with a smile. Her day had been thrown off, but Mr. Handsome had just made it much better.

"*Thank you. I guess there are some gentlemen in the world,*" *Mia said.*

"*Absolutely. Would I be too forward if I asked you to enjoy your coffee and muffin at my table?*"

Blushing, Mia lowered her head. She wasn't used to a man being this forward with her. It'd been a while, but she did check his hand for a wedding ring. When she didn't spot one, she lifted her head.

"*You wouldn't be at all. It's nice to meet you. I'm Mia,*" *she said, sticking her hand out.*

Jarel licked his lips. "It's nice to meet you, as well. My name is Jarel."

Mia shook her head as the memory flooded her mind. She couldn't believe Jarel did all of that and, in the end, was killed. Mia found his efforts admirable and hated the outcome of his story.

She was just thankful none of her sisters ended up taking the fall. Evelyn was alive, Jarel was no longer here to infiltrate their lives, their mother was free, and Matthew was in prison.

"I guess that was one secret he took to the grave with him," she said with a chuckle before dialing Hazel's number. She had to let her know what she'd just discovered.

"Hello?" Hazel answered.

"You won't believe where I'm coming from."

Knowing her sister, Hazel knew it was someplace she had no business being, but she fed into the hype anyway.

"Try me and see," Hazel said with a chuckle.

"The hospital Jarel's *fiancée* is at."

On the other end of the phone, Hazel slowly blinked as if that would help her comprehend what Mia just said.

"I'm sorry...his fiancée? When the hell did he get one of those?"

"Your guess is as good as mine. I thought I was going to check on his sister, and she was awake."

Hazel chuckled. "Surprised you, huh?"

"Heck, yes, but I'm glad she was up. The cousins I met aren't his cousins but his fiancée's siblings."

"This story just keeps getting crazier as months go by. Honestly, I'm not surprised that he was hiding being in a relationship all this time. She must've been the person he claimed we hurt. What's her name again?" Hazel asked.

"Evelyn."

"Evelyn...Evelyn," Hazel mumbled. Then, it hit her. "Her nickname must be Eve. She did used to buy from me. I wondered what happened to her."

"Well, we got our answer," Mia said. "Hold on. I'm about to order me something to drink from Chick-fil-A."

Hazel waited while she placed her order and couldn't help but shake her head. Knowing she played a role in someone's pain didn't bother her as much as she thought it would. Jarel and Evelyn were both casualties in the grand scheme of things. Had Jarel not sought his own revenge and let karma handle the sisters, he probably would've still been alive.

"Thank you," Mia told the man at the window and grabbed her lemonade.

Hating that the wetness from the cup was now on her hands, she opened her glovebox to retrieve some napkins. When an envelope fell out, her brows furrowed.

"Uh, hello?" Hazel questioned. "You still there?"

"Yeah, I'm here. Hold on. Let me park really quick," Mia said.

She pulled into the first empty space she spotted and parked. It wasn't often that she went inside her glovebox, but she didn't recall a white envelope being inside there the last time she did. There was nothing on the front indicating who it was for or from, so she opened it.

"What're you doing?" Hazel questioned.

"Someone put a letter in my glovebox, and I'm opening it."

Hazel sucked her teeth. "Here we go again."

Pulling the folded handwritten letter out, Mia immediately recognized the handwriting. The same penmanship belonged to whoever was leaving Teyona notes on her windshield. She read a couple of lines and chuckled.

"My life is a joke," Mia grumbled.

"Read it aloud," Hazel urged.

Mia cleared her throat and started from the beginning.

"If you're reading this, I'm probably no longer here. First, I want to apologize for making you fall in love with the man you thought I was."

Hazel gasped. "It's from Jarel?"

"Yes, and based on the writing, he's the one who was leaving notes on Tey's windshield."

"That motherfucker," Hazel hissed.

Mia was thinking the same thing. She sighed and continued reading.

"It was never my intention to cause you or your family any harm, but your sister hurt someone close to me. Evelyn isn't my sister. She's my fiancée. Yes, I was cheating on her, but for a good cause. The day she was supposed to meet up with Hazel, you happened to go in her place. That's how we met. The same pills your father prescribes to his customers are the same ones that made Evelyn sick, and I needed answers as to who gave them to her. Unfortunately, you got caught up in the mix."

"Wait. So, he's blaming us...well, me...for Eve being in a coma? That's not my fault. She'd been taking those pills for months. Wouldn't something have happened to her before now?" Hazel asked.

"Possibly," Mia answered, not one hundred percent sure.

"I can't believe he did all this because his fiancée wanted to lose some weight. Whatever happened to her was not our fault, Mia."

She wanted to believe that, but Mia thought otherwise. Evelyn would've never had access to the drugs from Hazel had Mia not been stealing them from the pharmacy. Whatever pills Karter sold her that day weren't the weight loss pills Hazel had given him or the ones Evelyn was expecting. It was a mishap on his end. One risky situation had caused their entire worlds to be flipped upside down.

"Yeah, well, I'm having a hard time believing that."

"What else does the letter say?" Hazel wanted to know.

Mia's eyes scanned the letter for anything else that stood out before making it to the end. Jarel didn't say much more aside from claiming they could've been together had this been another time in their lives. Mia laughed at that. She highly doubted it.

"Nothing much. I'm so glad we can finally put that behind us." Mia exhaled, stuffing the letter back inside the envelope.

"Same. No more liars, stalkers, and blackmailers. Have you talked to Teyona?"

"Not today. She's supposed to be going to see Mom, so I'm sure we'll hear from her," Mia said.

"Good. They need to clear the air. I'm about to get some painting done, so call me later."

"I will."

The sisters hung up, and Mia rested her head against the seat. The last thing she expected was a letter from Jarel providing the final pieces to a puzzle she didn't ask to put together. She couldn't turn back the hands of time, but she could do better from here on out.

Before pulling out of the parking lot, Mia glanced at the letter with plans to burn it later. Nothing from her past that could incriminate her or her sisters was allowed in their future.

EPILOGUE

"**P**ick up your feet, Grant. This is the first visitor you've had." The officer chuckled as he jerked Matthew's bound wrists.

No one had visited him except his lawyer, so he was surprised. He hoped it was Paula but frowned when he saw his brother. Annoyed, Matthew flopped down in the chair and picked up the phone.

"What you want, Joseph?" Matthew grumbled.

"I thought you'd be in a better mood to see me."

Matthew clenched his jaw. "It doesn't matter that I see you. I'm in here, and you're out there. Now, what's going on? Have you heard anything from Paula?"

"No. Her place is empty, and no one she usually hangs with has seen her either."

"Disloyal bitch," Matthew spat. "After all these years, she finally decided to leave me."

Joseph had nothing to say, at least not about his affairs. He came to deliver some bad news.

"They came and searched the storage units," Joseph said.

Matthew's expression didn't change. "Okay."

"The freezer was empty."

"Yeah…I know."

Matthew leaned back in his chair. Joseph didn't need to say anything else to get his message across. Years ago, Joseph had been the only one he talked to about Lawrence and Kimberly. During a moment of vulnerability, he slipped up and said where he put his body.

"So? You gotta tell me something, man."

Chuckling, Matthew shook his head. "No, I don't. A missing person is called a missing person for a reason. Did you think I was going to place him somewhere he could be found? I love you, but I don't trust anyone, not even my own blood."

Standing to his feet, Matthew placed the phone on the hook and asked to be escorted back to his cell. He didn't know why Joseph thought to even bring that up. They, whoever was still searching, were never going to find Lawrence's body. Matthew made sure of that.

Lying on his back in his cell, he thought about his life and how he schemed his way to the top. Not all his moves were janky, but enough were for karma not to miss him. He thought starting a family would make up for it, but he was wrong. He couldn't even do right by them.

As hard as he worked to provide for his family and build a legacy, it all came crashing down at his daughters' hands. They jacked Matthew for everything he owed them and their mother and weren't sad about it in the least. When it was all said and done, their scamming ways had to win. Claiming a victory over the man who ruined their lives was what sisterhood was all about.

WWW.BLACKODYSSEY.NET

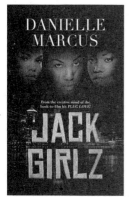

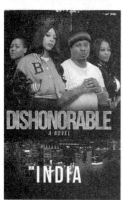

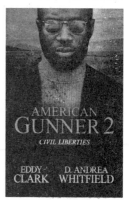